Lost and Loaded:
a Gun's Tale

a 509 Crime Anthology

Edited by Colin Conway

Lost and Loaded: a 509 Crime Anthology

ISBN: 978-1-961030-28-2

Cover Design by Zach McCain

Original Ink Press, an imprint of High Speed Creative, LLC
1521 N. Argonne Road, #C-205
Spokane Valley, WA 99212

Table of Contents

What is the 509?

Separated by the Cascade Range, Washington State is divided into two distinctly different climates and cultures.

The western side of the Cascades is home to Seattle, its 34 inches of annual rainfall, and the incredibly weird and smelly Gum Wall. Most of the state's wealth and political power are concentrated in and around this enormous city. The residents of this area know the prosperity that has come from being the home of Microsoft, Amazon, Boeing, and Starbucks.

To the east of the Cascade Mountains lies nearly two-thirds of the entire state, a lot of which is used for agriculture. Washington State leads the nation in producing apples, it is the second-largest potato grower, and it's the fourth for providing wheat.

This eastern part of the state can enjoy more than 170 days of sunshine each year, which is important when there are more than 200 lakes nearby. However, the beautiful summers are offset by harsh winters, with average snowfall reaching 47 inches and the average high hovering around 37°.

While five telephone area codes provide service to the westside, only 509 covers everything east of the Cascades, a staggering twenty-one counties.

Of these, Spokane County is the largest with an estimated population of 506,000.

*One man's trash is
another man's treasure.*

-    source unknown

Introduction

"Dude," Bobby Mathews said with a cocktail in his hand, "when're you doing another anthology?"

We were waiting for the 2024 Left Coast Crime awards ceremony to begin. Hundreds of authors mingled with other writers and fans of the genre. It had the feel of a Hollywood gala. Dressed-up attendees smiled and laughed with each other as they waited for the event to start.

Bobby's question was about my 509 Crime Anthologies. I'd assembled and edited three collections set in my fictional world of Eastern Washington. They were titled (in order) *The Eviction of Hope*, *A Bag of Dick's*, and *Back Road Bobby and His Friends*.

All hold a special place in my heart, but it was the second collection that earned me a bit of notoriety in the writing community. That anthology revolved around a missing sack of food from Dick's Hamburgers, an iconic Spokane eatery.

Upon our meeting at a previous conference, a well-respected East Coast author pointed at me and nearly shouted, "You're the *Bag of Dick's* guy!" Someone in her writing group had mentioned the name of my anthology which earned a round of snickers.

Entries into the trilogy of the 509 Crime Anthologies were by invitation only. I wanted to work with friends or people I admired in the writing business. A few of the authors who shared their work in the previous collections were James L'Etoile, Sarah Chen, Holly West, and Eric

Beetner. Naming all the participating authors here would make it feel like reading a phone book.

Some of the stories in those first three collections garnered recognition. Hector Acosta's tale in the first anthology ("La Chingona") was selected for *The Best American Mystery and Suspense 2022* anthology. Several other stories in the trilogy were listed in the BAMS' Distinguished Category.

"I don't think I'll do another anthology," I told Bobby.

"Aw, don't say that."

"They're a lot of work."

Bobby frowned, then sipped his drink. His gaze dropped to the nearby table I was hosting. "Where's your girlfriend?"

"She ditched me to sit with Wanda Morris."

"Understandable." Bobby waved at someone across the room. "I'll be right over," he called. His attention returned to me. "Before I go, you gotta make a promise."

"What's that?"

"If you do another anthology—" He held up his free hand to stop my protest. "I said *if*."

"If," I agreed.

Bobby saluted me with his drink, sloshing it dangerously close to the rim. "If you do another, you save me a spot." His smile was infectious.

"You'll be my first call."

He toasted me again. "That's all I'm asking."

***

Writing crime fiction is a lonely business which makes mystery conferences such a wonderful experience. At events like Left Coast Crime, Bouchercon, and Thrillerfest, an author gets to interact with existing fans, new readers, and other scribes through a variety of activities. Those events include discussion panels and hosted get-togethers. Some of the best exchanges occur in the hotel bar or during impromptu hallway meetings.

Topics of author-to-author conversations run the gamut from publishers to story ideas to industry scuttlebutt. These relaxed get-togethers are how new friendships are started and existing ones are continued.

The morning of the LCC awards ceremony, James D.F. Hannah caught me in the hallway during one of the breaks. He had a bag over his shoulder and a cup of coffee in his left hand.

I introduced my girlfriend to James, and she immediately adored the guy. What's not to like? He's a cheerful Kentuckian with an easy laugh. The three of us chatted for a while before James motioned at me with his paper cup. "This guy," he said to my girlfriend, "won't do another anthology. What's up with that?"

My girlfriend eyed me questioningly.

"They're a lot of work," I said to her before turning to James. "A lot."

"Yeah, but Joe, Nikki, and Frank were in them. I want to be in one, too. Feels like you're keeping me out."

"It's not just you," I said.

"Better not be." He grinned. "If you ever decide to do another—"

"I'm not," I interrupted.

"Maybe you should," my girlfriend said.

James smiled at her. "I knew I liked you."

"I'm not," I insisted again.

"All right, all right. I get it." James sipped his coffee. He glanced left and right, acknowledging folks he knew.

When his gaze settled back on me, he said, "Just so this is on the record, I want in if you do another."

"I'll tell you what," I said, "if I decide to do another, you'll be my first call,"

He toasted me with his coffee. "Was that so hard?"

***

As an author, I've made friends all over the world. Some are other writers while others are enthusiastic readers. I'm grateful to have friends in Australia, Canada, England, Lebanon and throughout the United States.

I've never met many of these folks face-to-face. It's the reality of our world today. We meet through email or social media and develop a relationship via the written word. It doesn't make them any less of a friend.

That's a perk of writing conferences—getting to communicate one-on-one with folks we only see once or twice a year.

Curtis Ippolito broke away from the group he was talking with on the afternoon of the LCC awards ceremony. He bit into an apple while he walked over. After introducing him to my girlfriend, we chatted for a few minutes. Curtis is an extremely nice and humble person. My girlfriend liked him right away. It didn't hurt that they were both from California.

He said, "I ran into James after a panel."

"Uh-oh."

"He said you might do another anthology."

"I think something was lost in translation," I said. "There isn't a next one."

"Maybe there should be," my girlfriend suggested.

"You should listen to her," Curtis said.

Before I could respond, my girlfriend added, "He says they're a lot of work."

"Oh, sure, I get that." Curtis took another bite from his apple. "Still, it would've been cool to be in one."

"I'll tell you what—"

His eyebrows raised. "Yeah?"

"If I do another, you'll be my first call."

Curtis toasted me with his half-eaten apple. "Now you're talking."

***

On Sunday morning, the day after the awards show, my girlfriend said, "Maybe you should think about it." She was in the bathroom doing what women do in front of a mirror.

I was sitting near the window of our hotel room, reading a book and occasionally spying on downtown Bellevue.

"Think about what?" I asked absently.

She popped her head out of the bathroom. "Another anthology. With James and Curtis, you've got two stories right there."

I closed my book. "Bobby Mathews said he wanted in if I ever do another."

"When did he say that?"

"Last night."

"Where was I?"

"Not at my table."

"Oh, yeah." She grinned. "Did I tell you how amazing Wanda Morris was?"

"You did. Repeatedly."

"Don't be jealous. You're still my favorite author."

I smirked. "You said Jo Nesbø was your favorite."

"I said he was the best." She sounded like a mother assuring her children that she loves them equally. "You're still my favorite."

"Uh-huh."

"If Bobby's in, you've got three stories." She disappeared into the bathroom. "You're halfway there."

"Not quite."

"If it matters, I think you should do it."

On the street below, a police car with flashing lights attempted to stop an old pickup. They turned the corner and vanished from sight.

"This feels like *The Godfather*," I said after a few seconds passed.

My girlfriend stepped out of the bathroom with a toothbrush stuck in her mouth. "Huh?"

"You know. 'Just when I thought I was out, they pull me back in.'" I did my best Michael Corleone impression.

"What's that?" She tilted her head back so toothpaste wouldn't dribble down her chin.

"*The Godfather*," I repeated. "Al Pacino. I think it was the third."

"Never seen it."

"You get the point, right?"

She rolled her eyes. "Don't be a baby. How hard could it really be?"

Before I could argue, she disappeared once more into the bathroom.

My gaze dropped to the street below and my thoughts returned to a possible fourth anthology. There was an idea I'd been sitting on for a couple of years. Something I thought would be perfect for another collection.

It had to do with a mysterious gun turning up in places it didn't belong.

Colin Conway
Winter 2024
Spokane, Washington

A Husband's Duty
Colin Conway

Marlin Hattenburg nicked his chin with the razor and a droplet of blood immediately appeared. He grimaced at his reflection but didn't stop shaving. Not while thick cream still covered most of his face. It wasn't the first time Marlin had cut himself and it likely wouldn't be the last.

While in high school, Marlin learned how to shave from his father. The old man used a razor, so that's how he taught his son. Marlin's friends, those who shaved, used electric razors. Marlin's father insisted *how* a man did something mattered as much as *what* the man did, whether that be personal grooming or a job.

"If you wanna be a ditchdigger," Marlin's father said, "be the best damn ditchdigger there is."

As soon as Marlin left for a stint in the Army, he tried an electric shaver. No longer under the shadow of his father, Marlin could be his own man. Unfortunately, the electric razor didn't leave his face feeling as smooth as the manual method. He stubbornly stuck with the electric shaver for several weeks before throwing it away and reverting to the way his father had taught.

Marlin cleaned his razor under the faucet before setting it in a plastic cup next to his and his wife's toothbrushes. A line of blood ran from Marlin's smooth chin and down his neck. He slapped water on his face, clearing away the remaining bits of cream. The blood came quicker now.

He dried his face, which left a smear of blood on the light gray hand towel. Sandra would surely squawk about that. What was new? She complained about everything lately. He couldn't remember a time when she hadn't grumbled about something he did. Maybe when they were first dating, but that quickly faded when they were married. In the years since, it seemed he could do nothing right in her eyes.

Marlin applied a torn bit of toilet paper to his chin. It immediately turned red. Before leaving the bathroom, he closed his terrycloth robe and secured the belt around his waist.

Sandra reclined in bed, her attention on the early morning news program. Her long blonde hair fell over her shoulders, and the bedcovers were pulled up under her armpits. Her eyes cut to Marlin, and she clucked. "Cut yourself again."

He shrugged. "Just a nick."

"It's 'cause your face is sagging."

Marlin frowned. Plenty of things sagged on her, but he didn't dare point it out. Any time he risked speaking up, she'd start in on how she wasted all the good years of her life with him. It wasn't like he made the best of those years, either.

He opened the closet door and removed his postal uniform. Marlin draped it over the back of a nearby chair, then dropped his robe.

"Don't know why it matters," Sandra said absently. "They don't care how you look." She was focused on a reporter blathering about some recent political polls.

Marlin remained silent. Years ago, he had explained his father's advice about doing a job to the best of one's ability to Sandra. Maybe she listened back then, but now she heard what she wanted.

He slipped on his postal carrier pants and light-blue shirt. Marlin didn't bother to turn around as he dressed. It'd been years since his wife looked at him in an adoring or sexual way. He wasn't in bad shape, maybe a little flabby around the middle, but compared to most men his age, Marlin Hattenburg thought he was doing all right.

When the news program broke for commercial, Sandra muted the television. "What's his face—the one with the turban?"

"At work?"

"Where else?"

"Harjinder," Marlin said as he slid his belt through the pant loops, still not looking at her.

"That's the one. He's got that God-awful beard, and no one says anything about it. Do they?"

Marlin never had a beard, but he didn't fault a man for wanting one, especially his friend. He didn't know if Harjinder wore facial hair for religious reasons. Marlin never asked since it was none of his business.

He sat in the chair so he could lace up his black soft-soled shoes.

The news program restarted, and Sandra turned the sound back on. The reporter smiled as she announced the Senate's proposal to cut the budget of some social program. Marlin wasn't paying attention when she mentioned the name.

He stood and wiped the creases from his pants. Next, he put his letter carrier baseball hat on and pressed the edges of the brim down. "Going to see him today?"

Sandra frowned. "Don't start with that nonsense again." Her eyes remained on the television.

Marlin nodded twice, then left the room without saying goodbye. He wasn't even sure his wife noticed him leaving.

***

A classic rock station played in the processing area.

When Marlin first started working for the post office, the tunes played on that station were from guys like Buddy Holly and Elvis Presley. Old fogey music. Songs that Marlin's dad listened to while barbequing on the weekends.

Something sneaky happened through the years; the station stayed the same, but the music improved. Acts like the Beatles and Jimi Hendrix got airtime, forcing out the rockabilly stuff. It wasn't the music Marlin grew up on, but it was close.

Then came the sudden realization that his favorite bands were filling the classic rock rotation. Gone were Buddy and Elvis. In their place came Peter Frampton and AC/DC. It took some adjusting to the disc jockeys referring to his favorites as classic rock, but at least Marlin got to hear them while he worked. Now, bands like Nirvana and Soundgarden were forcing his favorites off the oldies station.

Seemed to Marlin that most of what he loved was getting taken away from him.

"Looks like that hurt," Harjinder Singh said. He motioned toward Marlin's chin.

Harjinder was a tall man with olive skin. A tight black turban wrapped his head. Harjinder's wiry beard fell to the top of his chest.

Self-consciously, Marlin touched the bit of toilet paper on his chin. He'd forgotten to pull it off before leaving his car that morning. Marlin tugged it off now. "Just a nick," he said, the same comment he'd uttered to his wife earlier.

"Bleeds more than a nick."

Marlin touched his chin, then pulled his fingers back to reveal blood. "It'll stop soon," he said.

"Don't get it on the mail."

Harjinder and Marlin pulled trays containing letters from a storage rack and set them in their respective bins. Other carriers did the same, but they ignored the two friends. The bulk work of sorting and processing was done with machines at the distribution center. Feeding the machines was easy, mindless work, but Marlin never wanted to do it.

"I've got a new joke for you," Harjinder said.

"Save it for later."

Marlin pushed his cart toward the loading dock.

For his entire career, he'd walked a variety of mail routes throughout Spokane County. Marlin worked in freezing rain, blowing snow, and searing heat. None of the extreme weather bothered Marlin since it allowed him to be outside. It was fulfilling work, and he did it to the best of his ability.

As he aged and climbed the seniority ladder, various administrators suggested he apply for a Sales & Service position or maybe consider becoming a supervisor. Marlin politely declined. He didn't want to become a house cat—one of those workers happy to be indoors all day.

The closest he ever came to applying for a different position was a couple of years ago, after he broke his ankle falling down a set of icy stairs. While he recovered at home, Sandra gave him a daily earful about how hard the carrier job was on his aging body. She pushed him to leave the routes and be an administrator. Marlin appreciated how much his wife worried about his health.

Looking back now, he believed she just wanted him out of the house.

****

Marlin's last duty before he began his route was to pull the mail from the two collection boxes that sat curbside. Every branch assigned the duty differently. At this one, the responsibility fell to the carriers, and they rotated it on a weekly basis.

This was Marlin's turn.

He set a plastic tray on the ground before unlocking the first blue box. Only a handful of letters lay on the bottom. Marlin collected them and dropped them into the tray.

When he first started with the postal service, the blue collection boxes were everywhere in the city. That was before the overnight delivery services cut deeply into the post office's business. Long before anyone imagined emailing, which was another cut. Now the collection boxes were kept mostly around post office branches.

The service still moved a lot of correspondence, but these days it seemed to be mostly junk mail, utility and credit card bills, and holiday cards.

Carriers previously stored rain gear or winter coats inside the collection boxes with the mail. No one really did that anymore. All the carriers Marlin knew drove the small white trucks with roll-up doors in the back. They could keep their gear in their vehicles.

Marlin moved to the second collection box and unlocked it. The pile of envelopes was slightly larger here. He reached in for the letters and felt something hard. Marlin moved the letters and exposed a black revolver.

He stiffened.

It wasn't the first time he'd found something foreign in a collection box. In the past, he'd found partially eaten candy bars, brass knuckles, and a used condom wrapped in a pair of woman's panties. This was, however, the first time he'd found a gun.

Marlin stared at it.

If someone dropped it into a collection box, they probably used it in a crime. A robbery, maybe. Or a murder? Why else would someone get rid of a perfectly good gun?

Marlin collected the letters and dropped them into the tray. The gun sat alone at the bottom of the collection box.

He should leave it where it was and report it to his supervisor, Rueben Molina, who'd surely consult with the postal inspectors before alerting the local police.

Marlin secured the box, picked up the tray, and returned to the building.

***

The sky was clear blue, and the sun had reached its zenith. Sweat rolled down Marlin's back as he walked almost robotically through the various South Hill neighborhoods comprising his mail route. Had he checked the weather before leaving for work this morning, he might have worn his shorts.

Marlin worked in a daze; his thoughts clouded by an image of the abandoned revolver.

As a boy, his father taught him how to hunt. Marlin killed his first deer when he was twelve. His father's pride warmed his heart, but the animal's death bothered him. He knew hamburger and bacon, his favorite foods at the time, came from cows and pigs, yet seeing the death up close was shocking. He cried himself to sleep that night, unable to shake the memory of the life he'd taken.

Marlin kept his feelings to himself, though. Sharing emotions wasn't done in the house he grew up in. Not even his mother expressed hers. He continued to hunt with his father until he went into the Army. Every deer he killed resulted in a night of tears, but each one was progressively easier.

Entering the military, Marlin knew he might have to kill a man if war occurred, but he'd enlisted to be a mechanic. He figured he was more likely to spill oil than blood.

A kind, older woman on his route opened her door as he climbed the steps to her house. Marlin believed her to be lonely, as she often stopped him for several moments with benign chatter. It was no different today, except Marlin couldn't remember what they talked about. He simply smiled and nodded until it was an appropriate time to excuse himself. She waved him goodbye.

Marlin didn't own any firearms. It was his choice, but Sandra also forbade any guns in her home. He didn't mind her absolutism on the matter since he long ago decided he didn't want one.

Yet he wanted to feel the weight of the revolver in his hand again. Sandra would lose her mind if he brought it home. She wouldn't have to know about it, though. It could be his secret. Marlin didn't have many of those. Not like Sandra.

Marlin quickly pushed the thought away. Something inside him, an internal warning alarm, knew the danger of letting his imagination include thoughts of his wife.

He should have told his supervisor about the revolver before leaving. It was stupid not to. Reporting the gun to

Rueben would have stopped the bad thoughts pushing in from the edges of Marlin's consciousness.

He set his mind to do the right thing then. When Marlin returned from his route, he'd pull the mail from the collection boxes like he was supposed to do. He'd feign surprise at the sight of the gun and report it to Reuben.

Everything would be fine.

***

Marlin grabbed the revolver after clearing the collection boxes and slipped it into his pocket. When he brought the tray of afternoon correspondence into the branch, he excused himself and went to the restroom. He sat on the toilet for some time, holding the gun in his hands.

The manufacturer had engraved *Luger LCR* along the right side of the barrel. Underneath that they etched *.38 Spl+P*. Marlin had heard of a .38 Special but never held one. The molded grip felt good under his fingers. Marlin released the cylinder and discovered the gun held five rounds.

Using a piece of toilet paper to limit his fingerprints, Marlin removed each brass casing. Of the five, only three contained bullets. Two had already been fired. Marlin closed the cylinder.

He pulled more toilet paper from the roll and wiped down the gun, careful to clean every crevice so none of his fingerprints would remain. It wasn't too late to return the revolver to the collection box. He could leave it there overnight and report its discovery in the morning.

Marlin wrapped the gun in toilet paper and stuffed it back into his pocket. He left the bathroom and walked toward the exit, his hand hovering over the bulge made by the revolver.

Harjinder Singh saw him and waved. "Got time for the joke?"

"In a minute," Marlin said. "I need to run outside."

His friend nodded and headed toward the breakroom.

Marlin walked directly to his car and climbed in. He pulled the gun from his pocket and tucked it under the seat. He gripped the steering wheel and stared straight ahead for several moments.

Eventually, Marlin said to himself, "It's still not too late to do the right thing."

A knock on the window startled Marlin, and he jumped. His supervisor, Reuben Molina, stared at him, then motioned for Marlin to roll down the window. Reuben was a chubby man in his early forties. He meant well as a supervisor but often seemed disconnected from the needs of his staff.

When the driver's window lowered, Reuben asked with a grin, "You all right, Fish?"

Marlin hated the nickname. His father was a fan of *Zoo Parade*, a show that ran in the early 1950s, and its host Marlin Perkins. Throughout his childhood, Marlin and his friends watched his namesake lead *Mutual of Omaha's Wild Kingdom*. Marlin was proud of the name his father had chosen. He didn't want a nickname, especially one as dumb as Fish.

"I'm fine," Marlin said. "Just needed a minute."

"You don't look fine. Coming down with something?"

Marlin pointed at his stomach. "Feeling a little queasy."

"All right. Hope you feel better." Rueben patted the car's roof. "See you inside, Fish."

***

Marlin pulled into the empty garage. Sandra wasn't home. His imagination went to the worst scenario he could imagine—she was with Grant Ferguson again. Marlin didn't want Sandra to die in a horrible car accident, but that would be better than knowing she was wrapped in Grant's arms.

It wasn't like the guy was much better than Marlin. Grant Ferguson was a couple of years younger than he and maybe in a little better shape. Big deal. Grant worked the graveyard shift at the Amazon distribution center. His benefits and retirement wouldn't be better than Marlin's government pension.

Even though he knew of Sandra's unfaithfulness, Marlin couldn't divorce her. She remained the love of his life, and he knew full well he'd meet no one like her again. Especially not at his age.

Besides, divorce was a mortal sin. His mother explained to a young Marlin that a man would go to hell if he ever left his wife. She preached it so often he believed it without question. Marlin's father didn't bother correcting her, so it must have been true. The Hattenburg men never attended church, so his mother's view of the Bible was the only interpretation they knew.

When he was on his own, Marlin continued to avoid the church, and he never read the Good Book. That didn't matter, though. He still didn't want to go to hell.

Rationally, there could be plenty of reasons Sandra wasn't home. She might be at the grocery store, or perhaps she was at Target buying stuff they didn't need. Maybe she was getting her hair or nails done, or other services they couldn't afford.

None of those activities prevented Sandra from seeing Grant Ferguson earlier in the day.

Marlin reached for the gun but left it under the car seat. He was afraid he'd be tempted to use it if he brought it in the house. He'd surely go to hell for murder.

"Why'd you bring it home, then?" Marlin eyed himself in the rearview mirror. "Huh?"

He slid out of the car and slammed the door behind him.

***

Sandra came home shortly after six. She was dressed as if she might have had a job interview. Short white skirt, dark blue shirt, and white heels. However, her hair was slightly mussed and the lipstick she usually wore was gone. She carried a McDonald's bag in her left hand and a Target sack in her right.

"Sorry I'm late," she said.

"Where you been?" Marlin asked.

She lifted the two bags. "What's it look like?"

"All day?"

"No, not all day." She dropped the Target sack, then set the McDonald's bag on the counter. "I got a late start. Is that okay, Mr. Timekeeper?"

Sandra always pretended like Marlin didn't know the truth, even though he hinted she had a boyfriend. He didn't have the guts to say he had followed Sandra to Grant's house one morning after he called in sick. He followed Grant a couple more times after that, learning as much about him as possible. Marlin even looked him up on the internet. He learned so much about Grant Ferguson that it made Marlin sick to his stomach.

If Sandra found out he had followed her, she'd certainly file for divorce. Marlin would go to hell and not even be the one asking to get out of the marriage. It was one of the conflicts in the Bible that Marlin could never understand.

His mother explained it to him when he was a teenager. "God's reasoning isn't for us to always comprehend," she said. "We have to have faith." His mother didn't clarify her position any more than that, even though Marlin continued to say he didn't understand.

Soon after, Marlin's father pulled him aside and whispered, "A man's duty, especially a husband's duty, is to suffer in silence." He patted his son on the head and walked away.

Marlin didn't need to ask his father for an explanation.

"I already ate," Sandra said, "but I got you a Big Mac and some fries." She waggled the paper bag. "Your favorite."

Marlin hated McDonald's. He'd told Sandra many times, but perhaps she forgot. He wondered if Grant Ferguson liked McDonald's or if the Big Mac was his favorite.

Maybe Sandra got confused instead.

***

Marlin lay in bed that night as Sandra softly snored next to him. He stared at the ceiling with a heaviness in his chest. The only light in the room came from the blue display of the clock radio.

What if hell wasn't real? Marlin wondered. Life would be easier, that's for sure. He'd take the revolver he found and shoot Grant Ferguson without a second thought—right in the face.

Marlin smiled, but it quickly melted.

What if Grant didn't know he was doing something wrong? Maybe Sandra never told him she was married. She could have said she was single or divorced. For that matter, Sandra could have said she was a widow. She could be lying to both men.

Marlin should shoot her, then. If hell was just a figment of imagination that was. Heck, he could shoot both Sandra and Grant and be done with it. There'd be no repercussions if the devil wasn't real, except maybe prison.

If Marlin got a whip-smart lawyer, maybe he'd get away with it. The legal beagle could argue something about high passions or temporary insanity. Marlin's smile returned, but it was short-lived.

He wasn't willing to risk the chance of eternal damnation on a shifty lawyer. Especially since murdering one's wife had to be at the top of the sin list.

Although… Sandra committed adultery and that was considered a sin, too. Would her sin cancel his? Marlin always heard two wrongs don't make a right which probably meant no.

Sandra snorted once and mumbled, "It's a turtle." She kicked backward, and her heel hit Marlin's ankle. He didn't shake her or tell her to stop dreaming. He wanted to be alone with his thoughts.

Maybe he could use the gun and not kill anyone. Marlin was pretty sure threatening someone wasn't a sin. There was a whole slew of bad behavior the Ten Commandants ignored. Threatening could be a good option.

Maybe he'd just show the gun to Grant Ferguson. Flash the revolver and say something intimidating, like "Keep your dirty hands off my wife." Let the guy think Marlin was dangerous and that he should stay away from Sandra.

What if Grant didn't get scared easily? Marlin could shoot him in the leg. There wasn't a commandment against that, either. It was another one of those conflicts Marlin didn't understand. He could beat and intimidate a man and still get into the kingdom of heaven, but he couldn't steal. How was that fair? He didn't care since he wasn't interested in stealing.

Marlin felt lighter when he decided he could use the gun and not go to hell for it. Now he just had to figure out what that meant.

Sleep eluded Marlin for another hour.

***

In the morning, Marlin woke before the alarm clock. He buzzed with anticipation which wasn't good. He took a cold shower to calm himself. When the shivering didn't dispel his eagerness, he switched to hot water. That didn't help either.

Marlin needed to control his excitement, or he was likely to make a mistake. He closed his eyes and masturbated to memories of a porn movie he'd watched last month. Since Sandra rarely touched him anymore, Marlin had resorted to viewing free amateur pornography. It wasn't a particularly vulgar movie, just a couple claiming to be married and having sex in the woods.

Soon, images of a naked and sweaty Sandra underneath Grant Ferguson overtook the movie playing in Marlin's head. It didn't stop him, though. Instead, Marlin imagined walking in on them with the revolver clutched in his fist and how they'd cower before him, especially Sandra. He finished quickly after that.

Marlin fastened his robe around him before he left the bathroom.

Sandra sat upright in bed with the covers once again pulled to her armpits. The morning news show was on the television and the anchor bleated about a Hollywood starlet's recent drug problems.

"Didn't cut yourself this morning," Sandra said.

"Not today."

Marlin pulled his summer uniform from the closet and draped it over the chair. The news program went to a commercial, and Sandra muted it.

She said, "You were going to tell me a joke last night."

He glanced over his shoulder. "I was?"

"Something Harbinger told you."

"Harjinder," Marlin said. "Right."

In a moment of quiet guilt, Marlin tried to make nice with Sandra last night. He'd mentioned the joke his friend had shared. Sandra said she was too tired for it and played on her phone until she went to sleep.

"Tell me," she said, "before the commercials are over."

"All right." Marlin turned around and shoved his hands into the pockets of his robe. "A mother and daughter are talking over coffee. The daughter says, 'I'm dating someone new.'"

Sandra lifted an eyebrow but kept her attention on the television.

"The mother asks, 'Who?' and the daughter says, 'Bob the mailman.'"

"Doesn't Harbinger know any non-mailman jokes?"

"This is a good one," Marlin said.

Sandra waggled the remote at the screen. "Fine. 'Bob the mailman,' said the daughter."

"The mother gasps. 'He could be your father,' she says."

"He's old, is what you're saying."

"Just listen."

"I am." Sandra's eyes cut to Marlin. "Hurry up, will ya? They're back from commercial. How's the rest of it go?"

"So the daughter says, 'Mom, age is just a number,' to which the mother says, 'No, sweetheart, I don't think you understand.'" Marlin grinned as he waited for the punch line to sink in.

Sandra stared quietly at the TV. In a moment, her brow furrowed. "That's it?"

Marlin stared at her with an expectant smile.

"I don't get it," she said.

"Probably because you interrupted."

Sandra's face darkened. "Maybe it's because you told it wrong." She turned the television's sound on before Marlin could respond.

He turned to the closet and dropped his robe. "Yeah," he muttered, "I probably told it wrong."

***

Marlin drove to the edge of downtown and pulled into the nearly empty parking lot of an office building. He removed his phone and called his supervisor. He set his hand on an empty cardboard box he'd grabbed from his garage. Marlin drummed his fingers on the address label while the phone rang.

The call was answered after the fourth ring. "Rueben Molina."

"It's Marlin. I'm not feeling well this morning."

Rueben sighed. "Come on, Fish. I need more than thirty minutes' notice."

"I'm serious," Marlin lied. "I was barfing my guts out all morning."

"Is this what you were dealing with yesterday afternoon?"

"I think so."

His supervisor tsked. "What is it? The flu?"

"Food poisoning," Marlin said, "but I think the worst of it's over."

"You better not be faking so you can go golfing."

Marlin frowned. "When have I ever gone golfing?"

"I'm teasing."

"Maybe I should contact my union rep, let them know how you're jerking me around when I'm legitimately sick."

"Relax, Fish," Reuben said. "Geez. You need a day off, you got it. A little more notice next time would be nice, but you know I've got your back."

"I don't need a day off. Just an hour or two until I feel better."

"Why didn't you say so? That's easy." Reuben chuckled. "I'll have Harjinder get your route ready. Feel better soon."

"Count on it," Marlin said.

***

Grant Ferguson lived in a two-story McMansion on the Five Mile Prairie, about twenty minutes north of

Downtown Spokane. Automatic sprinklers watered the manicured lawn.

Marlin parked his car down the block from Grant's home. He rolled his window down slightly, then turned off the engine. He never worked this route during his career. It wasn't because he didn't want to; it was just how the cards were dealt. A guy could spend his entire career working in Spokane County and never cover all the routes.

Grant drove a red Tesla. Marlin found that out when he followed the man. The car was always parked in the garage, likely so it could be charged. Stupid electric vehicles, Marlin thought. It meant Marlin had no way of knowing Grant was home unless he went up to the house and rang the doorbell.

Mailboxes stood in clusters along the street, not next to the front door like most of the houses on Marlin's beat. That meant the carrier covering this route would remain with their vehicle whenever they came through the neighborhood.

The block was quiet. Likely most of the adults had gone to work, but there was certain to be one or two spouses who stayed at home like Sandra. That left Marlin to wonder about the absence of kids.

He knew one thing for certain: children no longer played outside like they once did. At the beginning of his career, kids were always running about when Marlin walked his routes regardless of the weather. Now he was lucky if he saw one on a nice day. No doubt video games and other bits of technology captured their attention and kept them indoors.

He reached under his seat and removed the gun. The weight felt good in his hand, but holding it made him feel guilty. He lifted his head and his gaze darted about the neighborhood.

The automatic sprinkles at Grant Ferguson's house continued to whir.

"You can do this," Marlin said to his reflection in the rearview mirror. "You're not going to hurt the guy. You're just going to scare him."

He cupped the gun like he was holding a wounded bird and studied it. Maybe he should remove the bullets, just to be sure he didn't accidentally shoot the guy.

Marlin opened the cylinder and reached for the first round. He stopped before pulling it out.

What if Marlin needed to fire a round but didn't have any? He did a fair amount of research on Grant Ferguson, but there was no way to tell if the guy had any martial arts training. Maybe Grant was a gun enthusiast and would greet Marlin at the door with a revolver of his own.

"This is a bad idea," Marlin muttered. His eyes lifted to the rearview mirror. "Right?"

His father's admonition came to him then. "If you wanna be a ditchdigger, be the best damn ditchdigger there is."

A husband, a good one, would stand up for himself, even if he was supposed to suffer in silence. He wouldn't let another man covet his wife. Hell, Grant Ferguson was doing a hell of a lot more than desiring Sandra. The guy was downright screwing her.

Marlin gripped the revolver's handle and felt powerful. He felt strong.

He slipped the gun into his pocket, climbed out of his car, and slipped on his postal baseball cap. Marlin hadn't changed out of his uniform, figuring it was better for any potential witnesses to see a mail carrier in their neighborhood than a random stranger. He grabbed the empty box from the passenger seat and tucked it under his arm.

Marlin walked too fast. Much quicker than a mail carrier would usually go. "Nice and slow," he said under his breath. "He'll either be there or he won't." He slowed his gait.

The sprinklers sprayed the pathway up to Grant's house and cold water splashed against Marlin's legs. He'd been sprayed by plenty of sprinklers over the years. His bigger concern was the possibility of a camera mounted above the doorbell. They seemed to be the rage with technophiles. Based on Grant's choice of vehicles, Marlin was certain there'd be one.

He kept his head down as he climbed the stairs, limiting what a possible lens could see. His heart pounded in his chest and blood rushed in his ears. Marlin felt light-headed. He should just turn around and go back to his car.

It still wasn't too late. Marlin could leave now and go to work. He could pretend he found the gun on the next pull from the collection boxes. Everything would return to how it was.

He lifted his head slightly and searched for a camera. There wasn't one. Why? Marlin wondered. Perhaps Grant wouldn't want his philandering caught on camera, yet his comings and goings would be normal. It was his house. Sandra's visits were the ones out of place.

The front door suddenly opened, and Grant Ferguson stood there with a questioning look. "Yes?"

Marlin couldn't do anything but stare at the man who'd been sleeping with his wife. Grant was taller than expected and his hair wasn't thinning like Marlin's. The man's smile was disarming. Was that what Sandra initially found charming?

"Is that for me?" Grant lifted his chin toward the box under Marlin's arm.

"Right." He held it out.

Grant accepted it and studied the address on top. His eyes widened when he read the addressee: Sandra Hattenburg. When Grant looked up, he noticed the revolver in Marlin's hand. "Hold on, now."

"Inside," Marlin said and waggled the gun. It was too late to turn back now.

Grant shuffled backward. "You must be Marlin," he whispered.

"Nice of you to know my name." Marlin shut the door behind him.

The living room was tastefully decorated. Expensive furniture, colorful art, and a wall of bookshelves. Marlin wondered when Grant had time to read.

"Listen," Grant whispered. "I'll end it today. Right now."

"Just like that?"

Grant nodded. "Just like that. I'm serious."

Marlin smiled. This was working out better than he'd planned.

"Grant?" An attractive woman Marlin had never seen stepped around the corner. She was several years younger than Sandra but had the same style haircut. The woman's hair was mussed, and her white shorts were unbuttoned. Her red T-shirt hung partially untucked. The woman's feet were bare, and a wedding ring adorned her left hand. Her eyes snapped to the gun in Marlin's hand. "What the hell?"

"I'm handling it, Ann," Grant said. His eyes remained on Marlin. "Right? We're handling it?"

"Did my husband send him?" Ann asked. Anger flared in her eyes.

"He's screwing my wife," Marlin said.

"Your wife?" Ann's gaze shifted to Grant. "You said we were exclusive."

"You're married," Grant said.

She threw her hands in the air. "You said you were okay with that."

"Enough," Marlin interrupted. He lifted the gun higher, pointing it directly at Grant's face. "Never again, okay?"

"You bet," Grant said. "It's done."

Ann slapped her hands together. "That's it. I'm so done with this situation." She stepped backward. "I'm calling the cops."

"No," Marlin and Grant said together.

"You don't get to tell me what to do," Ann said to Grant. Blossoms of red appeared on her cheeks. "Besides, it's not like he's going to shoot you now." She flicked her hand toward Marlin. "I'm a witness."

She took another step toward the corner and Marlin fired the gun. Ann crumbled to the ground.

Grant pulled the empty cardboard box tight to his chest. Fear flooded his eyes. "Why'd you do that?"

"There was no turning back," Marlin said. He fired the gun a second time.

***

Marlin carried the cardboard box away from his body as he walked back to the car. Some of Grant's blood had gotten on the top of it. Not much, but enough that Marlin didn't want to get it on himself. He forced himself to walk slowly with his head down.

He drove out of the neighborhood, keeping his speed to several miles under the posted limit. Marlin stopped in a gas station parking lot and tore the cardboard box into smaller pieces, careful not to touch any of the bloody parts. He didn't worry about ripping the address label off the box.

Marlin next wiped the gun with the toilet paper he'd wrapped it in yesterday. When he was satisfied no fingerprints survived, he wrapped the gun in toilet paper once more and put it in the coffee holder.

As he headed south, Marlin drove through various neighborhoods, tossing an occasional piece of cardboard box out the window. It took him a few minutes, but he got rid of the entire box by the time he neared the Monroe Street Bridge.

He thought about tossing the revolver into the river, but that would mean he'd have to leave his car. Anyone traveling over the bridge would see him, which would certainly lead to questions or someone remembering a guy throwing something into the water.

Marlin continued through downtown, taking the occasional left and right until he reached a semi-secluded spot underneath the freeway overpass.

He pulled to the curb and checked his various mirrors. He didn't see anyone walking in the area. Marlin grabbed the gun and its toilet-paper wrapping and threw it toward a cluster of low-lying shrubs. He misjudged the throw, and the gun bounced once before flopping onto the dirt. A portion of the toilet paper had come unwound and flapped in the breeze.

The gun would be easily found. Marlin glanced around again. He should get out and throw it deeper into the shrubs, but someone might see him.

What if the gun was found? Would that be so bad? Maybe the next person would use it to commit a crime and they'd get blamed for Grant Ferguson's murder. What about the woman he was with—Ann? Did she have children? Had Marlin just taken a mother away from her family?

Hell didn't feel like a figment of imagination now. He was sure it was real, and he was going.

Marlin slipped the transmission into Drive and slowly left the neighborhood.

***

Sandra was in the kitchen when Marlin returned home from work. He spent the entire day worried the cops were going to show up and whisk him to jail. During moments of rational thinking, he realized the cops would look to Ann's husband as the primary suspect.

Was it too much to hope the guy didn't have a good alibi?

Sandra looked up from the broccoli she was chopping. "How was work?"

"Fine," he said.

"You look more tired than usual."

"Didn't sleep well." Marlin stopped at the edge of the kitchen. "What're you making?"

"Chicken and vegetables. Nothing fancy."

"Do anything today?" he asked.

She shrugged. "Hung around the house. Did some cleaning."

Marlin eyed the living room. It did appear cleaner than he'd seen it in a while. His gaze swept back to Sandra. She didn't seem broken up. Perhaps she didn't know about Grant yet. Maybe she tried to call him, and he didn't answer.

If that was true, the cops were certain to call her and ask what she knew about Marlin.

"Get any jokes from Harbinger today?" Sandra asked.

"Harjinder."

She waved the cutting knife. "You know who I mean."

Marlin hadn't because he barely spoke to anyone today. His mind had been plagued by thoughts of hell. However, if the cops were going to contact Sandra with questions, he would have to make her think his day was normal.

"Harjinder has a lot of jokes about undelivered letters, but people don't get them."

Sandra cut another clump of broccoli, then looked up. "So he didn't tell you one today?"

"That's the joke," Marlin said.

"I don't get it."

"It's okay."

"Maybe you told it wrong."

"Yeah," Marlin said. "Maybe I told it wrong."

Leave The Gun…

Libby Fischer Hellmann

My first thought after I found the gun was the line from *The Godfather* after Clemenza and his crew killed Paulie: "Leave the gun, take the cannoli."

At the time Tony had said Clemenza was wrong. "How does he know there aren't any prints on the gun? Chances are good there were, you know? Even if someone filed off the serial number, there could be fingerprints on the barrel. And if the serial number is still there… well… it's way too risky. A hell of a lot smarter to take the gun and leave the cannoli. Right, sweetheart?"

I nodded. "Sounds right to me, babe." I didn't know the first thing about guns, and I didn't want to. Tony knew them well—he was the son of a mobster. I got nervous around them. What if the safety wasn't really on when he said it was? What if it dropped on the floor? Could it discharge accidentally? I shivered just thinking about it.

"On second thought," Tony raised his finger and pointed. "I'd take both the gun and the cannoli." Tony did have a sweet tooth. And he loved the subtle scent of rum that a real Italian bakery added to the cannoli filling. He even liked the pink tissue paper they wrapped them in before they slipped them into those little white bags.

Now, I had Lewis pull up to the International Coffee and Bakery, the only place in Spokane that sold the cannoli Tony loved. I asked Lewis to pick me up in twenty minutes and went inside.

The International sold the best pastries and sandwiches in town but wasn't at all pretentious. A few tables and chairs were grouped around a counter behind which you could watch them prepare the food. What made it special was a black leather couch and chairs in a corner that offered customers a place to "gather." There was also a small area with toys for the kids.

We discovered it, ironically, the day they diagnosed Tony's cancer in the medical building nearby. For the next two years we ordered cannoli whenever he was feeling up to it. Or took them home when he wasn't.

Mary Ellen, a redhead with a bright smile, was working the morning shift. "Good morning, Mrs. P. How's life treating you?"

I smiled back. "Not bad. You have any cannoli?"

Her smile turned conspiratorial. "Of course. Sit. I'll get them. The usual?"

I nodded and took a seat at a table in the back.

A moment later I was sipping a rich hot Arabica and digging into a cool cannoli. I sighed with contentment. Whoever said Spokane couldn't compete with the most sophisticated cities in the country clearly didn't know their coffee from their cannoli. I leaned back and slid both hands along the underside of the tabletop, a silly habit I'd picked up as a child.

I stopped abruptly. Something was stuck to the underside of the table. Something bulky. Wrapped in plastic. Wide strips of tape adhered it to the table. Duct tape? I felt around gingerly. What was it? I bent over as if to pick up my bag and snuck a peek. Something dark and metallic. My pulse sped up.

I picked up my canvas satchel, a roomy bag that doubled as my purse, and lifted it onto my lap. Then I picked at the end of one strip of tape with my fingernails.

It took a few minutes, but eventually I pried it off the table. I pried off a second strip of tape. Then a third. I glanced over at Mary Ellen. Her back was to me. I gazed around the café. Only one other customer. A sixty-something man who, when our eyes met, rose from his chair, hurried to the door, and walked out. I didn't know him. Probably just a "rando" as the kids today called them.

Finally, after pulling the fourth strip of tape, the package came loose. I dropped it into my bag and finished my coffee. I rose, went to the counter, and asked Mary Ellen to wrap two more cannoli. Then I made my way to the ladies' room. Inside a stall, I unwrapped my find.

It was a gun. Black. Small. Stubby. There was a name for it. Something "nose?" Yes. Snub nose. But how—and more important, why—was it taped to the underside of a table? I picked it up. It fit comfortably in my hand. A gun this small wasn't that intimidating. I could handle it if I had to. Still, I rewrapped it and shoved it into my bag. I had no need for a gun. I would get rid of it.

I paid for the cannoli and pushed through to the street. Lewis was waiting. He opened the car door, and I slid into the back. "We heading to the auction house now, ma'am?"

The Gold Rush, one of the only auction houses in Spokane, would be featuring a small Manet I had a hankering for. But I couldn't go now. The security check would pick up the gun. "You know, Lewis, I'm not feeling well. Let's just go home."

Lewis looked at me through the rear view. "Is there anything I can do, Mrs. P? Do you want me to call the doctor?"

I deflected the question and waved my fingers. "I'll be all right. I should know not to drink coffee on an empty stomach. Let's just go home." I settled in the back seat wondering where to unload the gun. I thought back to Tony. Maybe he'd had the right idea. Why choose between a cannoli and a gun when you could take both?

***

"Mrs. P" was short for Angie Williams Petrocelli, although that wasn't my birth name. Tony and I had moved to Spokane over twenty years ago, long enough to be considered locals. We bought a lovely house in the affluent Manito-Cannon neighborhood near Gaiser Conservatory, but we weren't the rich, flashy types. We tried to blend in and keep a low profile. Over the years I'd developed a discerning eye for fine art, jewelry, and other *objets d'art* and was known as someone who could reliably appraise almost anything. But I never charged anyone and was quick to say I was an amateur.

Concealing my actual *bonafides* wasn't easy. I'd majored in art history at Bryn Mawr and graduated near the top of my class. Afterwards I snagged an internship at Philadelphia's Museum of Art. Yes, the same steps Rocky climbed up in the movie. Two years after that I was offered a job with Nicholas Sheffield in New York. Nick was probably the foremost appraiser in the country. Over the next five years he helped me sharpen my ability to identify and appraise artwork and collectibles. When Nick died suddenly, the result of a motorcycle crash near his beach house on Montauk, he left me his business. Now people from all over the country—no¬, the world— trusted me with their valuables. I was making it.

Nick also taught me how to spot forgeries, a critical part of appraisals. Fake paintings are fairly easy to detect when you know what to look for. The age, weight, and quality of the canvas, the painter's brush strokes, the ink, the aging process. Even the painter's signature. Vermeer, Da Vinci, Botticelli, Chagall—their work has all been successfully forged. Helped along, of course, by various mysterious "fables" designed to enhance the appeal of the fake. The same holds true with jewelry and other valuables, although counterfeiting those required a different set of skills.

Which was how I met Tony. He'd walked into the shop in the West Village one rainy gray November afternoon with an umbrella in one hand and a box under his other arm.

"I'm Luke Caruso," he said. He was dark and well built, but it was those magnetic Al Pacino eyes that drew me to him right away. "You're the best appraiser in New York, and I want you to look at this necklace. I was told it was commissioned by Marie Antoinette before the French Revolution. Unfortunately, she was beheaded before it was finished."

At first, I thought he was going to make a pass at me. Many men did. I've been told I'm a "looker," with blond hair, green eyes, and a toned body. If that was it, though, he'd chosen the wrong collectible to lie about. I planted my hands on my hips. "The Affair of the Diamond Necklace, I presume?"

His cheeks grew crimson. "You know it."

"Any appraiser with half a brain knows about it." I shot him my best patronizing look. "And I suppose you just happen to have the real thing in that box." Despite those dreamy eyes, I was ready to throw him out of the shop.

He had the decency to take my comments without reply. But his enthusiasm clearly dimmed, and he seemed unsure what to say. This Caruso guy was either a rube or a con. In either case not someone with whom I wanted to deal.

"Check it out online," I said. "It's a convoluted story, but the bottom line is that poor Marie Antoinette, the Queen of France, was framed. By a con woman who strengthened the public perception of the Queen as a frivolous, extravagant spendthrift. The Queen's reputation never recovered. It was one of the triggers for the French Revolution and one of the reasons she was beheaded. And just so you know, the necklace was torn apart and the diamonds were sold off ... by the con woman. Of course, there are always rumors that the necklace somehow survived intact and was discovered in an attic, or behind a wall, or some such nonsense."

"Let me ask you something. If that was true, what would it be worth today?"

"Probably over fifty or sixty million, but—"

"May I show you what's in the box?"

I folded my arms. "Are you crazy? Who do you think I am? Leave now, Mister Caruso. And don't come back."

"What if I told you I'd been offered twenty million for it?"

"I am not a fence. Especially for counterfeit goods. Get the hell out of here."

He shrugged. "Well, I'll leave you my card. You never know." He smiled cheerfully and left the shop, his good mood surprisingly restored.

I was just short of rage, and it took me a while to calm down. The nerve! The chutzpah! To take me for a fence who dealt in forged collectibles. I crumpled the business card and threw it in the trash. Then I reconsidered. He was right about one thing. You never knew. I fished it out.

***

Two months after the holidays the registered letter arrived from Doyle & Phillips, a blue-stocking IP law firm on Park Avenue. The letter threatened prompt action unless Sheffield's made restitution of three million dollars to Mr. Conrad Fitzgerald for a forged Monet. Shock washed over me. Restitution? A forged Monet? Three million? I promptly called George Brinkley, the lawyer Nick had used for years. I still used him, but there hadn't been much for him to do since I took over. He told me to mail him a copy of the letter.

"I'll do more than that. I'm on my way over."

"Wait—I'm…"

I hung up, jumped in a cab, and was seated in his office in the Diamond District twelve minutes later. I handed him the letter. "What's this all about, George?"

George, a sixtyish man on the verge of retirement with a beautiful shock of white hair, read the letter. Twice. Then he sighed, picked up matches, and lit his pipe. He puffed a few times. My irritation grew. He was stalling.

"George?"

He exhaled.

I waved away the smoke. "Why do I get the feeling you're not surprised?"

"Because this happened before. About ten years ago. Nick swore not to do it again, but, well, you know Nick."

"So he found a fake Monet and sold it to this—this Fitzgerald for three million?" I'd believed Nick was scrupulously honest. Sure, he had an eye for the finer things in life, but I never thought he would stoop to a criminal act for them.

"Carol, where do you think the money came from for his motorcycle? Or the beach house?"

I was speechless. My world was spinning.

"We were able to resolve the situation with a few loans and a *nolo contendere* plea. Probation. And community service. I never thought—"

I finished for him. "But he did it again, and since I inherited Sheffield's, I'm liable."

He was quiet. "There is some good news."

"What's that?"

"By the time Nick's estate settles, there should be about a million left over."

"Great. So I only owe this guy two million, not three."

"I'm afraid so."

The bleakest part of a New York winter happens when snow has been shoveled to the curbs, where it turns dirty, gray, and crusty. That summed up my mood for the next few weeks. I had no idea how I was going to pay Fitzgerald. Believe it or not, although we deal in large amounts, my remuneration wasn't much more than a junior executive's. My savings were sparse, and my family back in Iowa had no money. I would need to file for bankruptcy, close the shop, and slink back home as a failure.

I grew desperate. I couldn't sleep. I lost my appetite and my confidence. I don't recall exactly when Tony and the necklace came into my thoughts. It might have been a dream, but the next day I was thinking about him. He claimed to have been offered twenty million for it. He'd probably exaggerated, but even if it was only worth ten, it would solve my problem. If he hadn't sold it to someone else. And if I was willing to break the law. I struggled with the ethics, but in the end, I had no choice. Nick had counterfeited artwork twice, and, for a while, it had worked. I went to my rolodex and thumbed to the "C's."

I met Tony an hour later at an Italian café in the Village. The seductive aroma of coffee brewing is almost better than the taste. I noticed the same box he'd brought the first time was under his arm. "I'm glad you called, Carol. It's lovely to see you again."

I had no hubris left. "I'm in a desperate place."

"If I recall, the last time we spoke you threw me out of your shop and told me not to come back."

I'd lost the nerve I'd summoned up when I called him. "I know. For some reason, though, I think you might give me some advice."

"I might." He smiled wryly. "Give it your best shot."

I explained the situation over coffee and cannoli. When I finished, he gestured to my plate. "So, what do you think?"

I frowned, confused. "About what?"

"The cannoli, of course."

"They're delicious. They don't have these in Iowa."

"Best pastry in the world. My grandmother made them from scratch. Took her all day to get the crust just right. But the filling is a family secret. If you forced me to tell you, I'd have to kill you."

I must have looked horrified because he added, "I'm kidding."

I gave him a wan smile. "So, what about my— situation?"

"It's a damn shame you're bearing the brunt of this. You did nothing wrong. Makes you think twice about the kind of man Sheffield was."

"You don't say."

He shifted. "As it happens, I might be able to help. But it will require some advance work." He paused. "And afterwards you'll have to close your shop, change your name, and relocate. Your own private WITSEC."

"WITSEC?"

"Witness Protection Program."

"Really? Must I?"

"Unless you'd prefer to spend a lot of years in a ten-foot cell," he said. "Hey. Look on the bright side. You'll have plenty to settle your debt. And then some." He leaned in. "And if you invest carefully, you'll have enough for the rest of your life. You could buy almost any piece of art you want. But your days of being an appraiser are over."

I sighed. "That's gonna happen no matter what I do."

***

Back at the shop, Tony carefully removed the necklace from its box and laid it on top of a velvet cushion on the counter. I gasped. The sketches didn't do it justice. It was stunning. At the neckline were three loops of diamonds and pearls with graceful pendants in each, and a larger one in the center. Beside the loops was a strand that looked like a braided diamond ribbon, which crossed at the center with tails and more pendants. To finish it off was another braid of diamonds, again with tails and pendants. Altogether it was said to have included 647 diamonds and weighed 2,840 carats, which was almost a pound and a half.

"Who made this?" I asked. "And when?"

"I don't know the answers, and if I did, I wouldn't tell you," he said. "But it's mine now. I've been working on the provenance story that goes with it."

I looked up. "That's easy. There are rumors that Marie Antoinette did indeed have the necklace and tried to get it out of France when she and Louis XVI fled during the Revolution. They didn't succeed, though. You just need to decide where they hid it."

"That's where I was headed." Tony smiled. "But if you look carefully, some of the diamonds are missing. It needs repair work. And cleaning. I was hoping you could do that. I have someone who's willing to fence it, so we're looking at a three-way split."

"Are any of the stones genuine?"

"A lot are. They're a mix of lab diamonds, cheap industrials, even a couple of flawed blood diamonds, I'm told."

"Then, how can you—I mean—why don't you sell it as a replica? There's a lot of that going on these days."

"Passing it off as the real thing is ten times the value."

"Yes, but replicas are legal."

"Carol—by the way, I hope you're thinking of a new name—let me say this kindly. Legal won't pay off your debts. But don't worry. I'll handle the upfront costs."

I let out a breath. "I don't get it. Why are you doing this for me? I hardly know you, or you me. We've never worked together, and yet you're willing to give me a third of the proceeds?"

He paused. "Let's just say I see this as a long-term investment." He boxed up the necklace. "I'm not getting any younger. And you have impeccable credentials. If you vouch for something, people listen."

I tipped my head to the side. "I'm still confused. You don't need me. You obviously know your way around this business. Maybe better than I."

"Don't sell yourself short. Your appraisal will add a few million to the price."

***

The next two weeks were a flurry of activity. We scoured the diamond district for cheap stones to replace the missing ones. Once they were set, I carefully cleaned and polished the necklace. Even though it was a fake, it glittered like sea diamonds, those tiny sparks on top of the waves that catch the sunlight. We researched and wrote a bogus provenance, which claimed the Queen gave the necklace to her favorite kitchen-maid when they fled, and it had been found under a floorboard in an old house near the Palace of Versailles.

Two evenings later we printed out the provenance then stopped for a pizza at Carlito's. We both drank too much wine and laughed a lot. Tony had a manner that wasn't overbearing or pompous, and I found myself attracted to him again. Afterwards he walked me home. I opened the door, wondering if I should invite him in.

"Aren't you going to invite me in?" A shy smile came over him.

"I was thinking of doing just that." He followed me in and closed the door. Then he took me in his arms and kissed me. It was a kiss neither of us wanted to end. So we didn't. We made our way to my bedroom where one thing led to another. It was the best sex I'd ever had. Afterwards, I lightly traced my fingers across his chest.

"I'm spelling out my new name."

He was quiet while I proceeded. Then, "I can't tell what it is, but it sure feels good."

"Angie."

"Nice. Last name?"

"Not sure yet. What about you?"

"Tony. I've always wanted to be a Tony."

"Last name?"

"Petrocelli."

"That's good."

"Hey, I have an idea." He gathered me into his arms. "Why don't you be Mrs. Petrocelli?"

I pushed myself against him. "Mr. and Mrs. Tony Petrocelli?"

"I knew you were the one from the minute I saw you."

"Even though I kicked you out of the shop?"

"It made me want you more. You were a challenge." He rolled over on top of me, and we made love again. I gave myself up to him. If Tony and I were together, I could handle anything.

***

George Brinkley said Harold Manstoff, the fence, lived quietly in Queens and operated out of an office supply company. When he wasn't fencing jewelry and art, he trafficked in small arms. We drove out, but Tony did the negotiating. I stayed in the car and never met the man. All I know is that by Christmas, we were rich, and my debt was paid. Tony changed his name from Luke to Tony. I became Angie. We bought a BMW, I dyed my hair brown, and we headed to Spokane just after the new year. We spent twenty glorious years together until he passed two years ago.

***

Now, I debated whether to dispose of the gun or keep it. Despite the occasional counterfeit or heist, the art world I came from wasn't particularly violent. An air of civility prevailed. But the world in general had become a more violent, unpredictable place, even in Spokane, so I decided to hang on to the revolver, at least for a while. I think Tony would have approved. Before I stashed it in the top drawer of my bedside table, I went online to figure out how to load, aim, and shoot. The gun turned out to be loaded. With two additional bullets. All I had to do was point and shoot. I never would, of course, but I felt empowered.

***

The first inkling that someone was following me came about two weeks after I found the gun. Lewis was driving me to the hair salon when he said, "Mrs. P., I don't want to alarm you, but the same car has been behind us ever since we left Manito."

"What kind of car is it?"

"Looks like an Acura sedan. Silver."

I shrugged. "That's a pretty common car, isn't it?"

"True," Lewis said.

"Maybe it's someone who just moved in. I spotted a moving van the other day."

"Just wanted you to know." Lewis had been with us over a decade. I'm sure he suspected something was "different" about us, but he never said anything.

That evening I walked over to a private auction at my neighbor's home. She was using an auctioneer from the Gold Rush whom I'd seen many times. We exchanged nods. About twenty or so people were gathered. The featured item was a tiny Van Dyke, the famous Flemish painter who was the court painter in England during the Baroque era. But there were other collectibles for sale. The auctioneer would start with them.

I retrieved a glass of chardonnay and a few canapés and walked over to a group of women with whom I socialized, more so now that Tony was gone. They were chatting about a new man in town.

"He looks very distinguished. Mustache, neatly trimmed. Gray streaks in his hair," Adele said.

"Speaking of trim, he is that also," Meredith giggled.

"I invited him to the auction tonight," Janice, our hostess, said "He promised to come." She looked around. "But don't all of you corner him at once, ladies." More laughs.

"Another refugee from California?" I asked. "What's his name?"

"I don't think he's from California," Meredith said. "He talks with a New York accent. His name is Simon Randall."

I didn't know the name, but my gut tightened. That happened anytime I ran across anyone from New York. I gulped my wine.

"He seems to know the art world," Janice cut in. "At least he spoke intelligently about Van Dyke."

Adele leaned forward. "There's a rumor he just got out of prison," she whispered. "Can you believe it?"

"No kidding." Meredith grinned. "A good-looking man, unattached, with a mysterious bad boy backstory. Could this night get any better?"

"There he is!" Adele said. "Janice, bring him over and introduce us."

Janice gave us side-eye. "Maybe I should auction *him* off. I could use a few extra bucks."

Everyone laughed. I wanted to go home.

Five minutes later Simon Randall was holding court and answering questions. He gazed at all of us, but it seemed his eyes lingered on me more than the others. I didn't pretend to think it was my beauty or sex appeal. I was almost sixty years old. Simon was good-looking, though, and he carried himself with grace. Was this the man Lewis said was following me? A man with a New York accent who may or may not have just been paroled from prison? I didn't like where this was heading.

"Why did you come to Spokane, Simon?" Adele asked.

"I was ready for a change. And I read that Spokane is one of the 100 most livable cities in the country. I'm a widower, and my kids are grown. Why not?" He glanced at me. "Are you ladies all native Spokanians?"

"We say Spokanites, Simon dear. All of us are locals except Angie." Meredith pointed her finger at me. "She's from Boston."

"An East Coaster," he said. "Where in Boston?"

"Brookline," I lied. Before we left New York, Tony found an identity theft "consultant" who created new histories for us, down to the hospitals we'd been born in. Passports, Social Security cards, even college diplomas. Still, tonight I felt naked.

Janice called us to the chairs she'd set up in the living room. The auction was about to begin. I headed to the powder room, then slipped out. I practically ran home. On the way I looked around for a silver Acura. There it was! Parked down the street. Simon Randall had been following me.

The next day an "unknown" call showed up on my cell. Twice. I stopped answering the phone. If the doorbell rang, I'd tell Vicky, my housekeeper, to say I wasn't home.

A week later I met Meredith at Vieux Carré, a delicious New Orleans restaurant for lunch. Adele, it turned out, had purchased the Van Dyke. After congratulating her, we discussed our mutual aches and pains and health fears like other almost-sixty-somethings. Then Adele cleared her throat. "We've all decided that Simon Randall has the hots for you, Angie. Did you notice how he kept looking at you at the auction?"

I shouldn't lie. "I did. But I couldn't figure out why."

"Don't be coy, dear. We all know when a man is interested in us," Meredith said. "After you left, Simon started asking us questions about you."

I tried to stay calm, but my pulse was pounding in my ears. "What kind of questions?"

"What you did. Where you did it? Did you have kids? Were you married? That kind of thing." Meredith finished her wine and ordered another. "Angie, Tony has been gone for two years. It's time."

"Not interested," I said. "I can't even imagine it."

"Well, if you don't want him, send him my way," Adele said.

"Sure, Addie."

Who was this man? Did he have anything to do with the necklace? After all these years had someone figured out it wasn't genuine? Was he really an ex-con? He could be a detective who'd tracked me down. Or an undercover spy. Even an art dealer.

When I got home, I did something I should have done long ago. I went online and Googled "Diamond Necklace Marie Antoinette." I gasped. A flood of "new" articles had materialized about ten years ago. My stomach clenched as I read.

A New York fence, Harold Manstoff, had been arrested in a high-end counterfeit operation. A phony diamond necklace had been sold to a member of the Spanish royal family. Six years after its purchase, they discovered it was a fake. The princess accused Manstoff of fraud. Manstoff claimed he'd only been the intermediary. He knew nothing about the necklace itself. He wasn't responsible.

The princess went to the FBI. They interrogated Manstoff. He refused to tell them where he'd acquired the necklace. They alternately bullied, threatened, and promised a lighter sentence, but he didn't budge. So the Feds charged him and tried to find the fabricators. But they hit a brick wall.

This was all news to me. Tony hadn't said a word about this "unraveling." He had to know. He was always online. I rarely was. Why didn't he say something? Was it because he didn't want me to worry? Who doesn't tell their partner about an event that could jeopardize both their lives? And why did Manstoff keep his mouth shut? Had he and Tony negotiated something to that effect? If so, what? Like a bouncing pinball, I rebounded between fear, anger, and curiosity.

A couple of photos online confirmed that Harold Manstoff was, in fact, Simon Randall. Younger, fewer wrinkles and less gray, but definitely him. He even had the mustache. Manstoff was sentenced to fifteen years and got out after eight. Which made it just about the time Tony died.

I didn't sleep that night. Or the next. I was on borrowed time. All he had to do was drop my new name to the FBI. The case was probably still open. What did they call them? Cold cases. Yes. But how had Manstoff tracked me down? What was his plan? It couldn't be good. Maybe he wanted to blackmail me. Or did he want me to experience the exquisite pleasure of prison, like he did?

I could call Tony's brother back east. He was still in the family "business" and could take care of something like this. Or... I leaned over to my bedside table, opened the drawer, and took out the snub nose. Maybe the fact that I found it when I did was a sign to deal with Simon myself. I raised the gun and pointed it at the wall. I imagined squeezing the trigger.

I couldn't do it. Fraud was one thing. Murder was something else. Not only was it morally repugnant, but it would probably get messy. Blood all over the carpets and floor. I'd have to dispose of his body. The gun, too. He was a big man. I was small. No way could I physically move him. And how would I get rid of the gun?

Twenty years had passed since we moved here. I'd figured we were safe. I even started getting blonde streaks in my hair again. Now, for the second time in my life, everything was on the line. Was the risk of exposure, arrest, and incarceration worth it? Even if Simon promised not to turn me in now, he could in the future. Which made Harold Manstoff, aka Simon Randall, an existential threat.

The next morning my cell chirped before nine. It was the same unknown number. I knew who it was.

"Good morning, Angie. I hope I didn't wake you. Simon Randall here."

"Hello, Simon."

"I'd like to meet with you today. Are you available?"

I swallowed. "Yes, of course. How about this afternoon? About two? Manito Park is beautiful this time of year. We can take a walk if you're up for it."

"Perfect."

"Good. Let's meet at the café on the other side of the woods."

"See you then."

***

The sun was warm, but the air was cool enough for a light jacket. A soft breeze scurried through the air. The only downside was the park landscaping crew, their mowers and leaf blowers whining at top volume. They showed up twice a week, usually around now. I tried to ignore the noise and walked briskly to the café.

Simon was already there, sipping something with steam rising from his cup. Probably a latte. "Angie. Thank you for meeting me. Can I buy you a drink?"

"Thank you, no. I just finished a cup of tea." I searched for something to say. "Isn't it a beautiful afternoon?" Lame.

"Certainly is." He smiled. "Summer is delightful here. Not too hot. Not too cold. Which way?"

I pointed to the woods behind us. "That way. Once we pass the sculpted gardens, there will be fewer people and, hopefully, less noise. Of course, I picked the absolute worst time for a walk. Sorry about the landscapers."

He shrugged.

We started walking. He matched my pace. I tried to calm my nerves with small talk. "How are you liking Spokane? Where are you living?"

"I love it so far. Such interesting people!" He paused. "I haven't decided where to live yet. I'm still downtown."

"That can get expensive." I bit my lip. When you have a third of twenty million dollars, who cares about your outlay?

"I suppose it could…" He broke off. We were quiet as we sauntered through one garden, skirted the other, and angled toward the woods.

"Beautiful," he said. "They do a fine job here."

"Yes, they do. My husband and I used to come here almost every day."

"I hear he passed a year or so ago. My condolences."

"Thank you. Two years next month, but who's counting?"

"You are," he said.

"I guess I am."

Simon was considerate, I thought. For a criminal. We were quiet as we reached the woods. I headed down a dirt path that was partially covered with leaves. Both of us spoke at the same time.

"Angie—"

"Simon—"

"Go on."

"No you go," I said.

"I need to confess something to you."

We kept walking.

"I know who you are, Carol."

I sucked in a breath. "And I know who you are, Harold." I slipped my hand into my jacket pocket.

"I figured you might. But that's only part of my confession."

I tightened my grip on the gun.

"I've spent the last year tracking you down."

"How did you find us?"

He waved away the question. "Not now. What's important is that when I located you, I flew out here to make sure it was you. I paid the price for the two of you. I was angry. Hell, I was furious. I was going to verify it was you, then tell the FBI where you were. When I got here, I found out your…husband was dead. And then I met you. After that I—I changed my mind."

"What do you mean? You hardly know me."

"I had a lot of time to look you up. Do my own due diligence. I ran the prison library and occasionally had online privileges."

"You've been spying on me?" I was shocked.

"I prefer to call it 'research.'" He brushed his mustache with his finger. "You're a classy lady. Smart. You know your stuff. And easy on the eyes."

I opened my mouth but nothing came out. What chutzpah! As if I was an object to be analyzed and priced. Once a fence…

"Look." He cut in. "We're both… well… you two had the right idea to come out here. It's a great lifestyle. I can see myself here. After I met you, even after only a few minutes, I knew. I don't want to turn you in. See—"

"Simon, or Harold, or whatever your name is, please stop." I took a quick glance around. Trees closed us off from the gardens, and no one was nearby. Just the drone of the landscapers and our footfalls on the path. "I'm sorry to disappoint you. But there's no way I'd allow you to have the power of life and death over me. Only one man did, and he's gone. How do I know you're not just feeding me BS, anyway? I'm not naïve. I don't relish waking up every morning wondering if this will be the day you betray me."

"I understand. Why don't we take it slow and see where things go? Pool our money. Maybe travel the world. You can trust me."

The final tip-offs. First, he wants to live in Spokane. Then he wants to travel the world. Capped off with *Pool our money* and *You can trust me*. He wanted to control the money. I'd learned by now that anyone claiming they could be trusted usually couldn't be. Tony would never say anything that dishonest. Now I was pissed. How dare he assume I would do his bidding? Or entertain the idea we could be together? Never.

"Simon, I'm afraid you wasted a plane ticket. Every time I think about you, my stomach roils. I don't need you, and I don't want you judging me for the rest of my life."

"But, Angie, don't you see? You really have no choice. We can make it pleasant, or—"

"Oh, but I do. Have a choice." Before I could change my mind, I pulled out the snub nose, aimed, and fired. He went down. I glanced back at the gardens. Had anyone heard the shot? The lawn mowers and leaf blowers were still droning.

I looked at Simon again. His windbreaker was growing red at the spot where his heart was. His eyes were open and glassy. I checked his pulse. Nothing. They'd find him today, maybe tomorrow. Time for me to go home.

An instant of rage can help a woman do wonders. I jogged home. I should have thanked him—he made it easy for me to do what was needed. Back home I removed the two remaining bullets. Then I put on gloves and wiped down the snub nose with Lysol. I slid it into a freezer bag and taped it up. I knew exactly what to do.

I dropped the bag into my canvas sack along with the tape and gloves and went downstairs. Lewis was in the kitchen, chatting with my housekeeper. I looked at my watch. "Lewis, could you drive me down to the International? I have a yen for a cannoli."

Do You See the Light?
James D.F. Hannah

John's behind the counter, sorting albums, when he clocks the kid slipping the forty-five into a backpack.

"Hey, you!" John says, his voice enough to cut through the Replacements song blasting from the speakers. The kid, a stringy-haired beanpole with a moon-landing complexion, jolts as though he's been hit with a cattle prod. He lets both the backpack and the record fall to the ground and races for the exit.

John, a lumbering dude who gets bored with his sneakers long before they wear out, is no speed match for the kid, who's already long gone before John even reaches the door.

Back inside the record store, John picks the backpack and the vinyl—a goddamn Taylor Swift single, of all things—off the floor, slots the single back into place among the rest for sale. He thinks how many times a week he catches someone trying to rip him off, and he tries not to think about how often the little fucks get away with it. The absolute shit he sees there, every day, it wears him out.

Then the guy in the clown costume walks in.

This clown goes behind the counter, oversized shoes honking with each step, helps himself to a beer from the mini-fridge underneath the register. Chugs it in long, thirsty gulps until the can is empty. A bead of sweat races from beneath the corkscrews of his tomato-red wig and cuts a path through patchy white grease paint coating his face.

John sets the backpack on the counter and gets his own beer from the refrigerator.

The clown's eyes are circled in black and riddled with thin red veins like trails on a map. Eyes saddled with sadness, and perhaps a small malevolence.

John drinks his beer and waits. He knows what's coming.

"Birthday party," Danny says. His tone's a soldier telling a story about war. "This little fuck tells me he wants a balloon dog. Changes it to a lion. Then a giraffe. Finally, he decides he doesn't like any of it, and he kicks me in the shins. I say something along the lines of if he doesn't calm his tits, I'll knock his tiny teeth down his throat. The parents get pissed, and I don't even make it back onto I-90 before the agency calls and fired my ass." He pulls the wig off, revealing a sweaty mound of dark hair streaked in white. "You oughta be able to hunt five-year-olds for sport."

John's heard this rant—or variations on it—before. They've known one another since childhood, when Danny had his own proclivities for shoplifting and other small-market crime. Then he left Spokane for five or six years, time he won't talk about now except to say he "worked for some Armenians."

Since he's come back, Danny's worked as a celebrity impersonator. He's barrel-shaped and built low to the ground, so he specializes in things like Fred Flintstone or late-era Elvis Presley. His Jake Blues from *The Blues Brothers* is legendary.

Mostly, however, he does clown work. Usually birthday parties, parents trying to share with their ill-begotten spawn what they incorrectly imagine is a cherished childhood memory—because people forget in the fuzzy time between childhood and becoming an adult that clowns are goddamn terrifying.

The thing is, Danny's got a nasty temper and hates almost anyone under the age of thirty, so he's also been fired by almost every entertainment agency in the 509. John's pretty sure today means it's every agency now.

This bad attitude keeps most of the world at arm's length from Danny. Everyone tells John he shouldn't hang out with him, but John can't bring himself to turn his back on his friend. Besides, John's own life is essentially the store, and he doesn't guess he has many friends to spare.

Danny jerks his chin toward the backpack and raises painted-on eyebrows as thick and dark as spring caterpillars. "What's that?"

"Caught someone trying to lift a forty-five," John says. "He bolted and left it behind."

Danny unzips the backpack and dumps the contents onto the counter. A cornucopia of minor-league shoplifting spills out: T-shirts with Goodwill tags, a dollar-store digital watch, syringes, condoms, a paperback book, loose pairs of boxers. Danny gives the bag one more good shake, and that's when the gun tumbles out on top of the underwear.

"Shit," John says.

Danny picks the gun up with hands still sheathed in white clown gloves. It's a small snub-nose revolver, with a two-inch barrel, matte black. He snaps the cylinder out and makes a low humming sound.

"Five shot with a round missing," he says. "Means they've probably used it. Today might have been your lucky day, Johnny boy."

John's face has the ashen pallor of a January morning. Like he sees the gun and then his own mortality.

"We should call the police," he says.

Danny brings the gun to his face and casually scratches his cheek with the front sight, scrapping off a streak of white greasepaint.

"Cops ain't gonna do shit. Just tell yourself now you got a free gun."

"What if the kid comes back for it?"

"What if he does? People don't argue with people with guns."

Danny helps himself to another beer. He's still carrying the pistol as he walks toward a door marked *Employees Only*. "Got anything new?"

John keeps unmarked stock in back. The room's stacked with boxes and loose collections of albums and singles, eight tracks and CDs and cassettes and random reel-to-reels.

He points to the stack of boxes closest to the door.

"Picked those up today. A place in the burbs."

Danny sets the gun on a workbench and pulls the lid off a box. He lets out an appreciative whistle.

"Pristine. Dust covers on everything. Nothing's faded, no busted corners. House look like money?"

"Looked like a house. Lady called me out of nowhere this morning and told me she was getting rid of her husband's collection. Said if I wanted it, to come and get it. I showed up and it looked like she was in the middle of a yard sale. Furniture was in the front yard. Clothes everywhere. She was basically giving shit away."

Danny slides an album out for closer inspection. "Five'll get you ten it all belonged to her ex and she got dumped and now she's unloading everything so she doesn't have to think about him banging his secretary on a beach somewhere."

Danny could be right, but John's not so sure. He's seen those scenarios, and this woman hadn't carried herself with a hyperactive need for vengeance. She'd felt distracted more than anything, her eyes staring into a distance well beyond what anyone else could see.

Distracted enough, she didn't notice the smell: a faint rotting stench wafting away from the house, carried by a warm summer breeze warning of rain.

A dead rat, caught in the walls, John had thought as he loaded box after box into the van. Or worse, a raccoon in the attic. A stink that would last for weeks.

Danny sets an album on a turntable. The needle kisses vinyl and a wail of slide guitar and the chug-a-chug of a harmonica explode like a runaway train down the tracks.

For the first time since he'd walked into the record store, the clown smiles.

Danny's a vinyl head, and vinyl heads specialize like it's a medical practice. Bootlegs or Irish punk or 12-inch imports of German techno or soundtracks to industrial musicals. Everyone has a thing.

Danny's thing is the blues. He and John have spent many a night here after hours, drinking and debating which artists were more obscure or who'd died more terribly. Blues performers had a tendency toward getting shot by jealous women.

John forgets about the pistol, the woman, everything else. He goes and gets two more beers.

The two men work through the collection, and the more they dig, the more interesting it becomes. Things shift from the usual labels and performers to unfamiliar and uncommon names. Some, even Danny doesn't know. Chicago and Piedmont and Delta and Texas and New Orleans, a geography of styles and sounds.

The storeroom is as windowless as a casino floor, and between this and the beer, they lose track of time. It's after midnight and they're down to the last box when John says, "You were awful casual about that gun."

Danny keeps looking through the records.

"This magician I knew, he had a trick called 'the magic bullet' that he taught me. Had an assistant who'd fire a gun at him, and he'd catch the bullet in his hand."

"What happened to him?"

"One show, he caught the wrong bullet."

Danny pauses. Eyes widen in reverential awe. He pulls free from this final box an album and holds it out toward John, his fingers ever so lightly holding onto the edges. He handles it with much more caution and care than he handled the gun.

The lettering on the cover reads *Steel Wheels at the Apollo*.

Jerry "Steel Wheels" Wheeler. A bluesman in the Fifties and Sixties. Unknown in America but an inspiration to every British guitar player who ever ripped off a Memphis or Chicago blues lick. His live shows had been legendary—raw and volcanic pools of barely constrained emotion, full of tales of misery and woe, of women who'd done him wrong and the injustices of the world. He did three-hour musical marathons while Springsteen was still learning guitar chords.

The rumor was, Wheeler had been set to play dates with The Rolling Stones back in 1972—their first tour since Altamont—when his bassist caught him sneaking out the bathroom window of the man's girlfriend's apartment. The bassist slit Wheeler's throat with a straight razor, which led to Stevie Wonder opening for The Rolling Stones instead.

"The only live album Wheeler did, and the company folded before it could run a full press order," Danny says. "I don't think more than a hundred copies even got made. This has got to be worth some money."

John pushes his chunky black glass frames up the bridge of his nose.

"A scratched copy with a torn cover went for mid-four figures last year," he said.

Danny cautiously slips his fingers into the cover. The corners of his mouth collapse.

"It's not there," he says. "The album's gone."

John sighs.

"Not surprised. People don't pay attention and stuff gets broken or lost. You see it all of the time."

Danny pulls his lips together tight, until they're nearly invisible.

"Not here, though. 'Cause this guy cared about this collection. Look how careful he was with it. He wouldn't have put the cover back empty." He taps at the cover. "I'll bet it's at the house. Sitting on the turntable of some expensive stereo system, and it's what he was listening to before he ran off, and the wife, she never bothered to check." A beat. "We could go. Go and get it."

"We can't ring her doorbell, middle of the night, and ask her for some album."

"Who said anything about asking for it?"

The cool detachment in Danny's voice catches John off-guard.

"Steal it?" John reaches for his phone. "We're done drinking. I'm gonna DoorDash us some cheeseburgers."

Danny grabs him at the wrist, squeezes enough to make John wince. To ensure he has John's attention.

"Hear me out," Danny says. "We drive there. She might not even be home. If she's not, we go in, grab the album, leave. She won't even know it's missing."

"And if she's home?"

"We go to Denny's and I'll buy."

John surprises himself by giving Danny's idea any consideration. He knows the album's worth five figures to the right person.

He could use the money. Rent's going up, and the collectible market's only getting tighter and tighter. He's not sure how much more he can cinch his belt.

He pulls himself free from Danny's grip, rubs his wrist.

"What do you do? Go bust a window?"

"Hell no. I'll pick the lock," Danny says.

"Where'd you learn to pick locks?"

"From the magician."

"Same one who was supposed to be able to catch bullets?"

***

They take Danny's car, a Ford Focus with mismatched doors and an oil leak, which is still better than John's ride, a panel van with the record store's name and logo plastered on both sides.

John drives, because he's more sober. A steady rain starts as they pull out of the parking lot, switching to a downpour on the interstate. The windshield wipers can barely keep up.

"What if she's home?" John says.

"What if she is?" Danny reaches into the front pocket of his polka-dot clown pants and brings out the snub-nose revolver. "This'll keep everything under control."

John's knuckles bleach white around the steering wheel.

"Why'd you bring that?"

"In case we need it."

"I'm not threatening this lady with a gun, Danny."

"A gun's not a threat, John. A gun's a promise. If the bitch is smart, she knows we pull the trigger, the gun's a vow. Like on her wedding day."

John wants to find a place where they can turn around, go back to the record store and tell themselves this was nothing but a bad idea left unfulfilled.

Problem is, with the gun resting in his lap, Danny doesn't seem interested in sobering up or thinking this through to another day.

John takes the next exit, and now they're in the burbs. Tree-lined sidewalks front emerald-green lawns and overpriced houses that all look vaguely similar to one another. John slows the car to a crawl, his eyes moving constantly from the phone to numbers on mailboxes blurred by the rain.

Danny rubs his hands across his twitching legs.

"Don't punk out on me now, John. This is our chance."

"Gimme a minute. Everything looks different in the dark, alright?"

He parks just before a short driveway that opens to a bright yellow house sitting beneath heavy shadows from nearby trees. It's a neighborhood where the world falls silent alongside the 11 o'clock news.

Danny reaches into the glove compartment and removes a small, zippered pouch.

There's no preamble. No pep talk. They get out of the car and rush up the driveway. Danny's barefoot, his clown shoes left behind in the car.

Halfway to the house, John considers there could be security cameras. They should be wearing masks. Of course, what's a mask matter when your accomplice is in a clown costume?

The warm rain soaks through their clothes. They go toward the rear of the house. A small backyard, most of it has been consumed with an in-ground pool and a concrete deck that's as shiny as an oil slick from the rain. There's a cover pulled loose over the long rectangular enclosure, rain and leaves and twigs gathered in the sagging center.

Under the shelter of the back porch, Danny takes tools from the pouch and goes to work on the door lock. A sliver of moonlight cuts through the clouds and lands on Danny, sweat and rain having streaked away portions of his makeup, making it look as though his face is melting.

John thinks about a quote he read, Lon Chaney or Boris Karloff or Stephen King, he can't remember who exactly: "Nobody likes a clown at midnight."

The lock clicks. Danny smiles. His teeth look as gray as tombstones in the moonlight.

"'Boom' goes the dynamite," he says.

The door opens into the kitchen, and they're greeted by the rank smell John knows from earlier in the day, but now it's in full force, an open-handed slap across the face.

Danny gags and buries his face into the crook of his arm.

"Fucking Christ. What died in here?"

John uses his phone as a flashlight, running the white beam ahead of them. The house is all but empty. No appliances on counters, no table in the kitchen. Nothing kitschy on the walls.

The living room's cleared out also. The only things left are photos on the walls. Standard issue family stuff, taken at studios or on vacations. In most there are three of them: the woman John met today, a man he presumes is her husband, and a child.

Time passes in the photos. The couple ages. The shapeless infant turns into a little girl, a mop of reddish blonde ringlets, her mother's eyes, her father's mouth. Mom's own hair changes, longer and shorter. Dad's hair disappears, and a paunch forms over his belt. Moments frozen, already gone before the camera shutter tries to capture them.

Then, time gaps, and the couple are alone on a beach, he's in a tropical shirt, she's in a linen dress, and there's a gritted-teeth nature to their expressions. There are more years lining their faces than should be. They wear perseverance like masks. Smiles screaming the lie of "we will survive this."

Danny says, "Let's check upstairs."

He takes a step toward the staircase. Without warning Danny gasps and chokes back a scream in his throat.

John's heart thumps double-time. His eyes scan the room, searching for a threat, not confident he'll even know what to do when he discovers it.

There it is.

A Lego piece. In full light it would have blended into the carpet. Now it's practically invisible.

John picks up the toy piece. That's when he notices the plastic tub a few feet away, tipped on its side and Legos spilling out. A lid beside it, "Amanda's Legos" written in black marker across the top.

Danny hops on one foot. He snatches the Lego from John's hand.

"Fucking kids," he says, and chucks the toy piece into the tub with the others.

John feels more drunk than ever. His insides churn like a boat on an unsteady sea. He knows it's more than nerves. The smell gets worse the further into the house they go. It somehow reassures him the house is empty; no one could sleep in this.

Danny's limp fades to nothing by the top of the stairs.

The second-story hallway is long and dark except for a blade of charged purple light through a cracked doorway at the end, music trailing out behind it. An electric guitar cries a plea for absolution. A man makes a wordless wail that feels like prayer.

John knows the sounds. It's Jerry Wheeler.

He needs a bathroom so he can go vomit. The light from his phone guides his eyes until he finds words etched across a door: "Amanda: Our Angel" in an elaborate script, and two dates below it. The first one, eight years ago, and the second, a year ago. Below that, "May God hold our baby in His grace."

At the end of the hallway, Danny takes the gun from his pants pocket and pushes the door open.

Light and sound and smell strike at the same time. Simultaneous explosions that overwhelm the senses. The light, a star at supernova. The sound, a thunder crash. The smell, the lingering of death.

John comes up behind Danny. The room's on fire from the humming light of neon signs hanging on the walls. One that reads "Better together" and another proclaiming "It was all a dream" and still another spelling out "This must be the place."

He sees two shapes in the bed. He crosses the room like he's swimming the English Channel, an invisible tide pushing him back. What feels like worms in his brain niggle him to turn around and run from the house.

Fuck the record, fuck Danny, fuck all of this.

Somewhere, amidst the neon glow, he notices the spilled bottle of wine, a kidney-shaped merlot stain as black as blood soaked into the carpet, white pills scattered around the edge like pebbles. John knows they're Xannies.

The woman's wearing a long nightgown. She's rolled onto her side, one arm stretched out to embrace the person beside her. A trail of vomit runs from her mouth, colors her pillow. Eyes closed and unmoving.

The man beside her is most certainly and definitely dead. His bloated features vanishing. A green pall flushes his skin, and dried red foam crusts his mouth and nose.

John hears a rasping noise. Air, straining to pass through vomit dried around the woman's nostrils.

"Call 911," he says.

Silence slams into the room like a butcher's cleaver. Danny's at the record player in the corner, the album in his hands. He looks at it as if it was a newborn child, his own flesh and blood.

"Alright, let's go," he says.

John's eyes grow large. "Did you not hear me?"

Danny checks the bed with a dismissive glance. "They're dead. Nothing 911 can do." He takes a step closer. Coughs and wretches. "The neighbors'll catch the smell in a day or so."

"She's not dead. If we call and EMTs ..."

"They'll do what? Save someone who sure as hell looks like she wants to be dead." He points to the man. "And that fucker's definitely gone bad." He wipes tears away from the corners of his eyes. "Can we get out of here? The stink is murdering me."

John turns off the flashlight on his phone, pulls up the dial pad. Thumb hits the "9."

Danny steps forward and knocks the phone from John's hand, sends it across the room.

"Have you lost your goddamn mind?" Danny says.

"We can't leave her here to die, Danny."

"Yes, we can, because if you call 911, they track your phone and cops'll ask what the hell we're doing here. You wanna do jail time for saving someone's life who's not interested in living?"

John thinks about picking up the boxes, the resignation on her face.

Her husband's body had been lying here in the bedroom, the smell John imagined was nothing more than a dead animal.

He hadn't been wrong about that.

Not really.

Danny touches his arm. "Are we good?"

John's got his hands on the album before he realizes what he's doing, wrenching it from Danny's grasp. He holds it over his chest like armor.

He inches past Danny toward his phone.

"I can't leave her here. Not like this."

The gun wavers in Danny's hand. "We can walk right the fuck out of here, John, and we can make some money, and ain't no one ever gotta know."

The tips of John's fingers press harder into the album, turn white as bone.

"I'll break it," he says. "I'll shatter it right here. I'm not letting this woman just die."

"She's already dead. As good as. Listen, if this is what you want, fine. But let's leave. Find a pay phone. Call from there. We can—"

John's foot taps against his phone. He bends to pick it up, his eyes staying on Danny as takes the phone back into his right hand, his left clutching the record firm.

***

Danny watches John—that motherfucker—bolt out the door.

He has a breath where he thinks about firing the gun. He doesn't because what if he damages the album? What if he's dealing with a bleeding-out John? Combine that alongside everything else, and what a fucking night this would end up being.

But he can't let John call 911. Danny knows he still has warrants sitting on him, and all it'll take is a cop asking the right question—like his name—and he's fucked. Plus, once the cops have him, the Armenians will know where he is two seconds later. He can't have that, not if he wants to keep on breathing.

So he chases after John, who's already vanishing down the stairs.

Danny can see John fucking with his phone in one hand, half-paying attention to it, half-checking what's coming ahead in an unfamiliar house. He keeps the album tucked into the crook of his other arm.

John hits the first floor and heads toward the kitchen. Danny can see John's phone screen. The call button green and ready.

Danny tells himself if he can make up these last few feet, he can get close enough to bust John upside the back of his head with the butt of the revolver. The way they do in old movies. Grab the album and give John time to cool down. See what the right thing to do is.

Or he can just take the album and leave him here. Fuck him.

Now John's in full stride, out the door and onto the concrete. He looks back over his shoulder.

His right foot splashes and slips in a puddle.

What happens next is a lesson in physics.

John's mass times his velocity equal the momentum of his out-of-control body sliding across wet concrete.

His arms flail as he tries to catch his balance. The album flies loose, lost in shadows. He fumbles his hold on the cell phone and it hits the concrete with a screen-shattering crash.

John tumbles forward. There's a fraction of a second at the lip of the pool where the world seems to hit the pause button. He almost catches his balance.

Almost.

Then the world unsticks again. John falls, smacks onto the pool cover with a slap. He rolls toward the center, tries to climb onto his hands and knees.

There's the first pop, and a pool cover strap snaps loose, whips through the night, and catches John across the face. John's nose explodes like fireworks of cartilage and blood and he flops face-down.

Danny makes a decision in that moment. He goes to one of the straps, attached to a steel buckle anchored to the ground. He flips the latch and the canvas strap flies free, and what tension there is on the pool cover, holding it over the water, slackens a little.

John doesn't move.

Danny repeats the action on another buckle. And another. He moves quickly around the pool.

John's weight sags the cover more with each strap set free.

Danny's almost done when John raises his head and looks at Danny. His face is a sea of red, and his eyes hold a tired awareness of what's about to happen.

The final strap.

Water rushes in and the cover envelops John like octopus arms, swallowing him in one bite, his weight dragging it and him to the bottom of the pool.

Danny stares into the dark water that looks like ink under the night sky. The rain's stopped, and everything is still except for bubbles rising to the surface.

Those don't take long to stop.

Danny thinks he's hallucinating when he hears a voice, tinny and as far away as a star, say something about 911, and what's your emergency?

John's phone.

Danny grabs it off the concrete. The screen's a spiderweb of glass, but there it is, a connected call to 911, and a woman's voice saying they're using GPS to get the location.

"Help will be on the way," she says.

Danny tries to hit the red button to disconnect the call, but the shards of broken screen only fall away under the pressure of his thumb.

He knows he's not hallucinating when he hears the sirens, or he sees the lights dancing in the distance.

Alright, get the album, and get out of here. He scans where he knows it flew when John lost it. He starts walking that section of the backyard.

He takes a step and hears the crack underneath his foot.

In the pale moonlight he looks down and sees *Steel Wheels Live at the Apollo.* The split in nearly perfect, between "Wheels" and "Live," dividing the album into two equal pieces.

Goddammit.

Danny runs for the car. Stops long enough to toss the gun over a fence into the neighbor's yard.

Cursing with every breath. All this shit, all for nothing. Wondering why he even bothered to get out of bed this morning.

The sirens scream louder and the flashing lights are practically heat on the back of his neck when he reaches the Focus. Pats down his pockets.

The first cop cruiser roars down the street toward him, the headlights catching him like a tossed net, when Danny remembers.

John had the car keys.

The Book Deal
Robert Lopresti

Ron Vernadsky stared down at the Spokane River, wishing he had the guts to jump in.

Not really, of course. Losing your job wasn't worth dying over. Even if you get fired in a particularly humiliating way.

Besides, while the sun had set there was plenty of light around, with most of it coming from the Convention Center, which loomed behind him like the palace of his enemy, the lair of the monster that would ruin his life—

Ron shook his head. He would never allow such overblown prose in a book he edited.

He was simply missing out on the biggest book deal of the year. That was not the end of the world. Just the end of his job, and most likely his career in the wonderful, high stakes, tear-out-your-guts-and-eat-them-with-bourbon world of publishing.

Behind him he heard the laughter and chatter of people who had spilled out of the Center, successful people who were having a better day than him, fellow attendees at the National Media and Book Conference.

Ron snorted. When he joined the biz, almost ten years ago, it was still called the National *Book and Media* Conference. Another decade and those antiquated objects stuffed with paper pages might be forgotten entirely.

Disgusted, he began walking along the pavement beside the river, away from the happy conference-goers.

They were all here: publishers, editors, agents, authors, would-be authors, publicists. All supposedly to learn about next year's attractions but really to tell the world about me, me, me. Vain, egotistical, self-centered bastards.

How he yearned to stay one of them. But that seemed unlikely.

The trip had been a disaster from the start. His plane was delayed for six hours at JFK. His luggage detoured to Atlanta, for reasons no one could explain. His hotel room was, naturally, a mile from the elevator and the damned key card only worked about every fifth or sixth try.

Whoops. He almost tripped. Wouldn't it be perfect if he fell in the river? People would think he had done it on purpose. Frank, his beloved boss at David & Dean, would probably rejoice in being able to cash in the return ticket.

A loose shoelace had caused this latest glitch. Well, that was one problem he could solve. Ron knelt down and—

Something was gleaming under a bush.

He pushed branches apart, peering cautiously in and— jerked back as if he had seen a snake.

It was a gun. A real gun. What sort of idiot would leave a genuine shoot-em-up bang-bang Second Amendment pistol under a bush in downtown Spokane? Was this some drop-off point for drug dealers or gang bangers? He couldn't believe he was using a word like *gang bangers*, even in his own head.

He looked cautiously around, half-expecting to see a mobster—or a cop—looming over him. People strolled beside the river, but none were close enough to see what he was doing.

What was he doing?

The gun was still there. Ron pulled out a handkerchief and gingerly removed the pistol from the bushes. Could a twig touch the trigger and make it go off? It would be the perfect end to a perfect day if he accidentally shot himself.

He tugged it out, making sure his body blocked the view of passersby. It was a revolver; even he could tell that much. Some of the chambers held bullets. Or were they called cartridges? When David & Dean published a crime novel, they always ran it past an expert, because nobody screamed about mistakes like gun nuts.

Ron shook his head. What was he supposed to do with the damned thing? Put it back? Drop it in a garbage can? He should take it back and call the cops. But strolling through the Convention Center with a gun seemed like a sure winner for Dumb Idea of the Day. He could call 911—

He froze. And looked down at the gun with new eyes. Maybe the nasty little thing could solve his problem.

If he had the nerve.

***

He walked into the Convention Center, sweating bullets, even though he had taken off his sports coat. He held his jacket awkwardly with both hands, wrapped practically in a ball. Everyone who saw him must be thinking *What's he hiding in there? A gun?*

In movies, heroes casually tuck a gun into their waistband but he had instantly rejected that thought. He would certainly have wound up shooting himself somewhere delicate.

The cocktail party was dwindling down in the lobby. So many happy people bragging about their latest deals. So many hungry people hunting for someone to make deals with.

No one was looking his direction, because no one wanted to attach themselves to a falling object.

He heard laughter and saw a group of people circling Chase Longwood. His nemesis.

Chase was his opposite number at SmartWelcherJames. The man who, according to rumors, was about to sign Nikki Gallo to a multi-book contract with SWJ.

Nikki Gallo was the hot target Ron's boss had sent him to sign. Frank had offered an ultimatum: *Bring back her signature on a contract or with yours on a resignation.*

The latter seemed the likelier outcome.

Nikki was nowhere in sight. If she had been Ron would have tried again to get past her handlers for a chat. She often traveled with a muscular bodyguard and, at this event, her agent Sherry Marmot, whom most publishers found more terrifying than a Seal Team.

But Nikki was sticking mostly to her suite this weekend, receiving selected visitors there. She only visited the peasants occasionally to make her videos.

Because that was what it took to be the hottest thing in literature these days: Nikki was an influencer. This beautiful young woman spent hours each day filming herself enthusing about products and places, which paid her handsomely for the mention. Her followers bought clothes, food, and beauty products she recommended by the millions and thousands of them flocked to resorts and theme parks she promoted. Next week hundreds of young women and a few men would be here in Spokane, filming themselves in the exact spots where their idol had appeared.

Nikki made the news last year when she shot a vlog standing near a cliff in Hawaii. A teenage boy had tried the same, slipped, and broke a leg. Rumor had it she complained that if he had died, she would have gotten more press.

Last month Nikki informed her followers—"the Nikksters"—of an exciting new discovery. "Books! They are the hottest thing. When I'm not filming for you, I have my nose in a novel or I'm reading history. They're cool and you know what? There's millions of them out there!"

Every publisher worth their martinis begged her to review their books—or at least claim that she was reading them.

A few days later she raised the stakes by announcing that she would be coming to Spokane for the Conference. Rumor spread that she wanted a book deal of her own. David & Dean was desperate to make the match.

That was because their rivals at SWJ had managed to land the biggest book of last year, a book with so much publicity baked in that it topped the bestseller list on pre-sale.

That volume had been not a literary masterpiece but the memoir of Pete Bartholomew, universally recognized to be one of the greatest shortstops in the history of baseball. (Not that there were many shortstops in, say, hockey.) But that wasn't what made his book a bestseller.

Bartholomew's girlfriend had been shot to death in his mansion. Their rocky relationship had involved restraining orders, police reports, and violence on both sides. If Bartholomew had still been playing, MLB might have shitcanned him, but he had retired before the bad news arrived. One more in a long string of lucky breaks.

The biggest of which was this: the cops never found the murder weapon. Bartholomew had spent the fatal day with friends who picked him up at his mansion and swore he had never left their sight. Coming home, he immediately reported finding the body.

The police—and just about everyone else—thought Bartholomew had killed her before leaving the house, but where was the gun? (And what gun? He had supposedly surrendered all of his weapons during an earlier legal settlement.)

When a reporter dared to ask if he had done it Bartholomew sneered: "If I had killed the... beauty, I would have used my bat."

That made every news feed in the country. His memoir, *I Would Have Used My Bat*, was the biggest book by a murder suspect since O.J. Simpson's *If I Did It*. It made SmartWelcherJames the go-to publisher for celebrity tell-alls (or in Bartholomew's case coyly-hint-alls) and made its supposed author a mint. The shortstop went to all publicity events carrying his favorite bat and many celebrities and some allegedly normal people had had their pictures taken with him and the mighty stick.

Bartholomew was supposed to be a major feature at the book show, but at the last moment the cops had brought him in for another round of questioning. His lawyer said they did it just for spite.

But his absence, combined with the gun from the bushes, might give Ron the opportunity of his career.

Now well past the partiers, he walked through the connector to the hotel, down the long hallway, and pushed the elevator button.

As he waited it felt as if the revolver was growing in the jacket he held, getting heavier and hotter. Wouldn't this—

"Ron!"

He jumped a foot.

Hustling down the hall was the one person in Spokane who actually wanted to see him. Wally Eick was an actor. Nobody's idea of star material but he had acquired a breakout role in a sitcom, playing a no-talent artist who cluelessly thought he was a peer of the painters who were the main characters in *Exposure*.

Ron had published Wally's light and fluffy memoir, *Exposing Myself*. It was selling better than he expected, better than some books that were even good.

"Having fun?" Wally asked as they entered the elevator. "This is great! I was just talking to Leonard about his Oscar win. Do you know he's got a book coming out?"

"I do. I even know who wrote it."

"And Nikki Gallo! My daughters love her."

Wally didn't notice Ron wincing.

"Are you gonna publish her?"

"We're pitching. She hasn't signed a contract yet."

"Well, you should definitely get her," Wally advised. "That book's gonna make a mint."

"Yeah, I should have thought of that."

"What's wrong with your coat?"

Ron blanched.

"This?" He held up the bundled jacket. "It got stained. Trying not to get it on my clothes."

"Oh. That's a shame. Hey, I'm on a panel tomorrow. Do you have—"

"Sorry, this is my floor."

Ron stepped out, praying Wally wouldn't suggest going back to his room for panel tips.

At the door to his room he awkwardly shifted the jacket and pulled out his key card. This time the damned door hadn't even locked properly. *Fantastic.* He needed to remember to complain at the desk tomorrow.

He took a quick glance around and saw that no one had slipped in to steal his suitcase, so recently arrived from its unexpected visit to Georgia. Ron placed the jacket on the bed, ever so gently, and went to the minibar. He selected a whisky. It vanished untasted so he had another one.

Then he unrolled the jacket. Sure enough, the gun was still there.

Why was he nervous? This was America. Didn't damned near everyone own a gun? Plenty of people would be terrified to be outside *without* one.

What was the law in Washington State? Did he need a permit?

It didn't matter. He wouldn't have it long.

***

Ron set his alarm for 5:45, an hour which at publishing conferences was more likely to be for bedtime than rising. This was necessary because Chase Longwood, along with his many other loathsome traits, bragged about being an early riser. He would be in the hotel gym by six.

When Chase opened his hotel door Ron was standing there with a smile and a leather bag, which normally held his toiletries.

Chase backed up, surprised, and Ron took advantage to enter.

"Ron! What the hell?"

"Sorry to butt in. I just need a few minutes. You'll have plenty of time to play with your dumbbells."

Chase went red in his handsome, patrician face. "What the hell is this about?"

"You're going to drop out of the bidding for Nikki Gallo's book."

Chase's jaw dropped. Then he laughed. "You're out of your mind. Now get the hell out of my room."

Ron smiled, trying to look confident. "Don't be hasty, my friend. Let me show you what I have in this bag."

"Oh, please do. I'm trying to imagine how you think you could bribe—Jesus!"

Rob displayed the gun without taking it out.

Chases's eyes were wide. "Are you crazy? Get out or I'll scream my head off."

"Relax. I'm not threatening you." Ron considered. "Well, I *am* threatening you, but not with the gun. Not to shoot you, anyway."

"Are you drunk? You're not making any sense."

Ron smiled confidently again, this time pretty sure he nailed it. "How about this for sense? For the last two months David & Dean has had investigators with dogs searching through the woods behind Pete Bartholomew's house."

"Trespassing? You've come to confess?"

"I said the woods, Chase. Your famous shortstop's property backs up to an undeveloped piece of parkland, remember? They showed it on every news show after the murder. The cops searched it for days and then gave up. We didn't."

Chase looked wary. "You're saying—"

"Four days ago a bloodhound named Cletus started howling next to a ditch. His handler dug under some branches and found this revolver. The lab experts confirmed last night that the fingerprints on it match those on your boy's autographed photos."

Chase's face turned a satisfying shade of pale. "You're bluffing."

"I swear I'm not."

"Why the hell would you bring the gun to Spokane?"

Good question, damn him. "A visual aid. Believe me, we have all the evidence back in New York, so even if you threw this in the river it wouldn't help."

"I'm not throwing it anywhere. I'm not touching the damned thing. But I don't believe a word of this."

"Fine with me," Ron said. "But your bosses won't be happy when it turns out their star author is convicted of murder. He's been a sensation by keeping people guessing, but when this comes out Bartholomew will be the latest victim of cancel culture and SWJ will look like a cross between a sucker and an accessory after the fact."

Chase's face was grim. "What's the deal?"

"Easy. Drop out of the bidding for Nikki Gallo's book. Let David & Dean get it and the gun and evidence stay in a safe."

Chase shook his head. "You call us an accessory. But your bosses are willing to let a killer go unpunished?"

"All's fair in the book trade. Besides, your bosses are fine with making him rich."

"They don't think he killed her," Chase said. "Frankly, neither do I."

Ron's jaw dropped. "Seriously? You must be only the people in the country who don't."

Chase shook his head. "You haven't heard Pete speak about her in private about her. He really loved her."

"Plenty of people kill people they loved. Haven't you ever read a novel?"

"More than you, I'm sure." Chase brightened. "You know what, Ron? Pretty soon you're going to be convinced as I am."

"And how will that miracle happen?"

"Because we can talk to Pete in person. Oh, you weren't expecting that, were you?"

Ron felt queasy. "I thought he was still being interrogated."

"The cops came to their senses. He's on a flight right now." Chase was smirking. "What's the matter? You don't want to brag to him about your mountain of evidence?"

"Look. Forget it. Do whatever you want." He turned toward the door.

"Stop." Chase was tall and muscular; Ron was neither.

"Get out of my way. I have to—"

"You try to blackmail me and—"

Ron pushed hard and Chase fell backwards, yelping. He bashed his head on the wall as he tumbled.

Ron didn't wait to see whether he stood up again. He grabbed the doorknob with the strap of his toiletries bag—no fingerprints!—and fled.

Cameras in the hallway? Probably. He kept his face down, hoping his average, ordinary appearance would work in his favor for once.

He ignored the elevator and took the stairs. Hunted animals avoid enclosed spaces.

Was he being hunted? He was a blackmailer, and a— what had he done to Chase? Should he call for an ambulance?

No. Self-preservation. He had to get rid of the evidence, which was that damned gun.

Down, down, down past the main floor he found an exit into a dim alley. There was a dumpster there. He could drop the gun in it and be rid of it.

But no. If Chase told the police what happened, they would surely look for the gun there. If Chase was able to talk…

Dawn was rising as he walked beside the Spokane River. Throw the gun in and be done with it—

Except a couple was headed toward him, dawdling by the riverbank, kissing and pawing at each other. Clearly they had had a better night than he had.

Ron walked away and found himself near the same bush as last night, or perhaps its twin. What did he know about shrubbery? He knelt as if to tie his shoe – that was how it all started! With a quick glance around, he opened the toiletries bag and tossed the gun down.

There. *Let it rot.*

A block further on he found a miraculously empty trash bin and stuffed his bag in.

If Chase told a tale there would be no evidence to back him up. Assuming Chase lived to tell anything.

Ron shuddered. Then a happy thought occurred to him. If Chase was, well, unfortunately out of the picture, wouldn't that leave David & Dean a chance to sign Nikki Gallo?

***

He ordered breakfast in his room. If the cops were going to arrest him, let them do it in private.

No one came.

He went to see Wally Eick doing his panel with four other minor TV celebrities. Afterwards when he told Wally what a fantastic job he had done, Ron realized he hadn't heard a word any of the alleged wordsmiths had said.

In the hospitality room, he heard tons of gossip but none of it about ambulances or police cars. Did that mean Chase was still lying in his room, and would remain there until the maid arrived to tidy up? What sort of tip would you leave the poor woman?

Ron spent the early afternoon looking for Nikki and alternately hoping and fearing to see Chase. Hoping he was still alive. Fearing the man would be after his hide.

The day's highlight was to be another cocktail party. This was a make-friendly-with-the natives event so selected Spokaners (Spokansters? Spokaneers?) would be in attendance. It was sponsored by none other than SmartWelcherJames, so if Chase, their prize editor, didn't show up questions would be asked. Ron dreaded going but refusing would feel like a confession.

Damn that gun.

There was a crowd in the lobby. He headed to the open bar to fortify himself with a glass of wine.

He took one sip and almost choked. There was Chase, tall and blond and self-possessed as ever, talking cheerfully to a small group of admirers.

Well. At least he wasn't dead. Alive to press charges.

Chase was chatting with someone who aimed a phone in his direction, obviously filming. When Ron spied literary agent extraordinaire Sherry Marmot nearby, in her trademark muumuu, he realized that the hand with the phone belonged to Nikki Gallo.

Then Chase saw him and grinned. "There he is! Ron, come over here."

Maybe he banged his head so hard he has amnesia.

The whole group turned to look at Ron. He tried a smile.

"How are you doing, Chase?"

"Doing great, Ron. I'm glad you're here. You can watch Nikki and I sign a fabulous multi-book contract!"

The influencer turned his way. She really was gorgeous. "Chase says you wanted my book so much you tried to fight him for it."

Ron tried not to blanch. "Oh, that's not true."

Chase laughed. "Well, he gave me a shove, but Ron doesn't spend as much time in the gym as some of us."

Oh. Ron relaxed. Chase was so vain he couldn't admit that a runt like Ron had laid a glove on him, so to speak. And now he was on record with Nikki's millions of fans.

What a comfort. He would be fired for failing to land Nikki, but at least he wouldn't go to jail for assault. Today that counted for good news.

And just like clockwork, here came the bad.

Chase eyes lit up. "There's the man! Pete, come over here."

Ron resisted the temptation to duck. He turned and saw Pete Bartholomew, the man he had recently accused of murder. The ex-ball player had a beer in one hand and was leaning on his famous bat with the other. He looked as smug and contented as a famous millionaire should.

"Greetings, all."

"Pete, you have to meet Ron Vermin. He's one of your biggest fans."

"It's Vernadsky," Ron said.

Bartholomew sipped beer and looked at him with mild curiosity. "Pleased to meetcha, Rod. You an author too?"

They'd already met. Ron had spent one evening in a gastro pub buying the man overpriced drinks and trying to persuade him to bring his memoir to David & Dean. Naturally he didn't even remember him.

And now the player instantly forgot him again, turning to Nikki. "And who's this?"

The beautiful influencer held out a hand. "Nikki Gallo, Pete. I'm a big fan."

"Glad to hear it." He held onto her hand for what felt like an uncomfortably long time. She didn't seem to mind.

"Maybe I could interview you later. My millions of followers would like to hear about your struggles."

Bartholomew's eyes lit up. "I'd love that. How about—"

"Speaking of struggles," Chase interrupted, unwisely. "I have to tell you the prank Ron here pulled on me this morning."

"We don't need to—" Ron muttered.

"He came to my room." Chase grinned. "Claimed he's had spies hunting behind your house for months. He showed me a revolver and said they found it in the woods and could prove it was the one you used to kill your girlfriend."

Bartholomew looked amused. "Bullshit. That was an automatic."

In the silence that followed Ron heard his heart thumping.

Then Nikki held her phone out toward Bartholomew. "Did you just confess to murder?"

The player went blank. Then he dropped his beer and lunged toward her. "Give me that, bitch!"

Ron and Chase both moved to block his path, banged into each other, and hit the floor. It was Sherry Marmot, super-agent, who threw her significant bulk in the way.

Bartholomew started to raise his bat, but a tall man grabbed his arm. "Stop. My name is Lieutenant Brand. We need to talk."

The player backed up, taking a deep breath. "Talk to my lawyer."

"Mr. Bartholomew!" the lieutenant shouted.

He moved through the party crowd, showing the hustle that made him an All-Star.

"Are you going to arrest him?" Ron asked.

The cop frowned and turned to Nikki. "Do you want to charge him with assault?"

"And stay in beautiful Spokane for a trial? I don't think so. Can't you arrest him for murder?"

"Not my jurisdiction. But I'll talk to the right authorities immediately." He glanced down at Nikki's phone. "I'm going to need that."

"Wait a damn minute," said Sherry.

"It's okay." Nikki smiled and held it out. "Just get it back to me as soon as you can, okay?"

The cop nodded and headed off.

"Are you sure—" Sherry started.

"Relax. It's synced to the cloud, plus I've got a second camera here." She touched a broach that dangled close to her low-cut top. "A girl can't be too careful."

"I don't believe it," Chase said.

They turned to him. Ron thought he looked like a victim of a terrorist attack.

"You really thought he was innocent," Ron said.

Sherry gave Chase a motherly tap on the shoulder. "I hope your contract with the bastard settles what happens to his royalties after he's convicted. Felons can't make money off their crimes, you know."

Nikki had removed the pendant from her necklace and attached it to her selfie stick. "This really happened, Nikksters! You just saw history being made. Rob, how did you do it?"

"It's Ron." He blinked. "Do what?"

"Trick that murderer into confessing. Incredible!"

"Oh." He shrugged. "Well, I put a lot of planning into it, Nikki. A lot."

"I'll bet. I want to hear all about it and I'll bet all my Nikksters do too." She gave him her brilliant smile. "Want to go back to my suite for an interview?"

***

The interview lasted past midnight—and no wonder she was okay with the cop taking her phone. She traveled with what amounted to a damned video studio. Ron was nervous at first but several bottles from her minifridge calmed him down.

By the end of the talk, Nikki seemed to have convinced herself, and no doubt her followers would agree, that she and Ron had plotted the takedown of Bartholomew together.

Ron was fine with that.

He watched, fascinated, as Nikki edited their talk and sent it out to the waiting world.

"Thanks so much, Ron. This is fantastic."

"I enjoyed it a lot."

She brushed her hair back, looking thoughtful. "You work for David & Dean, right? Sherry told me you were one of the top bidders for my book."

Ron felt his head buzzing as if he were in a jet taking off. "Absolutely."

Nikki nodded. "We'll talk to you in the morning. I'm damned if I'll sign with those accomplices at SWJ."

"That's great! I promise you'll be happy with us."

"Well, how could I disappoint a hero?" Her eyes went sleepy and sly. "Speaking of being happy, do you need to rush back to your room?"

***

Ron's phone alarm rang at 5:45, still set for his plan to sneak into Chase's room. Had that only been twenty-four hours ago?

He grabbed the phone. Nikki muttered in her sleep and turned over—and what an amazing view that was.

Better not let her see him in a pre-coffee mess. He would return to his room and make himself presentable.

Ron dressed quickly and left a note on a table—trying to hit the right mix of mush with looking forward to a business breakfast with Nikki and Sherry.

Out in the hall his phone began to ring. It was his boss. Thank God he could deliver good news.

"HI, Frank. I was gonna call you—"

"Ron! I can't believe it. You're amazing!"

Ron almost bumped into the elevator door. "I am?"

"Don't you know? Oh, that's right, it's still early over there. You've gone viral. Taking down Pete Bartholomew! Those bastards at SWJ will rue the day they outbid us."

"I'm glad it worked out," Ron said.

"And speaking of working out, the video looked like you and the Gallo girl were getting along."

"Uh, yes." Exactly how friendly did they look? "I think we'll be signing a contract."

"Unbelievable! Ron, you are justifying the faith I have always had in you."

Was this the same boss who threatened to fire him if he didn't score a contract? Everyone loved a winner.

"When you get back, we'll talk about the other book," Frank said.

Ron frowned. "What other book?"

"Yours, dummy! The one where you tell the world how you outsmarted that rotten right fielder."

"He was a shortstop—"

"Whatever. I hope they arrest him before you leave town. See if you can get your picture taken with the bastard, and we'll put it on the cover. The cover! We'll make you a great deal, Ronnie. Everything's gonna—"

"My agent is Sherry Marmot," Ron was surprised to hear himself saying.

Frank let out a squeal like a small animal in pain. "Come on, Ronnie. We don't need to involve outsiders."

"Catch you later, Frank."

He disconnected as he reached the door of his room. For once the stubborn key card worked like magic. This was the one day in his life everything was going right.

As he walked in his phone rang again. *Hell*. It was his wife.

"Hello, Bonnie."

"Darling! You're a hero!"

Hearing her use the same word as Nikki made him wince. "You've heard about it."

"It's all over the news and the social networks. My Mom's been calling, and the neighbors…"

He begged to get off. "We'll talk later, but here's the best part, babe. I'm getting a book deal of my own."

Bonnie screamed so loudly he had to yank the phone away from his ear.

When she finally ended the call, he dropped the phone on the bed and refused the temptation to join it. First, a shower and then the most important breakfast of his life.

Someone stepped out of the bathroom. A tall man slapping a baseball bat against his palm.

"Deal's off," said Bartholomew.

Mini Me
Mysti Berry

Trader Joe's in Lincoln Heights was busy, even by Trader Joe standards. Shopping carts jangled and the sliding doors whooshed, and customers nattered until the sounds all merged into a single sound that grabbed Gloria's attention and held it, even as she rang up products and dropped them in bags for each successive customer. She felt a weird pressure from the noise-beast and reached for her Closed sign, preparing a regretful expression for her next customer, but when she saw the woman, she froze.

Gloria's enemy had snuck up on her, and now she was trapped. Instead of escaping to the restroom for a quick break, Gloria had to serve the one person in the world she truly hated—her husband's "friend" from high school, Diane. The woman was five feet of seething resentment and cheap hair spray, and currently a petite but potent thorn in Gloria's side.

She flashed a rigid approximation of a smile in case her boss was looking and rang up Diane's items one by one. She stared at the items as she rang and bagged them, trying not to see the other woman.

Diane cleared her throat theatrically and said, "Your husband mentioned you were working here."

Gloria mulled over many responses, from the obscene to the confrontational, and chose silence instead. Diane was a very small, round person, so her choice to mimic Gloria's signature style of oversized, loud blouses was…unfortunate. The bright colors and small shapes just made her look shorter and wider, as did the expensive-looking satchel handbag that Diane dropped on the counter between them, open and precariously balanced, an even more expensive wallet sitting on the top.

Gloria shoved away the thought that her husband's neuroses shouldn't mean letting someone like this 'Mini Me' into her life. She gritted her teeth and finished ringing Diane up.

As she pulled the receipt from the register to hand over, Gloria felt a sudden wave of nausea.

She asked, "Is that Rare Beauty?"

Gloria felt dizzy from the familiar, thick scent wafting off the other woman. Gloria never wore her perfume to work, and never doused herself in it.

"Mmhmm. Frank mentioned it was your favorite. I love it!"

Gloria hated it now. One more thing ruined by Mini Me.

Diane handed over her credit card, a Platinum Amex.

She said, "Isn't it nice that we can get to know each other now that you two have moved in with your folks? I love catching up with Frank so much. He said you were bouncing back from losing your high-tech job."

Gloria held out the receipt, but when Diane grabbed it, Gloria didn't let go.

"I haven't forgotten that you tried to sleep with my husband after we were married. I will never forget that you tried to destroy my marriage."

Gloria said it loud enough to be overheard by the customer behind Diane.

Diane yanked the slip of paper out of Gloria's hand as her face and neck turned a blotchy red. She pulled so hard she managed to send her purse tumbling onto the floor at

Gloria's feet. Gloria stared at the purse on the ground. The wallet had tumbled out and was resting close to spilled coffee and powdered sugar.

"Jesus, Gloria, pick it up before it gets ruined by all that filth."

Gloria saw something small and black that had bounced out of the satchel and rested halfway under the counter. She pushed it farther back with her toe as she fetched the wallet, righted Diane's satchel, and returned it to her.

Diane huffed and pushed her cart hard out of the cashier's line and into the swooshing embrace of the sliding door exit.

Gloria realized she'd been holding her breath and exhaled. She helped everyone in her line in a sort of daze, and then closed her station for her long-overdue break. She grabbed her own purse out of the drawer underneath the cash register, and then slipped the object from Mini Me's purse into her own.

She retreated to the employee restroom and wiggled the door latch to slip into the stall with a Broken sign on the door. She was on her third cycle of pursed-lip breathing, feeling light-headed and wondering if the breathing was better for anxiety than a snort of Glenfiddich.

Everything today felt broken. Gloria had been laid off from her lucrative programmer's job four months ago, at the height of this year's layoffs. She couldn't get a new job anywhere without a degree, and probably wouldn't be able to until the layoffs across the country slowed down. Her resume was easy to ignore when hundreds were applying for every job.

Instead of enjoying the hustle and bustle of Seattle and a satisfying job coding for Microsoft, she was living with her husband at her parents' house, facing every ex that Frank had ever dated because apparently nobody else from his high school ever left Spokane. And she was working as a cashier because Frank couldn't work. He used to manage a coffee booth at swap meets, but once she was able to support them both, she encouraged him to quit and focus on his art.

Now that they were back in her parents' house, Frank didn't leave the house for days at a time. And when he did leave, it was to hang out with his high school friends, including Diane. At first Gloria thought he was just depressed about having to sell their condo and leave Seattle, but now it felt like he had completely reverted to the powerless teenager he'd been while living with his abusive parents. And Gloria had no idea how to bring him out of it.

Curious to see what she'd kept from Diane's purse; she pulled out the black zip pouch. It was too heavy to hold makeup or medicine. Intrigued, she unzipped it and found a little black revolver with the shortest barrel she'd ever seen, looking used but not banged up. She pulled it out and popped the cylinder and saw it had a few bullets. It could use a good cleaning.

She stared at it, wondering where Diane had picked up a gun, and what to do now that she had stolen it from Diane.

A gun is just a tool, her daddy had taught her. He'd taken her to the range when she was barely tall enough to see over the counter and taught her all the safety rules. His brief stint in the military left him with both the desire to keep guns in his house and the knowledge that without training, people can come to harm. She loved her dad's pragmatism, and wished he were still alive to guide her now. Gloria tucked the gun into its pouch and stashed it in her purse, pondering what kind of problem this tool could fix.

***

Gloria thought about Diane as she drove from the comfortable suburb to her own bedraggled neighborhood, devoid of comfort since at least the 1970s. She knew that no one understood her beef with Diane, or why she called her "Mini Me" behind her back. Well, Frank understood, but he didn't think the fact that Diane had tried to break up her marriage meant he had to stop being pals with her. And he thought she was jumping to conclusions every time Diane adopted a new facet of Gloria.

She parked in front of her parents' decaying ranch home and breathed a few times before dragging herself inside. She'd grown up in a much less wealthy part of Spokane than Diane and Frank. Dropping her purse at the door, she stowed in the fridge a few packages of expired food—tofu spring rolls and macaroni salad— that she'd salvaged from the store. Frank was stretched out on the couch watching an old anime. Gloria knew her mother was already asleep at 7:00 PM in the master bedroom. She slept a lot ever since her father passed away.

Gloria grabbed the remote off the littered coffee table and clicked off Frank's show.

"I never would have come back to the 'Kan if I'd known you were going to do…this."

He looked at her with a comical mix of high dudgeon and infantile hurt.

He said, "What did Diane do to you this time?"

"Mini Me—"

"Do you have to call her that?"

Gloria continued, "She showed up at my place of work today. In a shirt that looks like mine."

Frank raised both arms theatrically. "If I can't visit my friends, who can I see? At least you get to see people at Trader Joe's."

"Why are all your friends women? Who you slept with?"

Frank's eyebrow arched and his mouth twisted. "You know why."

Gloria felt the shadow of his past between them. It always showed up sooner or later, no matter how hard she tried to pretend Frank was okay now.

She tried one more time. "I have the right to keep her out of *my* life."

Frank stood up but stayed on his side of the room. "You earn the income, so you dictate what we do, is that it?"

Gloria felt her frustration crystalize into rage. "I know you're broken, Frank. It's a miracle you survived what your parents did, the abuse…I don't expect you to make the same money I do, that's not it. She…disrespected me when she made her move."

"That was when we first got married. She's different now. Married to a rich guy and everything."

"No Frank, she's exactly the same, except that now she's trying to become me in order to replace me."

"You're imagining things." Frank turned and headed to the basement door.

Gloria knew he'd stay downstairs for hours, jumping on the internet and chatting with Mini Me and who knows what other ghosts from the past. Again.

Gloria picked up her purse, hefted it and felt the weight of the gun inside, and then ran upstairs, her anger channeled into the beginning of a plan. She performed her nightly ritual as she worked it out in her head. Pajamas, dental hygiene, and bed, but she didn't crawl under the covers, she sat cross-legged, her purse beside her, and waited.

At last, she heard what she'd been waiting for: basement stairs creaking, followed by the sound of the TV and the soft groan of the couch as Frank settled in to finish his anime. Only then did Gloria pull out her iPad and begin her three-part plan.

First, break into Frank's email. It was easy to do; he'd been using the same password since college. She read the sugar-coated nonsense Mini Me wrote to Frank, clumsy prose full of words that she hadn't really mastered like "nonsecular" and "pedagogy." The last email invited Frank to meet her during Gloria's shift the next day, at a hotel restaurant near Trader Joe's; her sentences were full of flirty innuendo about the hotel being steps away from their rendezvous.

Two feelings seized Gloria at the same time—red-tinged rage that Diane was flirting with her husband, and shame that she was poking around in his private correspondence. She told herself that Frank's responses weren't flirty and shoved away the impulse to just walk to Diane's house in her PJs and shoot the woman in the head. Always aim for center mass, her father's voice corrected her. Not now, she thought. Just keep to the plan, the one that won't send you to jail.

The next step in the plan was easy. Gloria created an account that looked just like Mini Me's and sent Frank an email canceling the meetup. She was certain he wouldn't notice the difference between the letter L and the number one in the email address.

Finally, she logged back into Frank's email and wrote to Diane, accepting the real invite, but suggesting Upper

Lincoln Park as a better setting. She did this because it was closer to Trader Joe's; she could get there during a break. Surprising Mini Me with a loaded gun should scare her back to her upper-middle class life and out of what was left of her own, with Frank none the wiser.

***

Gloria trembled as she set out on foot for Upper Lincoln Park, her fingers running over the rough plastic butt of the gun in her jacket pocket, though it was still too hot to wear a jacket. Frank loved to tell the story about how he and his friends got drunk in the park as teens once. Now they were all grown up, and she needed Mini Me to start acting like it. Her dad's voice rose up, unbidden and this time unwelcome, chiding Gloria for planning to use a gun as a threat instead of a promise. Well, we can't always live up to our ideals, Gloria thought, and focused on her plan to scare Diane right out of their lives.

Gloria pulled on the restroom door, but it was locked, so she waited, leaning against the rough stone of the building on the far side of the parking lot, sweating in her unseasonable jacket. She was sure Mini Me would drive up and park without trying to hide anything, and she did, taking her time across the grass with her short legs and her lazy attitude.

With a deep breath, Gloria put a hand in her jacket pocket and stepped out from behind the building. Mini Me was on the swings and looked up. In the soft light of the early evening, Gloria felt a sense of security and satisfaction when the other woman's face changed from excitement to concern.

"Gloria?"

She didn't answer but walked quickly up to the swings and pulled the gun out of her pocket, keeping her arm close to her body and pointing the snub nose right at Diane.

Instead of backing up, Diane stared at the gun and moved forward. "You stole my gun!"

Gloria pushed her arm forward as if ready to shoot, and Diane backed down. When Gloria spoke again, her voice came out husky and trembling. "Stay away from Frank, or I'll make you stay away."

Diane held her breath for a moment, and then she burst out laughing.

"You don't get it, do you? *He's* the one you have to persuade to stay away from *me*."

Gloria repressed the urge to scream and instead took a step forward, keeping the gun pointed at the other woman's chest.

"If you want him, Diane, take all of him. The night terrors, the crushing insecurity, the way his parents literally hacked off his sense of self at the stem with abuse that no one should ever have to endure. Everyone in his life has used and abandoned him, and I swore, I swore an oath that no matter how fucking hard it got, I wouldn't leave him."

"Well excuse me oh mighty Joan of Arc of love. We were friends before he met you, and if we want to be friends now..."

Gloria felt her trigger finger twitch a little.

"You're using him to make yourself feel better than me. Once you've broken us up, you'll dump him because he's not rich like your poor sap of a husband. Please, save everyone the bother and just get out of our lives."

A voice so far back in her head she could barely hear it asked her what the actual hell she was doing. Gloria gritted her teeth and dismissed the voice.

She put her other hand on the gun and stretched her arms out, as if ready to fire. "Which is it? Leave your money train of a husband and take care of Frank for the rest of his life, or get out now, completely, forever."

"Or what, you'll shoot me? How would you explain that to Frank?"

Gloria heard a rustling and turned around to see Frank walking in his customary bearlike shamble.

Diane's voice was rich with triumph. "It didn't take me a minute to work out what happened and let Frank know. I told him to look for your email in his Trash folder."

When Frank saw the gun, he gasped. "Gloria? What are you doing?"

Her gun hand dropped to her side. She could barely see for a sudden rush of tears. Her throat ached.

"Frank, I can't live with her in our lives anymore. I've tried, I've really tried. But now I need you to choose—me or this cheap-ass imitation of me."

Frank held his arms out wide. "I choose to have a wife and an old friend."

Diane stood up from the swings and moved toward Frank. "She's the crazy one. You should have her committed."

Gloria watched Frank turn from her to Diane and back and knew he would never be able to choose. She loved him and hated him with equal intensity.

When Frank looked away from her and toward Diane, Gloria put the barrel in her mouth and pulled the trigger.

***

The sound was so loud, Diane and Frank just stood as Gloria slumped to the grass at their feet. Frank continued to stand, staring, as Diane moved forward gingerly toward Gloria's body.

Frank asked, "What are you doing?"

Diane turned on him, snarling. "She stole that gun out of my purse."

"Stop it, Diane. I'm calling the cops."

He reached for his cell phone as Diane ran back to him and pulled the phone out of his hands.

"That's my gun—I found it in a box of donations when I was volunteering at the Goodwill. My prints are all over it. I need to wipe it before you call the cops!"

"Why didn't you turn it over to the cops?"

"I needed protection from your crazy wife. And this way, I wouldn't have to tell my husband I had it. He hates guns."

Frank stared at Diane. His mouth worked, but no sounds came out.

At last, he said, "Don't forget the bullets when you wipe it for prints. If you dump it at the back of the Pull & Save, there's so much metal there, it would be hard to find again."

Frank turned his back on Diane and Gloria as the last of the daylight drained from the park.

A Gun in the Flower Bed
Jason Powell

By the time Steven Peiper realized he was being robbed, there really wasn't anything to be done about it. His hands were up as if a cop had warned him to freeze, but there were no police officers in sight. Four guys had shown up. The two he'd seen earlier were closest, out of arms reach, but just a few fast strides away. Both were showing knives and were positioned on the sidewalk so that either direction Steven might try to go if he decided to run would be cut off. If he decided to run.

The other two, each with one hand hidden in their pants pockets, almost certainly had knives as well. Or else some other kind of weapon. They were in the street, near the curb, Carla standing behind them, her expression unreadable. With his back facing the building behind him, Steven was stuck. Trapped. There were deceptively large gaps between the four men that could be closed without much effort. For all the good the gaps did, the men might as well have been holding hands around Steven in a circle. He stood up straight, therefore, letting his arms drop to his sides—accepting the situation. He wouldn't run.

The situation sucked but wasn't exactly unexpected. The whole day had been this way. The whole trip. Spokane, Washington was a fine place, but his excursion here had been the end result after a series of unfortunate events. This situation right now, was just more of the same. He'd been grinning to himself when he bought the ticket; practically giddy when he landed. Now he wondered if he'd ever smile again.

Steven stood there in the middle of the slowly rotating crowd like the center of a compass, resigned, shoulders slightly slumped. The fingertips of his left hand brushed against his own pants pocket; rubbing then pressing against the revolver nestled beneath the sweat stained denim. His eyes narrowed in a squint and swiveled between the eyes of the four men around him, meeting and holding them all for a second before moving on.

And he smiled.

***

The funny thing was that Steven didn't like guns. He wasn't naïve or political or anything like that. He knew that there was a time and place and circumstantial need for the things, but he never imagined a circumstance in his own life where one would be necessary. His was a world where most disagreements could be talked through. Where you could avoid being victimized if you just used caution and sense. A need for a weapon of any sort was unthinkable. He couldn't be blamed for not having foreseen this.

The fact was Steven should never have been there. Not there as in that spot on North Post Street outside of Spokane's City Hall; there as in any part of Washington State at all. He should've been at his home in New York City. Or at work at his pharmacy in New York. Pure arrogance had brought him all the way across the country, pursuing a fantasy. And a woman. Arrogance and ignorance. Some combination of those two things for sure, with the possible addition of loneliness.

He started down this path a couple of months ago. Steven was a tall, broad shouldered man with sun tanned skin and silver, white hair both on his head and face. It all went together well. With his facial hair trimmed and well-groomed, he'd recently been told by a woman, three drinks into their conversation, that he looked like an A.I. generated picture of Santa Claus as a young man. "Sexy Santa," she began calling him, after the fifth drink, though later she wouldn't remember that. Steven remembered though. It wasn't so much a stroke of his ego as a much-needed caress. Since Josephine left six months ago, he'd been more self-conscious; much more critical of his appearance.

Josephine. It was probably fairer to say that Steven had kicked her out than to say she left. Well, maybe not fairer, but maybe more accurate. Josephine left because Steven told her to, yes. Somehow though, that choice of words made Steven feel guilty, and he hated it. He *wasn't* guilty. Why should he feel bad about making her leave? It was Josephine who cheated. Josephine who lied. Why should Steven be the one battling remorse? Why should he suffer insomnia and a loss of appetite? He shouldn't. Yet...

It wasn't fair. It was stupid. But his mind needed a way of dealing with the loneliness, and apparently guilt was it.

He didn't just have to accept it, though. No. He could try and get over Jo the way most people get over their exes. Steven wasn't quite ready to create an account on one of those dating apps where you swipe left or right or whatever. Not quite that. For one, there's a big difference between being single and being available. He wasn't sure he was ready to be for another woman the type of man he had been with Jo. Infidelity is notorious for weakening the confidence of the cheated on. Lowering the quality.

More than that, though, the reason Steven wouldn't join a dating app, was because he and Jo had too many friends and coworkers in common. Too many people who'd offered an ear to her lies about why she and Steven were no longer together. Too many who believed her. A lot of those folks had dating app profiles. He didn't know exactly which people or which apps, but if Steven joined one of those sites just six months after he and Jo separated and one of those people saw it... well that would be all the proof they needed.

He knew he shouldn't care about that, but he did. So, no dating apps. But there were other ways to find new people. Safer, slower ways. There were new people on social media, weren't there?

Yes. There were. Steven had long ago created accounts on most of the major social platforms, though he never really used them. Now he became more active. More social. He interacted with the pages and people on his feed, commenting on sports and entertainment pages, liking the posts of women with nice profile pictures. In the search box on Instagram and Facebook he typed things like "single women NYC," with hashtags before or after each word, just to see what came up.

Then, two months ago: Carla.

It happened very organically. She'd liked one of his comments on an ESPN post about Lebron James and a minute later sent him a follow request. Her profile was public, so he searched her pictures and videos, and the dates they were posted, and it seemed clear to him that hers wasn't some scam account. There was a photo of her celebrating her 22nd birthday early this year, and photos much further down on her screen that went back to when she was a teenager. Steven couldn't believe it. A real, genuine, good-looking young woman, who liked sports, was sending *him* a follow request.

He accepted, of course. Right away. Well, he waited ten or fifteen minutes after she sent it, so as not to seem too eager; but after that, he scanned his own pictures to see if there were any he'd want to get rid of—photos of him and Jo for instance—then accepted her request. She messaged him before the day was over, he responded, and they talked every day for a week. Then two weeks. Then pictures were exchanged—current pictures to prove integrity. Then phone numbers. Weeks of social media turned to days of phone contact. Text messages led to calls and calls to video chats and then, finally, this: the invitation to Spokane.

As it happened, Steven knew a couple of people in the state of Washington. A married couple, Rod and Laura Veet, who both worked remotely for Google. Last week Steven called Rod, told him of his impending trip and accepted the hoped for offer to stay in Rod and Laura's second bedroom which sometimes doubled as an office. Rod was an old friend and he and Laura were kind, quiet people. They too were the kind to get along. So it was more than surprising that it was Rod who suggested the caution and Rod who had given Steven the gun.

*****

It happened earlier that day. After an anxious ride out to JFK airport in New York City, Steven boarded his plane, strapped in and immediately fell asleep. Which was a surprise. He usually had difficulty falling asleep on planes. As the owner of a pharmacy, Steven had access to any number of sleep aids, but this was one time he hadn't minded being awake. Nevertheless, he slept fast and long. He awoke, five or six hours later when the pilot announced their descent into Seattle, and the seatbelt light clicked on with a soft chime. He took his phone off of airplane mode and found a message from Carla. He responded, smiling despite the distracting speed of his pulse, then got off the plane and killed the half hour layover time till his short flight to Spokane.

The second plane landed at Concourse B in Spokane International Airport, to a busy but not crowded terminal. While Steven stood by the carousel at baggage claim texting Carla that he'd landed, a dozen people milling around, Rod appeared, wrapping him in a tight bear hug.

Steven freed his arms and hugged him back, then the two men chatted a minute about the flight. Steven, both pleased and surprised, asked about the surprise airport pick-up.

"We were never gonna let you take a cab, bud," Rod said. "You know that. We work from home. No reason we can't get you." Rod's voice was both smokey and smooth. The kind of voice you'd expect to narrate a documentary about the Second World War.

"Thanks man," Steven replied. "I was fine with taking an Uber, but this is much better." To his right, his bag showed on the carousel, and he tapped Rod's shoulder, excusing himself to go grab it. On the other side of the baggage claim area, Steven noticed two men, maybe in their early twenties, standing beside a backless medal bench, looking across at him. Both men were dark, and very thin, like professional marathon runners. One wore a baggy Jordan jersey from when Michael was on the Washington Wizards, which Steven found ridiculous and borderline blasphemous. But, if such an offense could be forgiven anywhere, this was the place.

The other man wore a plain, chocolate brown T-shirt over tan cargo shorts. Both articles of clothing looked as if they'd been passed down from a bigger, wider brother. Steven glanced at the two, then did a double take when he noticed their eyes watching him. After too long a beat, both men turned away looking pointedly in other directions. Steven, too, looked away, grabbing his bag and walking it over to where Rod stood waiting.

"Laura in the car?" he asked as Rod led the way toward the exit.

"No, no. She's home." Rod checked his watch. "Probably on a Zoom call right now. But I wanted to come get you by myself anyway. I had a question for you."

"Yeah? What's that?" Steven took a quick peek over his shoulder to where the two men had been. They were still there, beside the bench, watching him again.

***

What Rod wanted to ask was anything and everything there was to know about Carla. Steven had been expecting the question yet felt caught off guard. He showed Rod the most recent picture Carla had sent before Rod pulled out of the short-term parking out to the street. Rod took the phone in his hand, pinched the screen then handed it back, saying nothing.

Feeling anxious, Steven gathered his thoughts, figuring out how best to tell the story. Rod was a good friend and wasn't likely to judge him. Or maybe he was likely to, but it wouldn't change anything between them. He wasn't likely to think less of Steven. Still, it was important to Steven not to appear embarrassed when telling the story.

So, after a moment's consideration and preparation, he told Rod the history of his relationship with Carla. A truthful, albeit vague, barebones recap of the last couple of months. When he was done, Steven thought he'd done a decent job showing that a meeting with Carla in person was the natural next step.

But Rod wasn't satisfied. Or stupid. He wanted specifics. Details about Carla, about how their relationship progressed, and how it led to today. So Steven looked out the window at the airport and the surrounding area and told the story again, with detail.

Carla was the first to message. The two had both commented on a Sports Center post, with opposing views, and Carla had messaged Steven to make sure she hadn't crossed a line. He couldn't remember what her comment had been, but he understood that, read the wrong way, it might have been interpreted as insulting. The irony was that at the time she'd sent him the message, Steven had been on her page. Looking through her pictures, with a heavy focus on the collection from her trip to Cancun last year. When the notification showed at the top of his screen, he'd been both surprised and excited. Then surprised again by how smooth his response was. How bold.

Carla had messaged, "I hope you know I was kidding with that LeBron comment. Hope I didn't offend you."

And he'd replied, "If I lie and say that you did, will you try and make it up to me?"

He'd sent it and almost immediately, the status beneath it went from "delivered" to "seen." His pulse raced while he waited for a response, every second feeling like thirty. But then, after only a minute, she reacted with a heart and replied, "Absolutely."

Steven was much more comfortable, after that. He and Carla asked questions of each other and flirted some more. Carla knew that Steven was a pharmacist because of the photos on his page. Holiday parties or selfies with celebrity customers, that sort of thing. Carla's page was less obvious about what she did and so he asked.

As it happened, Carla was both an assistant manager in Sephora and an aspiring entrepreneur. She made scented candles in various shapes and designs and intended to start a business selling them. She'd posted a few via her social media but hadn't yet made a sale. She wanted to start a website for the business, but to do a website properly was expensive, and Sephora had never made anyone rich. So her dreams were still dreams for now, she said.

Steven, feeling both generous and opportunistic, offered to pay for the set-up of the website and first year's maintenance fee—a total just under $450—but only if she promised to let him be the first customer and gave him the candle in person. This part wasn't only flirting. It wasn't desperation either. It wasn't a gesture of a weak man trying to impress a beautiful woman. It was the action of a grateful man. Steven hadn't been feeling good about himself the last few months, and Carla had changed that; had given him some confidence back. Their conversations, the relationship they formed—Steven needed it. And he was grateful for it. So he made the offer.

Carla agreed, of course. She'd love nothing more, she said. If she had the money and vacation time from work, she would fly to New York just to hug and thank him. Steven, having both money and vacation time, suggested that he might come to her.

And here he was.

Rod remained silent though out the story and for two or three minutes after. While Steven had been speaking, Rod's eyes had been watching the road and the mirrors. It was clear he had been listening but unclear how he felt about what he was hearing.

Finally, his eyes still facing the windshield, Rob said, "So you flew halfway across the country to meet a total stranger?"

Which was unbelievable. Steven clenched his jaw, vibrating with irritation. After all the detail, all the explanation… The question, the tone of voice—it was like a slap in the face. "First of all," Steven said, slowly, "people fly across the country for strangers all the time. Second…"

Rod laughed—an insincere chuckle and glanced sideways at Steven. "Really? People do it all the time? That's your defense?"

"Second of all," Steven said loudly, talking over him, "she isn't a total stranger." Rod glanced at him, then back at the road, and shook his head. He was grinning but without amusement. "And third," Steven added, annoyed more by the condescending grin than the comment, "I don't need a defense."

Rod turned his head to face him, but Steven avoided his eyes. They'd cleared the airport roads and were rolling down a highway along brown and green fields with billboard signs spaced every eighth of a mile for everything from restaurants to home insurance. Steven watched the poles stream by without really seeing them.

Rod said, "Steve. This is me. You don't need to be defensive. You gotta admit this is crazy. You know nothing about this girl. Nothing real, anyway."

Steven opened his mouth to reply, but Rod talked over him. "And! She's half your age, unbelievably hot, yet single and free to talk to you every night despite the three-hour time difference. You're old enough to be her dad, for crying out loud. I mean, you're a good-looking dude, and a great guy, but you're halfway across the country. She agreed to meet you and doesn't really know anything about you either. Except that you have money and are extremely generous."

"C'mon man that's not fair," Steve said, offended. "Five hundred dollars isn't that much for people like us with decent jobs. You wouldn't loan someone five hundred for a good cause?"

"A woman I've never met who exists only on my computer? No."

Steven shook his head, frustrated. Rod was going out of his way to make this look worse than it was. Dumber than it was.

"Have you never heard of catfishing?" Rod asked staring at Steven.

"We've face-timed, Rod," she's not catfishing me.

Rod shrugged. "Maybe I don't know what catfishing is then. She may be the same person in the pictures she sent, but that doesn't mean she's the person she claims to be. You telling me it isn't at least possible that she lied about her feelings, or her motives?"

"What would be her motive, if not getting to know me better?" Steven asked, but already knew what the answer would be.

"Your money. Obviously."

Steven shook his head. He had nothing to say to that. Outside the window, the city of Spokane was beginning to take shape. Homes and businesses, parks and people. And Carla. She was out there waiting for him. For him, not his money.

Steven sighed. He was annoyed by this conversation, but he understood. Most people would find this weird. They wouldn't understand the chemistry. They couldn't possibly know that, somehow, Carla and he just… clicked. Like puzzle pieces. It was hard to understand because it was hard to explain, and he understood. So did Carla. And neither of them needed anyone else to.

The silence lasted for a minute or so and then Rod said, "Open the glove compartment." Steven turned from the window and looked at him. Rod nodded once, his eyes on the road. "Open it."

Steven frowned. What was this? Open the glove compartment? Why? What was he supposed to find in there?

The idea of a weapon in there flashed foolishly through his head. Why would Rod have a weapon in his glove compartment? Why would he have a weapon at all? It was impossible to imagine Rod owning a knife or a gun, let alone driving around with one. Confused, Steven reached forward and pulled the tab out.

Impossibly, nestled inside the small compartment, atop manuals and facial tissue, sat a black .38 snub-nosed revolver.

Steven didn't touch it. He couldn't have even if he wanted to. He didn't have brain power enough even to form words, so asking his brain to move his arms was definitely out of the question. After a few failed attempts, he finally managed to form a sentence of sorts.

He said, "What? What is this?"

"It's a revolver."

"Yes, I know. Why is it in your glove compartment? Why do you have it?"

"Found it," Rod said simply. "Couple of days ago. Not too far from a junior high school. I picked it up so no kid would come across it. They use the yard even when school's out. I didn't want to deal with the hassle of turning it in to a precinct or something, so I just kept in there." He waived a hand toward it. "Go ahead and put it in your bag."

"What for?"

"To take with you on your date later."

Steven couldn't begin to understand what was happening. Rod, the last person in the world he'd expect to have a gun, was casually offering Steven one to bring on a date. Why?

"Why, Rod? Why the hell would I bring a gun on a date? You want me to shoot her?"

Rod laughed. "No, no. Let's avoid you going to prison." He waived at the compartment again. "There are no bullets. Go ahead, pick it up. See for yourself."

Steven peered at Rod through narrowed eyes. If this was a joke, he didn't get it. But he could play along, wait for the punch line. Steven reached out and grabbed the gun. It was smaller than his hand but felt heavier than he expected. Holding it by the butt and turning it this way and that, Steven looked it over. All the chambers were empty. No bullets.

"This place isn't abnormally dangerous," Rod said, nodding at the windshield, indicating the city. "Definitely not compared to New York. I mean, don't get me wrong, there's crime; but it's not as if you can't walk around outside."

"Okay." Steven was still confused.

"But social media *is* abnormally dangerous," Rod continued. "Listen, I don't know what's gonna happen when you meet up with Carla. Maybe you'll hug and hang out or whatever and have a nice safe time." He turned his head towards Steven briefly then faced forward again. "But maybe, God forbid, this beautiful girl who should realistically be out of your league, only brought you here to scam or rob you. That's where the gun comes in."

Steven held up his free hand. "What am I supposed to do with an empty gun?"

"Scare her. Or whoever else tries to do the robbing. That's usually how it works. Two or three people working together on this scam. They corner you, force you to an ATM to take out cash; maybe have you Zelle them or Venmo them or something, nowadays. I'm not sure. Take your credit cards. When they show themselves, that's when you pull the gun. Scare them. Use the gun as a deterrent. The sight of it should be enough."

"I don't..." Steven started, but then couldn't think of how to finish the thought.

"Steve, I hope I'm being paranoid. I hope we'll be laughing about this later. You know what Laura said about you yesterday when we were talking about you coming here for a woman? I didn't tell her any of this by the way, my thoughts or worries. Anyway, she said that you were like a flower bed. Said flowerbeds are small parts of gardens where beautiful flowers grow. The garden itself is varied, green grass, dirt, rocks: that's the whole pool of men in the world, some good, some bad. But you're one of the parts that make women keep coming back. You and men like you—I guess that includes me—are the flower beds that make tending a garden worth it."

Steve turned away and looked out at the road again.

Rod said, "We both hope you end up with someone who appreciates that." He shrugged. "Who knows, maybe that person will be Carla. It's possible I'm wrong about all this."

"But you don't really believe you are," Steven said.

"No. I don't. If I am though, if you never need the gun, get rid of it. Hell, get rid of it even if you do end up needing it. Somewhere safe."

Steven put the revolver down on his lap above his knee and closed the glove compartment. Outside, the city crept closer as the road sped by. His meetup with Carla was planned for tonight. The plan was that she would tell him the name of a restaurant, based on where he was staying, and would meet him there around eight that evening. She got off of work at 6:30.

Talking more to himself than to Rod, Steven said, "We'll see."

***

By the time Steven realized he was being robbed, there really wasn't anything to be done about it. He'd been looking at his phone, following Google's navigation to O'Doherty's.

Irish Grille, when he realized he'd made a wrong turn. He'd gone left one street later than he should have and it would be easier to go back then circle around. Conscious of the heat and the fact that he was sweating, Steven hoped he'd be at O'Doherty's before Carla long enough to freshen up. Why had he worn jeans? He could feel the moisture clinging to his legs.

Abruptly, he turned around, intending to head back to make the correct turn, and behind him, a man in a Michael Jordan Wizards jersey was hurrying up the sidewalk in his direction. Their eyes met and the guy looked so startled, he broke stride. Steven kept walking and the guy seemed uncertain about something, as if he too had made a wrong turn. The two men passed each other, both giving the other furtive glances, and then Steven rounded the corner again, going back a block.

Later Steven would consider that it was his nervousness at meeting Carla, that had his mind moving so ridiculously slow. Nervousness both because it was the first time they'd meet face to face, and because of Rod's concerns. Nervousness distracted him and the only thing he wondered in that first moment was, "Did I know that guy? Was it a familiar face or just a familiar type? Thin young guys wore jerseys and athletic gear as casual clothing all the time in New York City. But good jerseys. Not the tragedy that was…

And then he remembered.

The guy in the airport. One of two. Steven turned and looked over his shoulder and the Wizards jersey had rounded the corner after him. There was no charade this time about being confused or lost. His eyes were on Steven and one hand was in his pocket, the other tugging at the cloth near the other hand, helping free it. What was happening? What was this about?

Facing forward again, noticing for the first time how little foot traffic there was around here, Steven looked for a place to go. From across the street and up the block, the other man from the airport hurried toward their corner. Then out of the front seat of an idling car stopped on the curb across the street, two more men. Steven held up his hands, still not certain what these guys wanted. But then the back door opened in the car and out came Carla,

She was stunning. Better even than her pictures. She stood by the car, her expression unreadable. The four men had formed a sort of semicircle around Steven: two in the street, two on the sidewalk. The weather was hot but a small steady wind blew, cooling the sweat running down his side. An empty single-serve Rolds Gold pretzels bag buffeted against a storm drain near where the jersey guy stood on the corner. Steven looked at him then at each of their faces, and there was no doubt what they were here for.

He looked again at Carla and caught something in her eyes. Was it guilt? Remorse? Steven wasn't sure, but whatever she was feeling, it was clear that she knew this was coming.

Feeling a finger of disappointment, even before the wave of fear or anger, Steven dropped his arms to his side. Rod was right. Another tragic love story. If this farse could be called love.

He sighed. A thing like this shouldn't happen to a man, certainly not twice. His shoulders slumped and the fingertips of his left hand brushed against the revolver.

And he smiled.

***

Earlier, Steven had intended to wear a cross-body messenger bag, that could be both casual and professional, but Laura talked him out of it.

"Why would you wear a bag?" She'd asked genuinely confused. "You're not going to work and you're not bringing her a gift or anything. What would the bag be for? You're not a woman." A reasonable question for someone who didn't know about the gun.

Laura hadn't been against his coming across the country for Carla at all. In fact, she said she thought it one of the more romantic things she'd seen a man do outside of a television show or movie. "Present company included."

The conversation about the bag happened as Steven was preparing to leave, and by then, Rod's concerns had taken route inside of him. Steven had gone back to the spare bedroom, dropped the bag on the bed, and extracted the revolver. He moved his wallet to his back pocket and stuffed the small gun deep into his left. When he was leaving, Rod lifted one eyebrow, and Steven gave a tiny nod in response. He had the gun.

Now, Steven smiled and stood at the middle point of the group, his back to the closed down city hall behind him. The two from the airport were on the far outsides of the half circle, the two from the car, the inside. They all looked at each other, maybe confused by the smile. Still, they moved slowly closer to each other and to Steven, tightening the circle. Carla stood where she was.

The Jordan jersey guy said, "You gonna come with us bro. Just down the street for a minute. Don't make us kill you." Steven didn't know what was down the street. An ATM? A bank? They might've been more successful with whatever they had planned if they'd waited until after the date. But maybe Carla lived around here. Maybe they didn't want her seen with him in a public place in case things went poorly later and he ended up in the hospital.

Or worse.

Steven still smiled but he was angry now. About a lot of things. Angry that he'd dedicated his life to aiding others and all he ever got for his trouble was screwed. He was angry about Josephine and about Carla. He was angry that Rod was right and the idea a woman like Carla was supposed to be wanting to be with him was so unlikely that Rod thought it was more likely a crime than true interest. Steven still smiled, but without humor, and it showed.

The men stopped moving. All four had knives out now but none of them were doing anything with them other than holding them out like an usher with a flashlight in a dark theater.

Steven reached in his pocket and pulled out the gun, switched it to his right hand. A heavy silence seemed to fall over the area, though no one had been speaking anyway. It was as if they all held their breath. As if the car stopped idling. As if the wind stopped blowing.

Rod's words from earlier came back to him, then. About what Laura said about men like him. Flower beds. The beautiful part. Maybe, but now he had thorns.

His arm hung to his side, the short barrel of the gun grazing his thigh. He didn't hold it up or point it at anyone. For one thing, there were no bullets, and if anyone of them looked at the cylinder, they would see right through. But also because it didn't feel necessary. The effect was made. The jersey guy began to walk backwards. The other one from the airport, moved slowly to his right toward the idling car, though he hadn't come from there originally. Or maybe he had before Steven had come back around the corner. Who knows? It didn't matter. They were all moving now. Everyone but the Wizards fan moving toward the car, all of their eyes switching from the gun to his face.

Carla was the first one to the car. The car was an old Ford four-door sedan with the windows tinted. She paused before climbing inside, looking back at him. The corners of her mouth turned down, making her look insincerely sad, like a circus clown. Her lips spread, as if she were going to apologize, but then she turned and ducked in and disappeared. The other three were inside a second or two after her. To his left, Steven could hear the

Wizard's footsteps pounding away around the corner. Steven didn't move.

Three car doors slammed, and the Ford pulled away from the curb and down the street, not exactly speeding, but fast enough.

Steven stood where he was, remembering the conversations he'd had with Carla. The messages and the phone calls and the FaceTime. He hadn't suspected this for one moment before his talk with Rod.

Steven crossed the street to a park, not bothering to check for traffic. Riverfront Park, the plaque on the gate said, open until midnight. He walked in and followed a winding path toward the water and a looming lighthouse. When he saw a woman walking a small white terrier near the gardens, he stuffed the revolver back in his pocket.

At the water's edge, Steven looked out at the lighthouse and thought about the last two months. Then the last six. Then, more broadly over his entire adult life.

Such a waste.

He stayed there, by the water, nearly twenty minutes before he was ready to go. He was no longer angry. He couldn't quite identify how he was feeling, but whatever it was, he was resolved. Done. Finished with this moment of introspection. Stretching, Steven took the revolver out intending to toss it in the river. The memory of the woman and her Terrier flashed through his head, and he looked around to make sure he wasn't being watched. There was no one around. Looking at the gun, thinking about how he used it tonight, he thought again about that woman and her dog, alone in a park at night. Had she seen him? If so, had she been worried about being harassed? Attacked?

Reconsidering, Steven turned away from the water and walked back toward the entrance. Using the bottom of his shirt, he did his best to wipe or smear his prints, though he couldn't figure how to do it properly while still holding it. He did his best though and made his way back to the gardens. Steven hadn't walked through the entire park, but he felt the flowerbeds were as unlikely as anywhere else in the park for a kid to go. Kids wouldn't be allowed and would probably have no desire to anyway. Standing behind a waist-high fence, Steven stuck a finger through the trigger guard of the revolver, then tossed it onto a bed of peonies. There it'd be most likely found by a park employee or gardener. Hopefully whoever it was would find a use for it. A purpose that helps them without hurting anyone else.

Laura's words echoed in his mind again and Steven scoffed, shook his head. An ironic smile creased his cheeks. After a while, Steven stuffed his hands in his empty pocket, turned from the flowerbed and walked out of the park. He checked both ways before crossing the street, then headed back in the direction he had come.

The Big Mess
Cindy Goyette

Why was Tate such a slob? The kid was smart enough to apply to Harvard but failed to understand that if he left dirty dishes in his room eventually they'd have a pest problem, not to mention a shortage of forks and spoons.

On hands and knees, Jill conducted her weekly sweep of her son's room. It was her Sunday routine when her husband Joe took Tate fishing. They'd come home to a spotless house, not even thinking to thank her. Acting like a magic genie had swooped in and performed a housekeeping miracle.

Headphones on, she was elbow deep separating a pile of dirty clothes on the floor when the cell in her pocket vibrated, alerting her to an incoming call. She answered, still gathering laundry.

"Hi, Mindy." She tossed a pile of darks into the basket.

"Have you heard?" Her friend was president of the rumor mill. But Jill appreciated her. Otherwise, she'd be clueless about the goings on in the world.

"Heard what?"

"Sydney Fisher was killed last night."

Jill stopped, holding a dirty gym sock in her hand. "What? No. Please tell me that's not true."

"Oh, it's true. He was murdered. Shot in the back."

Jill sucked in a deep breath. Sydney was in Tate's class. They'd been friends back in middle school but had grown apart over the years. Sydney hung with the shady kids while Tate's friends were all jocks. Sydney wasn't applying to Harvard. He would have been lucky to graduate high school. Still, he was just a kid.

Mindy kept talking, but her words barely registered. Instead, Jill's thoughts centered on Sydney's poor mom. Alice worked at the local diner which barely covered the rent of their one-bedroom apartment. A good mom, she slept on the living room sofa so Sydney could have his own room. Jill knew that because they used to be friends too. But like the boys, they now moved in different circles and had lost touch. Still cordial when they ran into each other but not part of each other's lives.

But they had one thing in common. They loved their sons. Would do anything for them. Alice must be a complete mess. How would she even go on?

"What happened?" Jill finally managed.

"Well," Mindy said, like she was sharing a juicy secret and not talking about a dead teenager. "There was a party at the Sandbergs. An argument broke out around midnight and Sydney was asked to leave. The kid was walking home when a sports car pulled up and one of the passengers opened fire. The witness didn't get a good description because it was dark. But the shooter wore a white hoodie."

Jill looked down at the white sweatshirt in her hand. Didn't every kid have one of those?

Where had Tate gone last night? Kenny Sandberg was Tate's best friend. If Kenny had a party, Tate would've been there. And he'd come home late. Just after one. Jill knew because she'd looked at the clock when the front door had creaked open and shut. She never slept soundly when Tate was out at night and last night was no different.

"I have to go." Jill disconnected the call before her friend could say anything more.

She glanced at Tate's closed closet door. Guilt sat heavy in her heart as she thought about opening it and searching… for what? She should trust her son. He'd never hurt someone, much less shoot an old friend. But he'd acted strangely that morning. He'd been moody and had snapped at her when she asked him if he'd had fun the night before.

She'd chalked it up to him being tired and angry that his father had roused him from a sound sleep to go fishing. Like most teens, he could sleep half the day away.

She had to check. Had to know. Otherwise, it would eat at her. Just a quick look would put her mind at ease.

Opening the closet door, she found another mess. Clothes piled high on the floor.

She pushed them aside, spotting a duffel bag in the back. Pulling it out, she laid it on her lap and unzipped it.

Inside, more dirty clothes. Did this kid ever put anything in the hamper? How was he going to survive when he went off to college and didn't have her to clean up after him? He was going to college, wasn't he? Not if he had anything to do with the shooting. She had to check. Had to make sure. She'd do anything to safeguard his future.

She pulled wrinkled T-shirts out, one by one, trying to convince herself that the bag wasn't too heavy for just dirty laundry. That something else wasn't inside weighing it down.

But her hopes were dashed when at the bottom lay a snub nose revolver.

***

When her phone chimed in her ear, Jill startled, forgetting that she still had her headphones on. Distracted by the gun in her hand, she took the call.

Mindy again. She jumped right in, not even saying hello. "Detectives are making the rounds. They're at Savannah Gunnison's right now. They're checking on everyone who was at the party last night."

The Gunnisons lived down the street. That meant their house was probably next. Jill balanced the heavy gun in the palm of her hand. She knew a little about guns. Her father had been in the military, and he'd taught her to shoot when she was a kid.

She popped the cylinder and counted the rounds. Only two when the gun held five. Even if one was in the chamber, she'd come up short.

A little bit of black gun powder colored the muzzle, indicating the gun had been recently fired.

Not good.

"Are you still there?" Mindy wanted to know.

The doorbell startled her. "I think they're here. I've got to go."

Jill hung up not waiting for an answer. Putting the gun back in the bag, she zipped it shut and took it with her. Stopping at the hall closet, she shoved the bag behind a row of winter boots.

Pausing at the mirror, she checked her reflection, wiping away the smudge of gunpowder on the back of her hand before opening the door.

***

There were two detectives from the Sheriff's Office. Both female. One short, one tall. All she could think of was how mismatched they seemed. She invited them inside once they showed their identification, admitting right off that she'd heard the news and was expecting them. "My son isn't home. But I doubt he knows anything. He would've said something if he did. He's a good boy."

One of the detectives raised an eyebrow.

Stop talking... stop talking... She always yammered on when she was nervous, and these women were trained to spot a liar. She had to tone it down.

She waited them out.

"Was he at the party last night?" the tall one asked.

She needed to be careful. She and Tate had to get their story straight before she said too much. "I'm not sure. He's eighteen. We don't keep as close tabs on him as we used to."

"But he knew the victim."

Jill bit her lip. There was no sense in lying. "Our little corner of Spokane is pretty small, so yeah, of course he did. I feel so bad for his mom."

"Does your son drive?"

"He has his license." Nothing they couldn't look up. "He sometimes uses the family car."

"Which is?"

Not a sports car, thank God. "A Subaru Outback. He and my husband took it to go fishing. And I drive a Prius, but Tate hardly ever uses it."

"Okay," the smaller detective said, handing Jill her card. "We'd like to talk to Tate when he gets home. Give us a call and we'll swing back by."

And ask about the gun. Maybe search the house. Jill took the card and nodded.

As she shut the door behind them, she knew what she needed to do. Any good mother would do the same.

***

Jill checked the time. She still had a few hours before Tate and Joe would come home.

Pacing, she placed a call to her son. He should have service, even if they were on the river. But the call went straight to voicemail. Tate only ignored her calls if he was hiding something from her. She tried her husband's phone, but he didn't answer either.

She couldn't wait to talk to Tate. She didn't have that kind of time.

They'd be out in the boat. She had no way to reach them.

Retrieving the duffle bag from the closet, she placed it on the counter. Under the sink she found a cloth and appliance cleaner. It removed fingerprints from the fridge like a charm. Donning rubber gloves, she handled the weapon, removed the bullets, and wiped everything down, including the empty casings. Afterward, hands still gloved, she returned the revolver to the bag.

Next, she threw the white hoodie and some other light-colored clothes in the washing machine and started the cycle.

Changing into black joggers and a black long-sleeved shirt, she slapped a ball cap on, picked up the bag and headed for her Prius.

She drove to East Sprague. The other side of the tracks some called it, although there were no tracks. But the houses became less and less desirable as the numbers on the streets went down. This, she imagined, was where criminals congregated. A perfect place to dispose of the gun. No way they'd be able to trace it back to her family.

Some miscreant would probably pick it up. Hopefully not a child, but children shouldn't be dumpster diving. Nobody should. But she knew people did.

Hopefully, a garbage truck would whisk it away and it would wind up in the dump before anyone found it. Never to be seen again by anyone. It would simply disappear.

Jill turned down the next street. Graffiti marked walls in nonsensical ways and trash and tents lined the streets. A homeless camp. Probably as good a spot as any. She slowed, glancing down alleyways, looking for the perfect spot.

She drove down a side road. To her left was an overgrown field. A van was parked at an angle, halfway in the street and against the curb, the engine running. She started to drive around it when a woman's scream stopped her.

Jill hit the brakes and positioned herself so she could see the open door of the van. A man wearing a grimy tank, and jeans had a small woman by the wrist and was forcing her inside. She kicked and screamed, but he seemed unfazed. She was half his size, and he had little trouble manipulating her.

Jill didn't have time to call 911. The opportunity to help the frantic girl was dissipating.

She reached for the duffel bag.

Not taking her eyes off the people in front of her, she blindly felt for the gun and pulled it out of the bag.

Adrenaline quieted her thoughts as she jumped from the car and leveled the weapon, aiming at the man's chest. "Let her go!"

The man stopped to look at her. He shook his head. "You don't understand."

Jill tightened her grip on the weapon. "Let. Her. Go."

He rolled his eyes, reached into the waistband of his jeans, and pulled out a weapon of his own, pointing it in her direction.

She hadn't thought this through.

Jill was not a badass; she was a self-described wimp. Squeamish at action movies, she preferred romcoms. Yet here she was in the worst part of town, holding a gun used in a homicide and facing down the barrel of another weapon aimed her way.

The woman twisted in the man's grasp, turning sideways and giving Jill a clear shot at the man. Her trigger finger seemed to have a mind of its own, like the gun was doing the talking and she had no control. Before she could reason with herself, she squeezed the trigger, and a deafening shot rang out. The bullet hit the man square in the chest and he collapsed onto the ground. She'd always been a good shot.

The woman stood over the man's body. Her mouth fell open and she ran a hand through messy hair as she stared hard at Jill and then at the man laying at her feet. Jill hoped shadows from her ball cap shielded her face from the girl. Even if she'd saved her, she didn't want to be involved. It might lead police back to the gun. To Tate.

Jill gave one last glance at the lifeless man in the street, jumped in the Prius, and left the scene.

***

Now she'd done it. If the gun wasn't a murder weapon before, it was now. She needed to get rid of it. Stick to the plan.

But it wasn't murder she'd committed; she'd helped that girl. Her father had taught her about self-defense.

And God only knew what that man would have done to that girl once he got her in the van.

What if the cops didn't see it that way?

***

With frequent glances in the rearview mirror, Jill drove off. Several streets over she found a mostly abandoned strip mall. The last store standing was a nail salon and massage parlor, but it had a closed sign in the window. It was Sunday, after all.

Jill circled around back and found an ugly green dumpster. Pulling beside it, she slipped out of the car, took the last bullet out of the gun, and wiped everything down once more with the rag she'd brought from home. A toss and metal hit metal as the unloaded revolver landed in the bottom of the container.

She expected to feel relief, but the knot in the pit of her stomach only tightened, horrified by what she'd done. The girl…, the gunshot…, the man falling…, none of it would leave her mind. She pocketed the last piece of ammo and got back in the car.

Three streets down, she found the dumpster's twin. She tossed the lone bullet in there, then found a third garbage can where she left the duffel bag.

Her hands were still shaking, and it was almost dark by the time she returned home. The Subaru was parked in the driveway. The detective's car blocking it in.

Had Tate already admitted to having the gun? Were they searching the house right now? Or had Tate been too afraid to call their attention to the missing duffel bag and not say a word?

Did her husband love her enough to cover for her? She was about to find out.

Inside, tension hung heavy in the air. Tate was red-faced, crying. Joe paced the living room as the detectives from earlier stood stone-faced. One of them had a pen poised over a pad of paper, ready to take notes.

When Tate spotted his mother in the doorway, he ran to her and threw himself into her arms. He was still a little boy in some ways. A man who could take a life in others. As he melted into her embrace, she wondered how she could ever think that of him.

"Sydney's dead." His words were muffled into her shoulder.

She patted his back. "I know, sweetheart. I'm so sorry."

Joe stuffed his hands deep into the pockets of his jeans. "The detectives want to search the house."

"I told them I had a gun," Tate said. "That I took it from Kenny last night. He was drunk and angry, and I didn't want him to do anything stupid."

"Probably the murder weapon," the short detective said.

"But it's gone," Tate said, stepping back and wiping streaming snot on the back of his hand. "I left it in my closet. It's not there."

Jill swallowed the ginormous lump in her throat. "How can that be?"

"Did anyone come by?" the other detective asked. "Go in Tate's room?"

"No," Jill said.

"Did Kenny have access to the house?" the taller one said.

"He had the garage code," Tate admitted.

Jill swallowed hard. It was at least something to throw them off her trail.

"And where have you been?" Joe wanted to know.

Lies swirled in Jill's head. A sick friend? No, too easy to check on. A drive? Not exactly a lie. "I had a few errands to run." Damn, they could check on that too. But the lie was already out. She couldn't take it back.

"We're going to have to do a more complex search of the house," the detective said. "Just waiting for the judge to sign the warrant."

Jill clasped her shaking hands behind her back. They wouldn't find anything. Still, she thought she'd hit the floor.

***

Now she had a much bigger mess to clean up. She knew the police would check her alibi. She had no receipts to prove she'd been shopping. There would be no video footage of her leaving a store. But they seemed focused on finding the murder weapon. By the time they completed their search, the events of the night before had become clear. Kenny shot Sydney over a girl. Tate, unknowing at the time that one friend had killed the other, took the weapon from his intoxicated buddy in an attempt to stop any violence from happening, not knowing that it already had.

And Jill, in her infinite wisdom, had disposed of the murder weapon. Protecting no one and screwing up the case.

But she couldn't admit to that.

Of course, the cops came up empty in their search. They left the house torn apart. She didn't even know where to begin to clean things up.

***

Jill spent the following hours putting the house back together. Exhausted, she poured herself a drink and settled on the sofa, putting on the eleven o'clock local news.

Joe and Tate had gone to bed hours ago.

The anchorman looked serious as he faced the camera and spoke in a deep voice. A photo of a man and a teenage girl filled the rest of the screen.

She recognized them both. The teenage girl was prettier than she remembered. The newsman's words explained why.

"April Jones, a runaway, was living on the streets. Drugs had changed her. Her father, Daniel, had been searching for her for almost a year when he found her this afternoon and tried to bring her home. He almost had her in his care when an unidentified woman driving a Prius pulled up and shot him for no apparent reason. Daniel Jones died instantly. The shooter has yet to be identified. Anyone with information on this senseless act is urged to call the police."

This was a mess even she couldn't clean up.

The Deserved
Frank Zafiro

Ronnie Rossovich stumbles up to the Spokane Transit Authority Plaza, his breathing ragged. He pauses outside, taking several deep gulps of air. He adjusts his sweatshirt self-consciously, ensuring his waistband is still covered. STA has security cameras and uniformed guards but no screening process. He doesn't even have to go inside. He can get his ticket from the automated dispenser along the outside wall and catch his bus at the curb.

With shaking fingers, Ronnie reaches out. He notices the red smear on the tips. Blood. For a moment, he wonders where it came from, then his hand raises to his chin. The fingers come away with another small smear.

It's from Pino, he thinks. Tiburon's knife nicked his chin.

Ronnie slides his hand inside his sweatshirt sleeve and presses the material against his chin to stanch the blood. With his other hand, he feeds a couple of bills into the ticketing machine. He is queasy. Not from Pino or the blood and not just from anticipation of what is to come, either.

He needs to fix.

After, he tells himself. He needs to be alert for this. He can't afford to nod off halfway through.

Ronnie selects the route and, a moment later, the machine spits out his pass. He shuffles to curb space that matches the bus line on his ticket. He keeps pressing the material to chin while he waits. The next bus is due in only seven minutes. The ride north is twenty-three minutes. There is no return bus, at least not one he'll have time to catch. He'll have to walk home.

That's all right, though.

After what he has planned, a long walk will do him good.

As he waits, the tense moments at the alley's entrance just minutes before are still sharp in his mind. He'd been walking in the gait that he always used, part shuffle and part scurry. The shuffle is to hide and the scurry is to pre-emptively flee. *Don't notice me*, the stride begs, *and I'll be past you and gone before you ever do.*

His heartbeat picks up at the thought of Pino Tiburon stepping unseen from the alley.

"I know you," Pino Tiburon had snarled at him. "You're Ronnie. The fucking snitch."

"No, I'm not," Ronnie had whined in return, which only seemed to aggravate the man more. He works for Laszlo Nagy. Ronnie thinks he is either dealing or enforcing, but his role isn't entirely clear. Either way, it seems a strange alliance for the two men, given their ethnicity. Then again, maybe the world was changing.

Tiburon's glare was withering. The scar near the outer corner of his left eye looked like an upside down question mark. Short and wiry, Tiburon exuded the kind of unbalanced danger that Ronnie made an extra effort to avoid.

Hurt people hurt people. Gavin's voice rang in his head. His friend was fond of saying that to explain some of the painful indignities the two of them endured at the hands of others. Maybe he was right but Ronnie suspected Tiburon simply liked to hurt people.

At Ronnie's denial, Tiburon's hand twitched. Ronnie heard the metallic *snick* and suddenly there was a knife in the man's hand. The sight of light glinting off the blade sent a sensation of cold water splashing onto Ronnie's shoulders and washing down his torso. His stomach fell.

"You ain't Ronnie?" Tiburon growled. "*No me digas mentiras.*"

"I'm not a snitch." Ronnie's words sounded weak and plaintive. Unconvincing.

"Ronnie Rosso-*snitch*," said Tiburon. "This is what they call you, no?"

"They're wrong. It wasn't me."

Tiburon watched him suspiciously through slit eyes. "People talking shit, huh?"

Ronnie bobbed his head, a burst of hope forming. "Exactly. It's not true."

Tiburon didn't move or say anything for several moments. Ronnie's hope grew. He took in a deep, wavering breath, waiting.

Tiburon's contemplation finally seemed to end. He shook his head slowly. "No, too many people saying so for it not to be true. I believe it. You're a fucking snitch." He jiggled the blade in his hand. "I oughta do everyone a favor and gut you, *puto.*"

"No," Ronnie whined. "Please, don't."

Tiburon's lip curled in disgust. "You sound like a little girl."

"I just want to live."

There was a time in the recent months since Gavin's death when that may not have been true. Heaps of guilt, day after day. Then, yesterday, came the glimmer of possibility that the weight of it all might truly be lifted. Now, he had something to live for.

You always did, Ronnie. You just didn't realize it.

He pushed Gavin's voice aside and stared beseechingly at Tiburon.

"Please," he repeated. "I'm sick. I need to fix."

The admission hung in the air. Tiburon's lip curled further, then dropped into a grimace.

"Fucking junkies," he muttered. His words were laced with hatred. He pressed his fist against Ronnie's chest, letting the blade tip rest near his throat. "You ever snitch on me or anyone I know and I'll give you a bright red smile below your chin. *Entiendes?*"

Ronnie nodded frantically. His chin brushed the cool, hard metal of the knife as Tiburon pulled it away.

"Get the fuck out of here," Tiburon ordered him.

Ronnie forgot shuffling and scurrying. He ran.

The long squeal of brakes and the sudden arrival of his bus pull him from his reverie. He waits for the departing passengers to exit the bus before climbing aboard. The driver gives him a suspicious look, but it is tinged with weariness, as if he expects Ronnie to be trouble but doesn't care enough to intercept it.

Ronnie finds a seat halfway back. He sits and stares out the window, waiting for the bus to pull away from the plaza. He can feel the sickness within him, knows that only some of it is his body crying out for the heroin. He rubs his upper arms, even though it isn't cold. In fact, the day had been uncomfortably hot and he'd worn his hoodie tied around his slim waist since late morning. But he is twitchy and can't help moving. Soon enough, he knows he'll be rocking in place, forcing back nausea and keeping his mouth clamped against moans of despair.

Stop it. You're so goddamned dramatic.

As if in answer to his own internal critic, he hears Gavin's soft, even voice again.

Practice self-kindness, Ronnie, the Gavin-in-his-head says. *You don't have to be so hard on yourself. Plenty of other people for that.*

Ronnie chuffs. There's no doubt this is true. Seems like everyone has it out for him. Gavin was the only person who ever showed him love. Not the romance novel kind, though Ronnie knows Gavin felt some of that, too. No, it was the simplest and purest sort of love. The kind that asks for nothing in return. The kind people mean when they say ride or die.

He doesn't know what he ever did to deserve it. Certainly no one else in the world felt that way about him. Ronnie likes to believe his own mother had loved him like that, at least for a little while. Back when he was still a baby, all cute and shit. Of course, if it were true, it certainly didn't last. Maybe he stopped being so cute or perhaps it was all too much work for her. Or, given how his own preferences for escape developed, maybe she had a dragon of her own to chase.

No matter how it went down, he ended up in a box outside a fire station, and she was gone. He never knew who she was and had no memories of her. Of course, it went without saying that he also doesn't know his father. Hell, odds were she probably hadn't known, either, if she was from the streets. For all he knew, Ronnie might have met either or both of them while out and about, scoring smack and trying to survive.

The fire station must have called child services, because into the system Ronnie went. He lived in a long string of foster homes, so many that he stopped unpacking his meager belongings at each stop. He just lived out of his backpack. It was easier that way.

Through all of that, most people didn't give a shit about him. Not the case workers, not the foster parents, and not the other kids. A couple of the foster mothers showed him some small measure of kindness on occasion. One of the foster fathers took a particular interest in him but that quickly turned dark for Ronnie. And while he managed to get along with most of the other kids, he accomplished this mostly by disappearing into the background whenever he could. That seemed to suit most people, since they didn't much care for Ronnie or what happened to him.

No, Gavin was the only one. From the day they met at a flop house in Browne's Addition, Gavin saw something in Ronnie. Something no one else saw. He never asked for anything back, either. Just Ronnie's friendship, which Ronnie was happy to give. He wished he could have given Gavin more, given him the kind of love Gavin craved, but he couldn't. Ronnie just wasn't wired that way.

It's okay, Ronnie, Gavin whispers. *You did all you could.*

Ronnie keeps the sleeve of his hoodie pressed to his chin. He settles back against the seat. The thinly padded surface seems to push back, and he can feel the hard metal of the gun in his waistband. He swallows thickly and stares out the bus window at the businesses that flit by.

I'm sorry, Gavin. But I'm going to make it right.

***

Finding the gun had been a stroke of luck. Whether that luck was good or cursed remained to be seen, but there was no denying the seeming providence of the event. Everything lined up perfectly.

He just happened to be hanging out near the light pole on First and Jefferson, near where the Hope Apartments used to be. He'd been dreaming of the time he lived there with Gavin. The tiny place didn't even have its own bathroom and yet those days seemed like a golden era to him now.

His reverie was broken when a thick-chested black man barreled around the corner.

Ronnie cringed instinctively, but the man had no interest in him. He blasted past Ronnie at full tilt, almost brushing against him. Several flecks of wetness sprinkled against Ronnie's face and the smell of the sweat, fear, and cologne washed over him.

A moment later, the man was five steps away.

Ronnie followed him, transfixed. He watched as the man fumbled briefly at his waistband. Then the dark metal of the gun appeared in his hand.

Ronnie dropped into a crouch. A surge of adrenaline flooded his body.

Without breaking stride, the man flicked his wrist, tossing the gun to his right. It cleared the high curb, struck the asphalt of the street with one surprisingly subdued *clack*, and slid under a parked car.

Ronnie stared.

The man redoubled his efforts, pumping his legs and arms. As the sounds of his footfalls receded, Ronnie heard the stamp of more approaching feet. He barely managed to turn his head in time to see a pair of uniformed cops skid around the same corner, one behind the other.

The first cop's gaze cut to Ronnie, lingering for a fraction of a second before returning to his quarry.

"Stop!" he yelled after the fleeing man. His tone sounded almost perfunctory, but there was nothing half-hearted in the way he continued his pursuit.

The second cop was heavier than the first and trailed behind his partner, doggedly running despite his inferior speed. Ronnie recognized him but couldn't recall his name. The cop had busted both him and Gavin for shoplifting about a year ago. It was only a misdemeanor, but Ronnie realized in that moment that the charge was still unresolved. There was probably a warrant for him. Ronnie tried to shrink into the pavement but the pursuing cop didn't even look in his direction.

The man they were chasing went around the far corner. A few moments later, the lead cop rounded the same corner. His plodding partner took another several seconds to do the same.

And then they were gone.

Ronnie's gaze snapped to the space beneath the parked car. From this angle, a sliver of black metal was visible near the tire. Ronnie stood. His heart pounded, almost as if he'd been running himself, like he was part of the chase. He tried to remain casual while he walked toward the car, glancing around surreptitiously. The street had a thousand eyes but none of them seemed to be watching him now.

If the cops come back, I'll show it to them. That's gotta be worth something. Goodwill, if nothing else.

The thought made him falter. The jeering voices that had been haunting him for months now rang in his ears like a chorus. *Ronnie Ross-o-SNITCH.* That was the jacket they hung on him. It didn't matter how much he denied being a snitch, the label stuck.

Probably because it was true.

And the truth was what got Gavin killed.

Ronnie stepped forward with renewed urgency. When he reached the car, he squatted down and felt around. His palm brushed against the hot asphalt briefly before his fingers found the metal of the gun. He grasped it, lifted it to his middle, and then untied the sweatshirt tied around his waist. He forced the gun into the folds of cloth, wrapping it. Then, hands supporting the sweatshirt, he stood and walked rapidly in the opposite direction the cops and the fleeing man.

What are you doing, Ronnie?

The question bonged in his head like a church bell, but whether it was his own voice or Gavin's, he couldn't tell.

***

He'd been crashing at Emil's place for almost two weeks now. The gaunt man in his fifties worked nights at the nearby grocery outlet. He allowed Ronnie to sleep on the couch and use the bathroom in exchange for Ronnie scoring his dope for him. It was an arrangement Ronnie didn't expect to last, but then again, nothing did.

He'd barely slept the first night he had the gun. Instead, he sat on the couch and gazed down at the weapon on the coffee table. The black metal of the gun stared up at him. He reached out and touched it but didn't pick it up. The weight of the pistol had surprised him. He supposed the fact it was heavy was a good thing. It spoke to the seriousness of what it was used for.

And what are you going to do with it, Ronnie?

His own voice mocked him, all but calling him weak. He didn't bother to deny it. He *was* weak. A drug addict. A small man at the bottom of the food chain in the dirtiest part of town in a dirty city. The worst part was that the vile rumors about him weren't rumors at all. They were true.

Did Gavin know? He'd often wondered. The conclusion he reached was that it probably didn't matter. Even if he had known, Gavin would have forgiven him. He would have understood. Just like how hurt people hurt

143

people, his friend knew that people like him and Ronnie did what they had do to survive.

Even snitch.

He didn't remember when the plan formed in his head. He felt like maybe it had always been there, hiding in the recesses of his mind, afraid to slip from the unconscious to the conscious, as if in doing so, he might suffer repercussions for having dared to even consider such an action.

Gavin wouldn't approve, he knew.

But Gavin deserved it all the same, after what happened.

When all of the whispers about Ronnie became open suspicion, it was Gavin who stood by him. Suspicion turned to accusation and, still, Gavin remained at his side. Even when Laszlo Nagy, who ruled their little corner of the drug world like he was Tony Montana, called Ronnie out as a snitch, Gavin never wavered.

He stood tall, the only one Ronnie could ever remember doing so. Ride or die. True friendship. True love.

Call it what you will, such beautiful things are never free.

In the end, Gavin found that out.

When two hard men piled out of a car to chase Ronnie down, it was Gavin who told him to run. Gavin who intercepted one of the men. Gavin who paid the price in the form of a beating. When Ronnie crept back into the alley almost an hour after Gavin covered for his escape, his friend was barely recognizable, barely alive. He called an ambulance but they weren't able to do anything for him at the hospital. In the end, like a junkie Jesus, Gavin paid for Ronnie's sins with his own blood, his own life.

The only difference? Ronnie was never forgiven.

As time passed, Gavin's death ate at him like an infection. His friend, his best friend—his only friend— died because Ronnie was a snitch.

There could be no forgiveness for that, he knew.

The realization of this truth brought him to another, harder one.

Forgiveness may have been unattainable but vengeance was not.

***

Finding the home address of a Spokane Police detective should have been more difficult than it was. Ronnie was surprised when it only took twenty-five minutes of stolen time on Emil's phone while the man was showering. He had expected such information to be jealously guarded but perhaps no information was secret anymore.

In any event, he doubted Detective James Morgan cared if people knew where he lived. The thick-bodied brute may even have welcomed a visit from anyone bent on revenge. Ronnie knew the man skirted the edges of what was legal and what was questionable. He'd heard stories. Not just threats. Vindictive focus that a regular person would call harassment. Interviews punctuated with violence. He even heard one about a long ride in the dead of night out into the middle of nowhere, followed by a gun to the head. That was one version, anyway. In other version, the person never came back from the trip. Thing was, almost all of the stories were repeated by someone who wasn't actually there. It was always a cousin, a friend, a guy or girl someone knew. The speaker's own experiences with Morgan were more mundane, if still intimidating. Ronnie suspected most of the stories were straight-up boogeyman tales, there to enhance the man's reputation and encourage cooperation among the criminal underworld.

Hell, it had worked with Ronnie.

So had having a possession with intent charge hanging over his head.

In any event, if someone ever showed up on Morgan's doorstep to get even for some affront, Ronnie figured the big man would see it as a free ticket to let loose with any and all violence he wanted to visit upon the challenger. After all, every blow would be within the confines of legality at that point. It'd be a solution to any violence-related blue-balls the detective might be harboring due to holding back from smacking people he felt deserved it but couldn't legally justify delivering.

Ronnie believed Morgan would love the opportunity.

Of course, if he saw Ronnie on his doorstep, he probably wouldn't even waste the energy. Probably just smirk and swing the door shut and go back to watching *The Punisher* on Netflix. That's how small, how insignificant, he saw Ronnie as being. Just a gnat whose only value was in the snatches of information he periodically provided.

That was okay with Ronnie, though. Because he didn't plan on knocking on Morgan's front door. Gavin deserved straightforward justice but his soul would have to settle for the stealthy kind.

***

The bus sways on its shocks as it turns a corner and glides to a stop. Ronnie's nausea is part motion-sickness and part withdrawal. He tries to ignore it. He is out of his seat before the doors clack open. His feet hit the ground and he is walking.

It feels strange to be back in the suburbs. He stayed in more than a few foster homes dotted across the city's residential areas, but the setting feels foreign to him now. Most of his life in recent years has kept him within the core of downtown, part of an ecosystem very different from how people live out here. He thinks someone might notice him, see how out of place he is now, how he is nothing but a downtown rat out of his element. But no one pays him a second glance as he shuffles and scurries along.

The cut on his chin has stopped bleeding, though he checks it every few steps to be certain. His destination is only a block away now—a massive collection of mid-to-higher end apartments large enough to be its own village. From what Ronnie read on Emil's phone, they have their own gym and even a small convenience store that is for residents only.

Thankfully, though, access is not restricted. No guard shack, no gate. Just a roving security patrol that Ronnie hopes is as inept as most of the others he has encountered.

No wannabe cops tonight, he prays silently. He already has to deal with the real thing. That will be more than enough.

Ronnie slips between the buildings, a shuffling shadow in the darkness. When he reaches the parking lot nearest Morgan's apartment, he scans the parking stalls for Morgan's police-issued muscle car. It isn't there. His first reaction to its absence is dismay. He looks for painted markings on the pavement of the empty slots but there are none. First come, first served, he wonders? He doesn't think that would matter to someone like Morgan.

The detective would have *his* spot and woe to anyone who parked in it.

Then he spots the row of small garages on the other side of the lot. Ronnie hustles over, resisting the urge to look left and right to see if anyone's watching. He can't act suspicious, can't be noticed.

The one-car garages are marked with a placard above each that corresponds to an apartment number. Morgan's is the second one from the corner. Ronnie risks a peek through the dark sliver of glass, cupping his hands against it to peer inside. It is difficult to see any detail, but one thing is clear—there is no vehicle inside.

Morgan isn't home.

Ronnie's apprehension kicks up a notch. He turns away from the garage and retraces his path. It takes only a few steps before he realizes this works best for him.

If Morgan is out working, he might return soon. He'll be tired. Less aware. It will work better than his original plan to call the man and say he had an urgent tip to share. Get the detective to leave his apartment, then ambush him on his way to the car.

No, this is better.

Ronnie settles behind the carefully manicured, four-foot bushes, his back to the wall. The gun presses against him, reminiscent of when he'd been waiting for darkness in the downtown doorway. He leans forward and fishes the weapon out. He hefts it in his hand, feeling the weight. He wants to think that it feels good, feels right, but the truth is that the pistol feels foreign in his grip. He wonders if he could ever become accustomed to carrying it.

I don't need to get used to it. After tonight, I'll never have to touch it again.

He lets his weight push against the hard siding of the building. Through the thin branches and small leaves of the bushes, he can see the empty parking stall. Morgan's path from there to his apartment leads directly past Ronnie's position. The nearest light is mounted at the corner of the building, but the halo of yellow it casts falls short of the place he has chosen. It isn't dark but it is dim. Dim enough that no one will see him huddled there, waiting.

Especially not Morgan.

He envisioned it all in his mind. As Morgan passes by, Ronnie stands up, bringing his arm clear of the bushes. Does he squeeze the trigger immediately? Put two rounds in the back of Morgan's head? Or does he pause? Savor the moment. Maybe wait for Morgan to turn to face him so that he knows who visited this vengeance upon him. Hell, maybe the man will even beg for his life.

No, Ronnie realizes. That won't happen. Morgan isn't the kind of man who begs.

He should know why this is happening, though.

Shouldn't he?

Or was it enough that Ronnie would know?

Minutes pass. Become an hour, then two. Or so it seems. He resists the urge to check his small flip phone, worries that it has only been a short time and his body is trying to surrender already, to make him a failure at revenge, too.

He feels nauseated and tries to breathe past it. Instead of images of Morgan and the flash of a gun muzzle, Ronnie thinks of the beautiful, hateful ritual that his life centers around. Sees the spoon. The flame. The shriveling balls of cotton. He feels the sweet sting of the needle. The moment of anticipation. The rush of relief as he lowers the plunger. The brown concoction sluices into his veins.

And then… floating. The only time this world feels right for him.

He misses it. Yearns for it.

After, he reminds himself.

After.

His legs cramp and he carefully and quietly shifts to stretch them. His tailbone aches. The entire time, his mind goes round and round. Back and forth between visions of fantasy—some of revenge, some of fixing—and realizations of hard reality. Every trip around the topic, he lands back on one simple thing: he is here.

He's doing this.

This isn't you, Ronnie.

Gavin's voice is so clear in his mind that the sudden thought makes him start. He shakes his head as if to dislodge it. Before he can formulate a response, a wash of headlights and the rumble of an engine catch his attention. The lights drop away suddenly, then the dark silhouette of a Dodge Charger rolls into his view. The car glides through the parking lot and continues until it stops in front of the second garage. The car door swings open, but no interior light kicks on. It's not until the man exits, that Ronnie is sure it's Detective James Morgan. He sees the his unmistakably rugged silhouette in the dim ambient light.

Morgan makes short work of opening the garage door and pulling the Dodge inside. The red of the taillights flash briefly and the engine's growl is cut short.

Ronnie tries to swallow.

Can't.

Ronnie hears the muffled thump of a door being eased shut, then Morgan appears outside the garage opening. He extends his arm outward toward the garage's interior in the universal motion of clicking a car fob. However, there is no beep or flicker of lights. From this distance, Ronnie barely hears the slight plastic clack as the door locks snap into place.

He must have had mechanics disable the horn and light function when he locks it.

Ronnie doesn't have to wonder why. Morgan may have used loudness to his advantage on plenty of occasions but Ronnie knew he used silence and camouflage just as often. Hell, it was how he caught Ronnie, all that time ago.

Morgan lowers the garage door. Ronnie's heart hammers in his chest as the detective gives the door a tug to make sure it's secure, then turns and starts in Ronnie's direction. Morgan is carrying something is his hand. Ronnie can't immediately tell what it is.

It's a gun. He's ready. He knows.

Ronnie tries to breathe, tries to calm himself. He blinks several times and looks more closely at the approaching man. After a moment, he can see it's not a gun. It's only a bag of some kind.

Ronnie shifts the gun to his left hand. He wipes his sweaty, shaking right hand across the front of his hoodie. Morgan's confident strides cover ground quickly, more quickly than Ronnie wants. He wants Morgan to slow down, just slow down. Give him more time to think, to get ready.

Morgan reaches the end of the walkway and pushes the bag into the trash can situated there. The action is fluid and powerful, no movement wasted. Then Moran turns and heads down the walkway in Ronnie's direction. A splash of light makes it possible for Ronnie to see the hard lines in his face. His impenetrable expression is the same as always, as close to a real life Clint Eastwood as any man Ronnie has ever known.

Ronnie takes the gun in his right hand again. Wiping away the sweat did little good. The pistol grip feels slippery in his palm.

Morgan steps closer. Despite his solid frame and the boots he wears, his footfalls are almost inaudible on the concrete.

The magnitude of the moment washes over Ronnie. His legs are rubbery and he has no strength in them. He doubts he can stand. A moment later and it doesn't matter, because there is no time left. Morgan is there, he is two steps away, now one, and then he is past.

Tears slide down Ronnie's cheeks.

You weak, pathetic fuck! Do it for Gavin!

Ronnie raises the pistol without standing. His breath flutters in and out. He draws a bead on Morgan's back, peering through the twigs and leaves he is hiding within. His vision disappears into the deep black of the detective's T-shirt.

Do it!

And then Morgan stops.

Ronnie watches him, squinting down the trembling barrel of the gun. His own breath stills, like a deer who has heard the hint of a nearby predator.

Morgan glances around slowly, scanning. When his gaze passes over Ronnie's hiding place, a shiver runs up Ronnie's spine, making the barrel dip and bounce even more. He imagines Morgan stomping toward him, covering the few yards between them in great loping strides, reaching into the bushes and yanking him out by his throat, holding him in air like a trembling rabbit.

Ronnie closes his eyes, pressing them shut with ferocity, then forces them open again.

I need to do it. Shoot him. He's the reason Gavin is dead.

His finger nestles again the trigger.

Morgan's gaze passes over his hiding spot a second time. His eyes seem like they are perfectly capable of penetrating the brush. Yet, Morgan continues on, looking elsewhere. His pause and glance around have only lasted a second or two, Ronnie thinks, but it feels like forever.

Forever.

He's had forever to shoot.

But he doesn't.

Even when Morgan turns around again and shows Ronnie his back, even when he is that vulnerable, Ronnie can't squeeze the trigger. He has no faith in the bullets. They will tumble uselessly from the end of barrel or splat against Morgan's back like bird shit. All he will do is anger Morgan and have to face retribution.

He is too afraid.

Morgan trots up the stairs to his apartment. There is a brief jingle of keys and then the detective disappears inside.

I'm a coward. I'm nothing but a junkie and a cow—

Another voice intercedes, always calm, always loving.

No, you're not, Ronnie. Don't say that about yourself.

He closes his eyes. He can see Gavin's gentle smile.

You're a good person. That's the truth. Deep inside, you're still a good person.

Ronnie lets the tears spill out of him. They run hotly down his cheeks. He cries in silence for several minutes before he has the strength of will to rouse himself and slip out from the bushes. He staggers away on unsteady legs half-numb from sitting. His chest is leaden. The gun dangles from his right hand, weighing heavily, causing his shoulders to slope to that side. He waits until Morgan's apartment is out of his line of sight before he musters the courage to get rid of it. He spots a white pickup with big tires in a parking stall. As he nears, he flicks his wrist, hurling the gun away. It strikes the asphalt and hops once, disappearing behind the front tire. It is an echo, a rhyme of how he found it himself.

He is glad the gun is gone. He wishes his empty hands would bring him some relief but they don't. He is still the same person, the same weak, pathetic snitch who got Gavin killed and didn't even have the balls to avenge him, or even try to live a better life. Make something of the gift Gavin gave to him.

Ronnie trudges toward the entrance of the complex, his vision blinded by his tears. His rising nausea reminds him of what he needs to do, and soon.

You can still live that life, Ronnie.

Even Gavin's hopeful nature can't disguise the futility of those words.

You're a good person. That's why you didn't shoot a man in the back.

"Keep telling yourself that," Ronnie mutters.

Ronnie curls his fingers into fists and keeps walking, headed back to where he came from.

Shots
Claire Booth

"Tina. Tina! *Tina!*"

Our chant grew louder and then dissolved into hoots and laughter. Tina, tiara askew, tossed back the shot and wheezed toxic Fireball fumes before she found her breath.

"You guys have to go easy on me. We've only done one bar."

The nine of us all swayed to the left as the limo turned at the Sherman Street intersection. Tina bumped against me and turned it into a hug.

"I'm so glad you could make it, Rayna."

"Me, too," I said.

"How long do you get to stay?"

"Just for the wedding. I have to be back to work on Monday."

"You staying with Misty?"

We both looked at my younger sister, sitting at the other end of the stretch and talking animatedly with another of our high school friends.

"No. They 'don't have space.' Brock has a big work project going on in their spare room, apparently. So I'm staying with Mom and Dad."

And that made me feel like I always did when I came home to Spokane. Like a kid. With all the bad—and okay, admittedly some of the good—that came with it. The familiar friends stuck in their familiar roles, jostling against one another as the limo turned another corner. There were two women I didn't know, colleagues from

Tina's paralegal job at the law firm. Otherwise it was the same old gang. Thank God I moved away.

The champagne in my flute sloshed and I leaned in the opposite direction to keep it from going overboard. Misty caught my eye from down the length of the bench seat and smiled. My kid sis was looking good in a tight turtleneck shirt and flowy pants instead of her normal T-shirt and jeans, but how she wasn't dying in the summer heat was a mystery. Her bangs were new, and she'd switched eyeliner to a color that better suited her blue eyes, but otherwise she was holding steady. Not so for me.

My light brown hair was now short, almost a pixie cut. My boyfriend Mason had been surprised and thought it was sexy as hell. Tina had been hysterical and thought it would ruin the bridesmaid photos. But since I got it lopped off two days *before* she called and asked me to be in the wedding, I was left guilt free. And, let's be honest, more than a little perversely pleased. She didn't need to get everything she wanted.

***

Sweet shit, there'd never been this kind of place when I lived in this cow town. Techno thumping and people grinding and some hot bartender wearing Tina's crown. And absinthe. Fuuuck . . . it probably wasn't the real thing, but it was summery green and it twinkled at me like it had something to say. At least the third glass did. I couldn't remember if the first two had been talkative or not. I put this one to my ear, but then felt it getting taken out of my hand.

"Okay, Rayna," my sister said. "I think that's enough. You're at the point you're confusing your orifices."

I squawked in protest and got a patronizing face pat in return.

"Give it back. Or drink it yourself," I told Misty. "You need to start having a good time."

"I am." Misty smiled again. Even through my haze, I registered the lie. If she were really having a good time, she'd be giving me the shit-eating grin she was known for, not this bland face-bending.

I poked her cheek. Her makeup came off on my finger and I saw a purplish spot underneath. She moved away, trying to take my drink with her. The pretty green became my focus again. "Come on … You're Mother Hen-ing us. You don't need to. We have a driver. Have a few drinks."

Misty laughed. "Yeah, so I can be hating life tomorrow with the rest of you?" At least, I think that's what she said. The music was so loud, I had to read her lips.

"If you're going to be that way, make yourself useful and go get Tina's tiara back."

She stuck her tongue out at me. "I have a boyfriend. I'm not going to go talk to a guy."

"It's the bartender. That's his entire function. To get talked to. Plus, he's nice to look at."

"You have a boyfriend, too."

I was about to tell her that asking for the return of a five-dollar plastic crown wasn't infidelity when a big ol' farm boy shoulder-bumped me on his way off the dance floor. From Misty's reaction, I didn't keep my balance very well. She grabbed me and we both staggered back into Olivia, one of the bridesmaids I didn't know. My absinthe splashed all over her and all three of us started groping for napkins and tissues and anything else we could find.

Then the farm boy came back, face as red as a Yakima apple and plowing through people like he was on a winter wheatfield. Nobody else paid any attention. Until he threw the first punch. The assaulted, a too-skinny guy wearing too much denim, went down like a bag of bricks. And I was the only one who noticed. I swatted at Misty, but she wouldn't turn from the wreckage of Olivia's blouse.

The farm boy followed him down, hitting him in the face again and again. Two other men threw themselves on the attacker and started giving it back. That was the stone in the pond. The crowd washed away in all directions as the bartender started yelling for the bouncers. Misty finally noticed just as a bunch of other farm boys waded in.

Tina shrieked. It was, I grudgingly gave to her, a very efficient bid to redirect attention where she believed it belonged. If she dared swoon, though, I'd throw a punch myself. I could do it, too. I was starting to sober up something quick. I grabbed Olivia's right arm and Misty grabbed her left. The other five bridesmaids were already headed toward the door, dragging Tina with them. People all over the club were yelling and pushing. The fight in the middle of the dance floor was turning from a beatdown into a full-on melee. The strobe lights made the whole thing seem like a bad stop-action film. Then shit got real.

I saw a flash of silver at the exact moment a loud pop overlayed the thumping music. The guy holding the gun raised it even higher but before he could get another shot off, a hammy fist came at him from the side and hit him in the temple. He crumpled and dropped his weapon. The puncher dove for it. He got to it just as his shirt bloomed red. Instead of picking the gun up, he slumped onto the original shooter and stayed still. Oh, God. I shoved Olivia toward the door and followed, looking over my shoulder at what I prayed wasn't a dead man. The skinny denim guy approached them, arm extended. His gun was black. I could barely see it, but I sure heard it. Then other gunshots came from over by the DJ booth and the music died.

We were almost to the door. Misty was Herculean in her sobriety, dragging us both and not letting go as we got pounded by the panicking crowd. I didn't know if we were going to make it out. Then I heard sirens. That only made it worse. Now the fighters wanted to get away, too. They scattered like roaches. And the crowd reacted as if that's exactly what they were. Screaming, shoving, trying to get away as they darted through the crowd. If only we could've stomped them under our shoes. That was my last thought before I ended up on the floor.

I was hit from behind with so much force, Misty lost her grip on me. I spun and went down hard on my knees. I couldn't see anything except people's legs. A guy in blue Chuck Taylors kicked me in the side. I almost vomited. Somebody yanked on my purse strap and pulled me up. I rode the press of people out the door and into the street.

People fled in all directions and there I was, a long-distance runner and I couldn't get my legs to work right. I staggered around alone on the still-hot asphalt without a clue of what to do. And then, the sweetest sound I've ever heard. A shriek, from down the street. And yes, I was aware enough to note the irony.

I started toward hysterical Tina and the limo as another mess of people burst out of the building. Suddenly Misty and Olivia were next to me. I had no idea how I ended up outside before they did. All I knew was that my knee hurt, and the blue and red lights now washing over First Avenue made my head want to split open.

Misty hustled us to the limo, panting that we had to get out of here. She'd been so calm the whole time, but now she seemed panicked. Tina held open the car door and then followed us in. Everyone else was already there. The minute the door slammed, the driver hit the gas.

"Shouldn't we stay here?" Olivia asked. She had a scratch on her cheek and bloodshot eyes. "We're witnesses. The police will want to talk to us."

We all watched Tina's mouth become a thin line of stubborn. "We only saw what a bunch of other people saw, too. They can talk to the police. I'm not spending the rest of my bachelorette night at some scuzzy police station."

"Well, I'm sure as hell not going to another bar," said our friend Ava. She and Tina had been best frenemies since high school. They were in a good patch right now, which was why she'd been granted bridesmaid slot number eight. From the look on Tina's face, that offer was about to be rescinded.

"I'm not having my night ruined by a stupid fight. We're going to go somewhere else."

"It wasn't just a fight. People got shot," Olivia said. "I think somebody might've died."

I looked at her. The expression on her face said she'd seen the same thing I had. Maybe we should've stayed and talked to the police. But honestly, all I wanted to do was go home, take a bunch of Advil, and quietly crawl into bed. And pray my parents were already asleep. Jesus, it was high school all over again.

I glanced around the car. Opinion seemed to be divided. Some people were still dazed. Casey was crying.

Alyssa and Hannah were pushing for another bar. Misty, sitting at the other end of the limo, was pulling out her phone. I cocked an eyebrow at her. She mouthed Brock. She sent a text and her phone rang within seconds. She talked for a minute, then held out the phone. "Everybody say hi to Brock."

We half-heartedly helloed and then went back to not making a decision on our next stop. Until Ava unexpectedly came through.

"How about Satellite Diner? It's still open. And if Alyssa still wants booze, they have that, too."

Everyone stopped talking. We all turned to Tina. She pouted for a minute, then bowed to the inevitable because she was as drunk and suddenly hungry as the rest of us. "Fine. That does sound good."

I smiled at Ava. With that stroke of genius, she might've just moved herself up into slot number seven.

***

I stumbled in the fastest, so I made it to the bathroom first. Christ Almighty, I had to pee. I locked myself in and since there was no hook, held my purse on my lap. It was all lumpy, probably from getting battered around at the club. I wiped the bar floor scum and Misty makeup off my hands and opened it up to rearrange things. And there, lying on top of the penis-shaped drinking straws I'd planned to hand out at the next bar, was a gun.

It was an ugly little thing, black and short. It was a revolver, even I knew that much, its cylinder a wheel of destruction waiting to be spun. Was it the same one I saw the denim man shoot? Dear God. Someone—maybe him—must've stuck it in my bag during all the pandemonium. Now it lay there, staring at me. I used some toilet paper to pick it up enough to see that it still had bullets in it, and gaping holes where some should be and weren't. Then I carefully put it back down. I don't know how long I stared at it. I sat there, the seat protector sticking to my sweaty ass, and tried to think it through.

I didn't move until someone banged on the bathroom door. It startled me so badly I almost dropped the whole damn purse. Then I cinched it closed and rejoined everyone. They were at two tables in the back, arguing about which menu items would soothe upset stomachs. Except Misty. She was on her phone again. She startled as I peered over her shoulder.

"Don't look at me like that." She nudged me away. "Brock's just worried."

Ava scoffed. "Everybody's boyfriend was worried. One 'I'm okay' text took care of it for all the rest of us."

My first thought: Ava actually has a boyfriend? My second: I agree with her—Brock was keeping too close tabs on my sister.

I looked around for an empty chair. There weren't any. But the scene from a step back was ridiculously priceless. Alyssa's skirt was ripped—she was trying to safety pin it and order a tray of shots at the same time. Casey's face was splotchy and mottled red. Olivia's shirt was stained all down the front and she smelled like licorice. And Carmen, the other paralegal, had a bruise starting to form on her cheek. She saw me looking.

"Is it getting bad? It really hurts."

And Tina thought my haircut would be what ruined the wedding photos. Ha. I resisted the near overwhelming urge to point this out. Instead I told Carmen it was barely visible, a lie everybody immediately endorsed. Except Tina, who just averted her eyes. And Misty, who wouldn't look up from her damn phone. I plucked it out of her hand.

"I want to take a picture. Your camera's better."

Her look said bullshit, but I didn't care. I took a few steps back and started snapping. Then I walked toward the front of the place looking for a spare chair. And reading Brock's texts. It was what I'd expected. He was on his way. No more fun with the girls. Misty's evening was over. I pocketed the phone, grabbed a stack of napkins off the bar and a hoodie off the back of a chair and kept walking. Out the door and right on Sprague Avenue. Straight down to North Division where the railroad bridge crossed it. Stepped in front of Brock's car on the otherwise deserted street. Finished the thought I started in the bathroom, block hopped until I found a Dumpster, and still made it back to Satellite in ten minutes, not even winded.

A chair by the bar had opened up. I grabbed it and slid it to our table just in time to see Tina trash her wedding diet and order a bacon-loaded omelet.

There was one last shot left on the tray. I declined. I'd already had mine.

A Spy's Night Out

Puja Guha

Two spies walk into a wedding venue . . .
Sounds like the beginning of a bad joke.

Thomas Dubois grimaced. Under normal circumstances, he would have enjoyed visiting a place like the Northwest Museum of Arts and Culture in a vibrant town like Spokane, Washington. The area nearby was stunning, and he was nothing short of a museum geek. His favorite pastime at university had been to wander into one of the plethora of Paris museums. With his student card, admission was free, and he could check out a single wing. He read every label, stared at each brushstroke, and departed. Some of the best times ever.

But today was not one of those days. He felt more like Will Smith in *Independence Day*, dragging a heavy alien's body across the desert on the Fourth of July.

I could have been at a barbecue, he imagined himself shouting to the universe at the top of his lungs.

Instead, he forced a smile onto his face and walked around the main lobby of the museum building. The two full walls of windows drew his attention away from the upcoming drop, but only for a moment. In the distance, Mount Spokane stood out as an immovable masterpiece, several deep shades of green from the base with a snow cap on top. Thomas found himself staring at it as his hands made minor adjustments to the tablecloth at a high-top next to the northeast facing window. He fluffed the flowers in the centerpiece, at the same time tacking the coin-sized wireless Agency listening device to the base of the vase.

The muscles in his upper back and torso released the tiniest bit. Securely placing the first bug always made him feel better. As did looking at nature, especially mountains. Mountains predated all of humankind—including the gods of even the most ancient religions. They had stood for centuries, for millennia.

And will stand long after. Regardless of whether today's op goes horribly wrong.

Or perfectly right.

Whatever that meant when it came to spy craft. He was here pretending to be part of the venue coordination staff at the museum. For the wedding of Elise Fisher and Wayne Cartwright.

Or more importantly, the niece of Jonathan Fisher. Officially a wealthy global investor who ran a holding company with real estate and agriculture investments all over the world. But in the Agency circles, that name came with different descriptors.

Cocaine mogul. Ultimate scumbag. Bond villain. Take your pick.

Better yet choose all of the above.

Thomas certainly had. In his past six years at the Agency, he had never felt as compelled to go after a target as he was today. Everything Thomas had learned about Jonathan Fisher since the start of this assignment had bolstered his view that Fisher was a villain the likes of Joker in *Batman*. A psychopath so deeply rooted in his own version of reality that he believed the world to be a skit set up for his own amusement and personal gain. All humans were savages, so why not exploit them? Trample on their backs, take their money and all their dignity. Make them dependent on substances only he could provide so they would constantly come back for more. Crawling on their knees and willing to pay any price, regardless of the consequences.

Thomas moved across the room, checking each of the subsequent tablecloths. The sun caught the various shades of green outside, and he wished more than anything he was out there. Hiking on Mount Spokane instead of stuck inside on a risky op.

It's summer. They could have had this wedding outside.

If only. Then he wouldn't be here on the eve of his grandmother's birthday, instead he'd be celebrating with her and the rest of his family at his parents' estate in southern France.

Yup. He could have been at a barbecue. But, instead, he was hoping to execute step zero of two hundred and seventy-eight for the Agency to gather enough intel on Jonathan Fisher to stop his next major round of drug shipments. And, eventually, maybe, they might stand a chance of sticking him in jail where he belonged. Or a hole in the ground. Thomas wasn't picky. As an independent intel organization, the Agency was often confused with the much larger and better-known CIA, but they still had plenty of experience making people disappear. More experience than Thomas liked to admit, even to himself.

But that didn't matter today. This was a good mission. For once, he could be confident the Agency was one hundred percent in the right. Although Thomas wasn't green enough to believe the Agency might be able to make a difference. He'd seen too many targets get away scot-free. By striking a deal with the higher ups—something that enabled the Agency to supposedly catch an even bigger fish. Or by vanishing into the wind before the wheels of bureaucracy and justice could do enough to catch them in the act.

But we have to try. Even if it's a long shot.

Especially when it's a long shot. No risk, no reward.

Thomas caught the eye of Santiago, one of his team members, also posing as a member of the venue's staff. He didn't know Santiago well, but he was something of an Agency legend. An Agency field operative who had retired several years earlier, then been pulled back in to support one of his former mentees. Petra Shirazi, also a former field officer, twice over, with a stint in Research in between. Now dead after an op in Iran had gone sideways. As far as Thomas knew, one of the Agency's board members had convinced Santiago to return as an Agency trainer and instructor. So that no one else would suffer Petra's fate. Santiago had finally agreed on one condition. He refused to be on a first name basis with any of his new recruits. So now he went by Santiago instead of his first name, Carlos.

Clearly there was a lot more to that story, but Thomas was content to let it lie. He was lucky to have someone with Santiago's experience on his team. They weren't ready to recruit a new operative yet, but he'd convinced Santiago to be part of the op from the get-go. Necessary experience for when they would identify and bring in the new asset over the next few months. Or so he had claimed.

Whatever it took to get the job done.

But this is a good mission.

Thomas clung to that fallback. If he had to lie and cheat for a chance to bring Jonathan Fisher to justice, he would do it. No holds barred. For all the people who had suffered because of the drug trade all over the world. His ex-girlfriend was an addict. When they were together at university in Paris, he remembered her trying cocaine for the first time. He was an athlete so had abstained, but he hadn't raised any objections to her sampling it. Their relationship was already on rocky ground—he was three years older and six months away from graduating. He wasn't ready to factor their relationship into his plans after school, and so they had parted ways amicably at the end of school. By that time, she was using regularly—a couple of times a week, as far as he knew. They'd met up on occasion after that—when they were both in the same city at the same time. The hookups were fun and casual. Never any discussion of the future.

But four years into his time at the Agency, he had finally started to wonder. They had seen each other on and off for so many years. What if there was a future there, but they were both just too scared to admit it? He was on his way to Marseilles to visit her—to ask her if they ought to give something serious a shot—when it happened. The phone call that had changed everything.

"Aucune idée comment te dire. Son copain est mort..."
"...une surdose de drogue..."
"Elle est à l'hôpital en convalescence..."

He would never forget those words. Her brother's voice, intermixed with static as the train passed from a 5G zone on the outskirts of Paris into a 3G zone in the countryside. He had stopped by to borrow her fancy KitchenAid mixer so that he could make pavlova for his girlfriend that weekend. And found his sister Anya with some guy she was seeing, both half dead on the couch.

Thomas blocked out the rest of the phone call. Anya survived the overdose, but her boyfriend hadn't. Thomas had visited her in the hospital, and when she got home, sent her a card, but any further contact was too painful for either of them. He was so grateful to the universe that she had survived, and he bore her no ill will. But that memory was what first brought him into Jonathan Fisher's orbit.

Two years later he had finally received this assignment. They had a long road left ahead of them, but he planned to nail Fisher to the wall. Or go down trying. Whatever came first.

Thomas finished placing his last bug, then turned around and did a quick survey of the room. Golden hour had just begun and the whole room glinted and shone with the effect of the sun coming in through the floor-to-ceiling windows. The sky blue and indigo floral arrangements sparkled. The venue was ready, as were the Agency's special provisions. It was time to start on the journey to make Fisher pay.

***

Ten minutes later, Thomas walked into the staff bathroom. He went to the third stall and shut the door. He opened the trash receptacle, removed the bag, and underneath found the package he was looking for. A black plastic bag with a mesh oval pouch inside it. Something that would normally house toiletries or jewelry. But when he unzipped it and removed the packing paper around it, the matte black surface of a Ruger LCRx 38 revolver looked back at him. A local asset they worked with had bought it in a street deal and had delivered it the night before as part of the museum's cleaning crew. Thomas checked the cylinder. It held five rounds, and one was empty.

He swallowed and clicked the cylinder back in place. Given where the gun had been procured, he especially didn't want to know what had happened to the missing round.

Doesn't matter. I'm not going to have to use it.

Like many intel operatives, Thomas wasn't a fan of guns. He preferred handling his ops with more finesse. Less chaos. He believed firmly in the motto that if you had to pull the trigger, everything had already gone sideways. Past the point of no return. But he also knew better than to ignore a worst-case scenario.

He placed the pouch and bag back into the receptacle, along with the regular trash bag on top. With both hands on the grip, he shifted the Ruger between them, sensing the difference in weight distribution from his regular Glock. He raised it to eye level to imagine what it would feel like to fire—although he sincerely hoped it wouldn't come to that.

Can't imagine why it would.

But operations often went in ways you couldn't predict. He holstered the gun on the inside of his suit jacket. The jacket had been specially designed to mask the silhouette of a gun, so when he emerged from the stall and checked his reflection, the revolver was invisible. Thomas washed his hands and headed back toward the kitchen.

He picked up a tray of hors d'oeuvres on his way into the main lobby, pasted a smile on his face, and began walking around as the first set of guests arrived. The wedding party and family were taking pictures on the grounds below—basking in the continued glow of golden hour. Thomas spotted Jonathan Fisher's stiff posture from the window as he waited for a group of four to help themselves to the mushroom puffs on his tray. On the opposite side of the atrium, Santiago was also serving guests while they waited for Fisher to arrive.

They didn't have long to wait, although it felt like ages.

Patience. Half the battle in the spy game.

Maybe even ninety percent.

That's what most ops came down to. Staying alert, but not overly paranoid, while waiting for a target or a source. Anticipating the most opportune moment for an intel drop. Standing still while nothing happened—in the hope that everything would happen according to plan.

Fisher walked into the venue fifteen minutes later. He stood at just under six feet, with a lean build, sharp features, and salt and pepper notes running through his light brown hair. As in almost every picture, his expression looked grim.

Couldn't even fake a smile at his niece's wedding.

Thomas stopped himself from rolling his eyes. Fisher was no fan of Wayne Cartwright, a fact plastered on all of the Agency's intercepted communications related to the wedding. Not wealthy, prestigious, or powerful enough. But he and his brother ran independent businesses, both of which were extremely successful. So, Fisher hadn't been able to force that opinion onto his niece. He'd simply had to content himself with being a wedding guest, rather than the one in control. Not something he was used to.

Serves you right, asshole.

Thomas could think of a few better expletives for Fisher but shoved them aside. He didn't have time to get distracted thinking about the purpose of the operation. Not now that Fisher was here. He had to focus on the target.

He discarded the almost empty tray in the kitchen and picked up a fresh one with elaborate sausage rolls. Upscale pigs-in-a-blanket. Also, Fisher's favorite.

Before heading back into the lobby, Thomas checked his phone. The Agency cloning software was active and ready. All he had to do was trigger it when he was within a foot of Fisher's phone. Most likely, the security software on the phone wouldn't allow for ongoing access, but it would enable the Agency to capture a real-time immediate picture of all the downloaded apps, emails, and messages on the phone. A snapshot in time, but far better than what they'd been able to get thus far. Most importantly, Thomas was hoping the hack would capture details to narrow down which of Fisher's investments were legitimate and which were merely part of his cocaine supply chain.

Tray in hand, Thomas marched back out into the museum main lobby. Fisher was at a high-top across the room, chatting with a man Thomas recognized as Claude Bello. Fisher was a repeat investor in Bello Holdings, which ran real estate investments all over West Africa. Nigerian royalty, if Thomas remembered the description in the Agency file correctly. As far as the Agency had been able to gather, a large chunk of Bello's investments were above board, but that didn't mean they weren't also involved in Fisher's side dealings.

If this hack can get Bello's info too, we'll be golden.

Thomas approached the two men, deep in conversation. Bello's deeper Nigerian intonation contrasted with Fisher's posh British accent. As if he needed the whole world to know he went to Eton within a half second of meeting him.

"Spicy pork puffs," Thomas said as he reached them and held out the tray. With his other hand, he reached into his pocket and tapped the two volume buttons on the side of his Android phone with his thumb.

"Lovely," Fisher said. He took a napkin and two puffs, and then Thomas turned toward Bello. The Nigerian was about twenty years younger than Fisher, in his mid-thirties. He and his brother were slowly taking over more of their family business. From what Thomas had read, Claude was the engine behind a major expansion of the company's investments. Thus far though, he seemed completely aboveboard. But then the Agency had yet to identify how Fisher got his cocaine shipments from South America into Europe. Their supply chains could be anywhere.

Thomas waited while Bello helped himself to a puff. "Would you like some more?" He turned back toward Fisher, counting the seconds in the back of his mind.

Ten, nine, eight...

"Don't mind if I do."

Three, two, one...

Phew.

Thomas waited a few moments longer as Bello decided to take a second helping as well. Then, with a polite smile, he moved onto the next high-top on the left, working his way around the room. He tapped his left ear and nodded when he and Santiago crossed paths again.

So far, so good.

Even thinking that made Thomas worry about jinxing it. For a former engineer, he'd found that becoming an intel operative had made him extremely superstitious. Or at least superstitious enough to know that anything that could tip the odds in his favor—however irrational or illogical—was worth having. Within reason anyway.

The rest of the wedding celebration went by smoothly. Thomas finished his shift serving hors d'oeuvres and moved on to supervising the tables for the buffet dinner.

A buffet dinner? Fisher must have had a heart attack.

Thomas couldn't help but chuckle as he watched the suffocatingly posh English gentleman stand in the buffet line.

Just looking at his face makes this whole thing worthwhile.

Not that any of it had been an ordeal—not yet anyway.

But it isn't over until the fat lady sings.

He still had no idea what the reference to the fat lady was, but Will Smith still had the right idea. It wasn't time to celebrate yet. Putting Fisher in that hole had a million or more steps to go. But for tonight, all he and Santiago had to do was finish up their shifts, head to the rendezvous point, and call it there. Then focus on the monumental task of combing through the junk they had downloaded to find the real information.

Easy peasy.

***

By the time Thomas finished stacking tables at the end of the evening, he was completely exhausted. The last guests, including Fisher and Bello, had long since gone home. He'd taken a couple of breaks and made sure the sync to their phones had activated properly. Santiago had the same software as backup, but in this case, they didn't need it.

"Thanks for all your hard work," the event planner— an attractive blond woman who looked like she was in her early thirties—said. "Really appreciate all your help."

"My pleasure." Thomas flashed her a smile. If he weren't on a job, he would probably have asked her out. She had certainly tried to flirt with him, until she noticed his wedding ring. Just part of his cover, but a drawback, nonetheless. His persona tonight was anything but a flirt or playboy. He was reliable, hard-working, and didn't stand out in a crowd. All in line with the off-the-rack Macy's suit he was wearing.

He walked through the museum grounds toward his parking spot on his own. Santiago would head to the safe house separately.

Thomas drove toward the East Sprague neighborhood, where he was supposed to discard the gun, switch cars, and head to the safe house. He didn't know much about the neighborhood—only that it was slightly seedier than the main parts of the city. The Agency usually handled local supplies, including cars, weapons, and other necessities via local assets. Compartmentalization was the key. A gun supplier couldn't reveal details of an op if they didn't know them. The more distance between the field operative and the supplier, the better.

He followed his GPS and parked in a side alley. The area was indeed more run down than most of downtown, but Thomas had seen worse in some of Marseilles' better neighborhoods. He stepped out of the tan Corolla and shut the door, wondering why the Agency reps had chosen this area for a car swap. Street lighting was minimal, and it felt empty. Too empty.

Glancing down at his phone, Thomas checked the GPS for where the other car—a red Honda Accord would be. He was half a block away when he heard it. A few steps ahead of him, to his left. A kid—probably no more than in his late teens—stepped out into the alley. Knife in hand.

"Hands up! Give me your wallet and phone. Now."

A mugging?

Thomas's eyes widened. Of all the scenarios he had planned for as part of the op, he couldn't have dreamed this one up. "Look, kid. I don't have anything valuable. But I'm going to hand it over nice and easy."

He leaned over and placed his wallet on the ground. There was nothing valuable in it anyway. Not worth risking a shootout when all he had to do was get to the safe house.

Besides, he's just a kid.

"I gave you my wallet."

"Your phone, too."

Thomas frowned. His phone had all the intel they had just gathered on Fisher and Bello. One thing was for sure—he could *not* hand it over. "You don't want my phone. I'll be able to track where it is. You won't be able to use or sell it." He kept his arms out to the sides and stood back up slowly.

"Who do you think you are? Think I don't have a plan for that? Hand it over now."

"I'm afraid I can't do that."

Here goes nothing.

Thomas placed his foot behind the wallet and kicked it up and forward as hard as he could. The leather popped upward less than a foot, then skidded forward over the asphalt. The kid lunged toward him, knife in hand.

Thomas had enough training to know he wouldn't be able to get the gun out, take aim, and fire before the kid got to him. In close quarters, without the time to respond, the knife would beat the gun nine times out of ten. So, instead, he sidestepped and shoved the kid in the shoulder, angling his push downward. He had a few inches on the kid to play to his advantage.

The kid stumbled and caught himself on his hands. The knife clattered as it fell from his grasp. Thomas grabbed his opportunity and pulled out the revolver. "Stay down, kid."

But even in the dim lighting, Thomas could make out the kid reaching for the knife again. He angled the gun upward half an inch and pulled the trigger. The shot cracked through the air, hitting the asphalt a few inches behind the kid.

"I said stay down!"

Thomas backed up, grabbed his wallet, and bolted. He rounded the corner at a full sprint, jumped into the Accord, and revved the engine. The tires screeched as he took off down the street.

About a mile away, he pulled over at a stop sign. He wiped the gun for prints, walked three steps to a trash can, and chucked it in. Then without looking back, he took a roundabout route toward the safe house.

As he made it inside, he wondered if he'd done the right thing. The gun ought to have been disposed of more securely—at an Agency locker as planned, or in the river at the very least. But ops sometimes demanded a split-second decision and he'd chosen to protect the intel. To get it off the street as soon as possible.

As for the Ruger, he'd returned it to its roots. It had been traded on the street. And to the street it would return. Eventually. He had no doubt about that.

He kicked off his shoes and plonked down at the dining table where a silver Agency-issued laptop was waiting for him. He hooked the phone up to the computer via a USB cable and opened the software to review the files. In his bones, he knew the intel was within his grasp. He would identify one of Fisher's supply sites, find a vulnerable point, and get an asset in play. Someday, he would pay for all the people he had hurt. Cocaine addicts all over the world. And for Anya.

Task one of a million to taking Fisher down.
Here we go.

8-Hour Detour

Curtis Ippolito

The sky's been brightening for the last hour but it's when the sun pierces the horizon, beaming its radiation dead center through the Econoline's bug-splattered windshield, that Jake Dwyer's convinced he's having a heart attack. See, Jake realizes he's been driving east the past four hours. Not south, straight down the 5 as planned. He'd been popping rest stop speed to keep him awake through the night, and it did its job, he supposes. A little too well as the night stretched out like a ribbon for hours before him—keeping his attention locked on his headlights and the road. He can't remember seeing a road sign that would have alerted him, a billboard, nothing. Nothing until the sun shining right in his fucking eyes. Suppressing a string of curses, he steals a glance in the rearview mirror to find his two compatriots still dead asleep.

On top of this epic fuck up, the camper van begins to sputter. The gas gauge hasn't read true since the Baja California camping trip last year, but even still, he thought he had another hour's worth of gas. Turns out, he fucked that up, too.

Kyle and Jaycee are not going to be happy.

The sputtering transitions to a hacking cough that would prompt anyone over 60 to update their will. "Shit." Jake lets off the gas. Eases the Econoline to the shoulder. The tires crunch over loose gravel as he brings the van to a stop, the green road sign for Exit 280 glaring back at him.

"What's going on?" says Jaycee in her vocal fry that's a million times sexier in the a.m.

"Jake, man. Why are you pulled over?" her boyfriend Kyle adds.

Jake doesn't answer, doesn't look in the rearview. He slams the van into park. Drops his forehead to the steering wheel. He leaves his dumbass melon of a head there until he feels a soft hand squeeze his shoulder. Jaycee.

"Where are we, Jake?"

Lifting his head, he mumbles, "Somewhere east."

Before Jaycee can reply, Kyle says, "Spokane. We're right outside of Spokane." He drops his hands and phone to his lap. "That's four hours out of the way. What the hell, Jake? It was a straight shot down the 5. How did you end up in Spokane?"

"We're out of gas, too," Jake says.

Neither say anything. Not even a low grumble. Then Kyle gets tangled in his blanket while trying to get out of bed, making a production out of freeing himself. He smacks the kitchen counter with his palm, storms out the side door. Jaycee gives Jake an awkward smile, then turns to join her boyfriend outside.

Jake hasn't even lifted his ass out of the captain's seat when he hears Kyle ranting. He can't make out entire sentences, but a few choice slams do reach his ears. *Irresponsible. Selfish. Moocher.* The trifecta of put-downs that have dogged Jake his whole adult life. He's really done it this time. Kyle's one of the chilliest dudes he knows, and if he's this pissed, well, shit's not going to be as easy to paper over as drinking the last beer or coming up empty on his share of gas money for the thirteenth-thousandth time.

Jake has no clue how to fix this one. Four hours out of the way. Which means he gifted them with an unplanned eight-hour detour and an empty gas tank. Eight-hour detour and an empty gas tank is basically Jake's life motto, he thinks.

While Jake snickers about that, Kyle tears the door open and practically launches himself back inside the Econoline.

"This is what's going to happen," he says. Jaycee enters looking sheepish, making eye-contact only with the floor. "Thankfully, *I* refilled the gas can, which should be enough to get us into downtown Spokane. Once there, we'll park and Jaycee and I will catch up on work while you get money to pay for the gas to get us back on course."

"How do I do that?" Jake asks, his tone too innocent sounding, even to his own ears.

"Here's a concept: get a job!" Kyle yells. "Whatever it takes, man. I want a hundred bucks by the end of the day or we're leaving your ass here."

"But we're going to San Diego so I can see my brother."

"And it's your fault we're stuck here," Kyle says.

"I mean, the gas gauge—"

"Fuck the gas gauge. Fuck your constant excuses."

"Jake," Jaycee says sweetly. She touches his forearm. "We really need you to come through this time. You know we love you riding with us, but…you have to pull your own weight for once."

Jake senses he can't wriggle out of this one. He's never seen Kyle so pissed.

"Let's get this rig into town and go from there," Jake says.

The three-gallon, in-case-of-emergency gas can did indeed get them running again and into downtown Spokane. Barely. After parking in an all-day lot across from a 76 gas station for seven bucks, Kyle and Jaycee whipped out their laptops and chased Jake out of the camper van.

Jake doesn't know where he's headed, but for a split second he wishes he too had a cushy graphic designer or social media manager job like his friends. Bank some money working from anywhere. Then he quickly dismisses that bit of moronic jealousy. Sure, a steady paycheck would be nice, but he didn't bounce from his foster parents' house at sixteen, leaving behind his foster brother, Drew, only to get a job. He promised himself he'd see the world and he's done his dead level best to do so—North America and tons of Mexico, at least. Besides, work's for suckers. It's a construct, a societally accepted form of enslavement. Freedom. That's what Jake's about. So, while he finds himself in a pinch this time, it won't last. Never does. He's made it to his mid-thirties with no debts, no responsibilities, and very few regrets by staying loose, going with the flow, and not giving a damn what anyone thinks of him. He'll get a job this once, cause getting booted from the Econoline would be way more hassle than doing a day's worth of work.

He passes a fancy restaurant that's closed until dinner and a women's health center. Across the street is a dispensary with a healthy amount of foot traffic for—he checks his watch—8:30 a.m. No judgement. A joint would be the shit right about now.

Ten minutes later, he finds himself on 3rd Avenue. The sun is deceptively hot, making him whip off the

Padres hat his brother gave him and wipe his temples with the sleeve of his shirt. He approaches a red brick building with garage-style glass doors running the length. It's a closed brewery, but then a sign across the street and up a way catches his eye. DICK'S HAMBURGERS. He snickers. Their slogan below is, *Buy the Bagful.* Jake howls. "Buy a bagful of dicks! Genius."

He finds himself on Dick's side of the street without even knowing he crossed 3rd. Appears the place just opened or is set to by the line of easily a dozen people long is waiting at the order window. Jake feels a wave of nostalgia roll over him. He connects that the burger joint with its walk-up window, outdoor seating, and the building's vintage look reminds him of the Fosters Freeze in San Diego. The place he'd take his younger brother Drew to grab a cheeseburger and a Butterfinger Twister whenever Jake rolled back through town those first few years after leaving. They'd be surrounded by families. Fathers and mothers having dinner with their kids. And you'd think the brothers of no blood relation should've felt pangs of longing for having no true families of their own, but that was never the case. Not for Jake. They caught up on the time they'd been apart. Drew would tell him how he was doing school. What girls he had crushes on, that sort of thing. Those times at Fosters were the moments when Jake felt the most like an honest-to-God big brother.

The aroma of beef, grilled onions, and melted cheese coat the air. Goddamn, he could really go for a cheeseburger. That's a no-go though thanks to no dough. Whole reason he's out here. To find money—rather, work for it. Gag me, he thinks, rolling his eyes. He turns his back to the burger joint. There's a paint store directly across the street with a Help Wanted sign in the window. Jake exhales a huge sigh, crosses the street.

The inside of the store is empty save for two people. A gray-haired grandpa looking dude wearing a red employee's vest is handing a sandwich board to a middle-aged white guy who's likely homeless, going by his weathered appearance and clothing. Jake glances at his own clothes, decides he shouldn't judge.

"Walk up and down the sidewalk, or station where there's traffic going by—whatever, really," says the paint store employee to the man. "Come back in at noon and I'll give you a voucher for lunch. End of the day, a hundred bucks is yours."

The man nods, shimmies the sandwich board onto his body, and walks past Jake out the front door without making eye-contact or saying anything.

"Help you, young man?"

Jake steps up to the counter. "Saw the help wanted sign in the window. Hoping that you didn't just fill it." He looks toward the front door, bows his head.

"That's the job… Tell you what. I'll give you the same deal I gave that gentleman. We've been slow of late, so two sign holders might bring in more traffic."

"Thanks. Appreciate that." Jake has his moments of charm. Especially when money and a free lunch are in the offering.

The employee, whose name is Bob, holds up a finger before leaving Jake. He goes through a door and comes right back with another sandwich board. Same as the middle-aged dude's. Says, "Paint Your World with Premium Color. BOGO on select 1-gallons."

"So just come back at noon and you'll feed us lunch?" Jake asks.

"Not me." Bob flicks his chin. "Dick's. I'll give you a voucher for a burger and fries."

"Sounds like a plan." Jake grabs the sandwich board and heads outside.

***

"Glad we don't have to spin arrows or juggle a sign like some dorky circus act," Jake says to the other day laborer, Chuck.

Chuck shrugs. "Hundred bucks is a hundred bucks. I'd do this every day if they offered."

"And a free lunch, don't forget. How is it, by the way? Dick's."

"Best burger in the state."

"Nice." Jake turns on a heel and heads down the sidewalk away from Chuck.

Each time he approaches Chuck on the return Jake questions whether he should say something, get a conversation going, but nothing comes to mind. After a while, his head gets lost in the predicament he's in with Kyle and Jaycee. Then to seeing his brother. Things he wants to do while in San Diego.

A couple hours on and they've lured two customers into the store. Or maybe they each drove here to buy paint anyway. Jake's taking credit either way.

"Think we can go inside to take a leak, or should I go around the side?" Jake asks.

Chuck thinks on this for a second. "Better play it safe and stay outside."

"Cover me then." With that, Jake wrestles the sandwich board off and rests it against the paint shop building. Around the side he finds a small Dumpster to piss behind. While he goes, he wonders if he should've used the paint store's phone to call Kyle and tell him he got a job, has gas covered. Dismisses that. Then he asks himself why he didn't just call his brother, ask him to send Kyle the money. Nah. No reason to expose himself as chump to his little bro. Still, it would be nice to wrap this day up, gas up the Econoline, and get on their way. Day's not even half over yet and Jake's feet are sore and his legs are aching. Whoever said earning a buck wasn't easy has Jake's agreement. He zips up and returns to his post.

The next two hours absolutely drag.

Thankfully Chuck announces when it's noon. Jake doesn't carry a phone or a watch, so he wasn't sure how he'd know when it would be lunch time. The men get their vouchers from Bob and head to Dick's. Bob told them they wouldn't have to wait for their meal in the line, which is snaked around one side of the building. Instead, Chuck and Jake go to the back of the burger joint. Jake pokes his head inside the open door, gets a face full of grill steam.

"Anyone back here?"

The manager—Ramon—appears, greets them. He takes the meal vouchers and returns in no time with two to-go bags. A cheeseburger and fries for each of them. Ramon also hands them each a can of ice-cold Coca-Cola.

Somehow, they find two seats among the crowded wooden picnic benches out front. Neither man speaks while they eat. This must be what eating in the military is like, Jake thinks. Shoving food in your face as fast as you can to get back to work in the measly 30 minutes your commanding officer gave you. Or, in this case, Bob. Jake means to ask Chuck about himself, but opts not to as the man is head-down, showing no intention of talking.

Chuck finishes first. He gathers his trash and tucks it neatly into his take-out bag. Jake chews on his last bite, notices the mess he's made. Bits of lettuce dot the table, drips of ketchup are everywhere, and so many greasy napkins he's tucked in the slats of the table.

"Meet you back there?" Chuck says.

Jake nods. Over his shoulder, he watches Chuck toss his trash in an open-mouthed trash can, then walk across 3rd. It takes Jake a few minutes to clean up his mess. He wonders why he's even doing it. Usually, he'd leave the task for someone else, someone who's actually getting paid to clean it up. Jake gets a weird feeling. A sense of pride, maybe? He's working a job. Clearing his own table. If only Kyle and Jaycee could see him now.

He's chuckling to himself as he walks his trash to the can. Dropping it in, something catches his eye. Something dark. Something so black it stands out from the rest of the refuse. Intrigued, he reaches in and touches the item. It's a gun. Jake straightens up. Whips his head side-to-side to make sure no one is looking. All good. He locates his take-out bag, and in two swift motions dumps its contents into the can, and grabs what appears to be a revolver by the grip and shoves it into the paper bag.

He quickly crumples the bag around the gun and speed-walks away. Jake knows dick about guns. He thinks it's a snub-nose. I mean, he thinks, it does have a stubby barrel.

It's not until he's two blocks down, away from Dick's and the paint store, that Jake stops. Ducking into an alley, he shields his body from street view before pulling out the gun.

A snub-nose all right. Jake opens the cylinder. Five bullets. One round's been fired. Probably why it was ditched in the trash. He's about to pop the cylinder closed, but pauses, an idea forming. Jake tips the gun on its side. The five remaining rounds cascade into his palm. He shoves them into his pants pocket. Whips the cylinder closed with a snap, tucks the gun in his waistband, and wonders what he has on his person to conceal his face.

***

The Dick's take-out bag fits snug over his head. Thank goodness for small ears.

Jake's ducked behind a row of bushes across the street from the dispensary. His heart hammering in his chest, sweat pouring from his armpits and back. He's not a thief. This is new territory for him. Not that he hasn't stolen anything before. He's just never used a gun, never committed armed robbery. He's a veteran at sneaking cans of food, toiletries, even camping supplies. And countless packs of cigarettes back when he smoked and before stores locked them up. He sees himself as an opportunist. This is something different, though, and has him equally thrilled and freaked the fuck out. Considering the line of people he saw here earlier, the tip jars alone should cover the $100 he needs to give to Kyle for gas. If Jake can get even one budtender to open their drawer, he may be able to pay their whole way to San Diego and then some. They'd discussed summer in Yellowstone.

"Fuck it." Jake squeezes the gun's grip through his shirt and takes off across Monroe Street toward the dispensary. There's no line, and the absolute kismet kiss: no security guard in sight. Slipping through a row of concrete pylons guarding the doors from a drive-in, he rips open the glass door and flies inside. It's an open floor plan with counters hugging the perimeter, gleaming white tile floor set out before him.

"Everybody listen and no one gets hurt!" he yells, aiming the revolver at the ceiling. Three budtenders duck behind the counter and their customers hit the floor. Two women scream and a dude says, "Fucking hell." Blood pools so fast in Jake's ears that's all he hears—then it's only his own pounding pulse. He darts to the counter, gathers up three plastic jars each more than half full of cash. With his free hand he transfers handfuls of the bills to his pants pocket, his fingertips brushing the bullets he removed from the gun.

Head on a swivel, he tries to keep track of the customers and the budtenders. And even though he punched out generously sized eye holes in the bag, it's twisting on him, one eye hole damn near at his ear now. He needs to get one of the budtenders to open a register to really put this job over the top. Toss in some pre-rolls, too, while they're at it. Then, out of the corner of his unobscured eye, Jake sees a flash of movement. The door to the back room opening.

An older Black security guard tucking in his shirt enters the showroom. Dude immediately realizes what's happening, reaches for something on his belt—probably a taser, please not a gun—and rushes Jake.

Adrenaline floods Jake's blood, controls his next action. He bolts for the front door. Sneaks a look over his shoulder to see the guard on top of him. Right before Jake can slip through the concrete pylons, the guard grabs ahold of his shirt, tugs. Jake freaks, pinwheels his arms— hears and feels the revolver make contact with the guard's face. The sickening smack gives way to Jake's freedom. The guard goes down hard. Jake races out of the parking lot and is around the corner before the guard can even try to get up.

He runs and runs. Faster than he's ever run before. Cash still clenched in one hand, squeezing the life out of the gun in the other. The revolver's weight suddenly draws Jake's attention. Heavy as a boat anchor, even without ammo. And so many thoughts racing through his brain. Kyle's dismissive words from earlier. What Chuck and Bob will think when he doesn't come back to work. Jake's own doubts of whether he's truly a fuck up like everyone says.

None of that matters, he tells himself.

He came through.

The opportunist lives to fight another day.

Jake makes it to the opposite corner of the parking lot, folds over, winded. He spots the Econoline. Shining like a beacon. Never knew the meaning of that saying until now. Gulping hard for air, he stuffs the fist of cash in his pocket, surveys his surroundings. He's in the shadow of a two-story brick Baptist church. At the front door he sees two concrete planters, rushes over. They're planted up with pink flowers and a lime green conifer of some kind. Jake shoves the revolver into the planter, desperately covering it best he can with the mulch. He looks behind him. No one coming. He brushes his hands off on his jeans. Pulls out his rolled-up Padres hat from his back pocket and eases it back on his head while jogging across the street to the Econoline. He's fairly confident he scored enough cash to cover gas. He only hopes he has enough extra to take his brother to Fosters Freeze for a cheeseburger and a Twister when he rolls into San Diego.

A Good Samaritan
Rob Phillips

When Josh Tasker climbed into his 2008 Ford F-150 pickup, his sights were set on Seattle. From there his plan was to get on a ferry in Bellingham and head to Alaska. That should get him far enough away from Madeline and her controlling family. It would give him some time to think about things. About their relationship, if there still was one. And their future. Again, if there was one.

Tasker had been out of the Army for nine months, after serving for twelve years as one of the elite fighters with the U.S. Army Rangers. He had served overseas in Iraq and had been in Afghanistan when President Biden pulled all US troops out of the country.

Maybe he had changed during his time overseas, but Madeline definitely had. When he finally got home to Montana, she seemed not all that happy to see him.

They had dated for two years and were married just before he was sent to Ranger training school. Madeline's parents never really liked him. Or that's how it felt. They wanted a Montana boy who was going to stay home, settle down and start making grandbabies. The family cattle ranch would be theirs someday.

Tasker had worked on ranches growing up, around cattle and horses, and that experience made him realize that life wasn't for him. And he told Madeline that. She was fine with it. Or so she said. But with her at home in Montana, and him fighting for their country overseas, sometimes not able to call or communicate with her for days, even weeks at a time, the relationship slowly crumbled.

Could it be saved? He didn't know. What he did know is he needed to get away and think about it. The fight they had had was a doozy. She threw her wedding band at him, and said it was over. Then she walked out to her car, jumped in, and drove off. To her parents' ranch, he assumed.

He picked up the ring, put it in his pocket, walked into their bedroom, put some clothes and a few personal items in a duffle, grabbed the $1,765 dollars he had in an envelope taped under a drawer in the bathroom, and headed for the door.

He left behind his cell phone and the one credit card he owned. He didn't need either.

As he drove west through Montana, past Bozeman, Butte and then Missoula, he thought about everything that occurred to get him to this moment. The fight with Madeline had been perplexing. They seemed to be getting along fine when he returned home, but there was an underlying coldness there.

Tasker wasn't a big man. He stood five-feet-ten inches tall, and weighed 176 pounds, depending on what he had eaten for dinner. He had dark brown hair, cut short, but not Army short. He had let it grow some and liked the idea of not being identified as a soldier the second someone saw him.

His eyes were almost black, and they were set in what some people described as a "nice" face. Tanned, rugged, but with kind eyes and an easy smile.

In street clothes he looked like just another average guy. Average height. Average build. But take his shirt off and Tasker was impressive. His six pack was going on seven, and his pecks and biceps were rock hard. He worked out every day on the weights, and, as some bad guys had learned over in the desert, he wasn't one to be messed with.

Besides his strength, Tasker had lightning-fast reflexes and moved with grace and athleticism. All those attributes had made him a Ranger the members his team envied and admired. If they were heading into a fight, they wanted Tasker to be the soldier standing next to them.

After stops in St. Regis for gas and some coffee, he finally made his way into Idaho. He listened to the radio to try to get his mind off things, but all he could do was think about Madeline. How could everything have gotten so out of whack?

He wondered if she had found someone else. Or, if her folks had finally made her come to her senses about being married to someone who didn't have any desire to be a cattle rancher. Some cooling off time would be good for sure.

Daylight was fading when he was coming into Spokane. Tasker was getting hungry. He needed to eat something.

He spotted signs on the freeway for McDonald's, Taco Bell and a couple other fast food places, but quickly decided that the last thing he needed during his drive through Washington was a rampant case of diarrhea. So, when he saw the exit for downtown Spokane, he pulled off the freeway. Surely in town he could find a restaurant or diner where he could sit down and have a decent meal.

He pulled through town slowly, looked up a side street that was lined with buildings housing different businesses, and spotted a sign that flashed "café" in bright green letters.

"That'll do," he said to himself, and turned for the little restaurant.

As he walked through the café door, a bell over his head tinkled, which made some of the people sitting at booths and tables turn and look. A slightly overweight woman of about fifty with bright red hair and a sour look on her face walked over and asked, "How many?" The woman was wearing a matching set of green pants and top that made her look more like a doctor's office nurse than a server.

Tasker looked around, saw that he was still standing by himself, and said, "Just me." He gave the woman his best warm smile. It seemed to help.

"I didn't know if more were joining you," she said apologetically as she hustled down an aisle between some tables and booths.

Tasker followed and sat in a booth next to a window when she stopped.

"Would you like some coffee?" she asked with a smile.

"Please," Tasker said as the waitress placed a menu in front of him.

"The special tonight is meat loaf," she said. "And from what I hear, it is pretty good. I'm not much of a meat loaf person. Ate way too much of the stuff growing up. But all the customers like it."

"Thanks," Tasker said. "Let me look at the menu, but that does sound good."

The woman hurried off to get the coffee, and returned with a steaming cup, along with a glass of ice water, and set both on the table.

He had a personal philosophy against ordering the nightly special at restaurants because he figured the special was made up of meat or ingredients that were approaching their spoil date, with some possibly beyond. So, he rarely ordered the special. But tonight, he rolled the dice. Meat loaf with mashed potatoes sounded like the perfect dinner.

"You sold me on the meat loaf," Tasker said when the redheaded waitress returned. She scribbled something on her little order pad, asked what kind of dressing he wanted on his salad and hurried off again.

As he waited for his dinner, Tasker looked out at the buildings and sidewalks. He'd been to Spokane before, but it had been more than a decade ago. He remembered he liked the city back then and from what he could tell it hadn't changed that much.

There were some of the typical businesses in the storefronts on the street including a hardware store, a dress shop, and a donut shop. But others were empty. One of the empty buildings had some graffiti sprayed on it, with what looked like some kind of gang writing. Billings didn't have much trouble with gangs, but he knew in the bigger cities around the country, they had become a problem.

A few people walked along the streets, but as it was getting close to dark, most folks on the sidewalks were hurrying along. He spotted a young couple walking up a side street, carrying an infant in a car seat.

Didn't most people walk a baby in a stroller? Whatever. Tasker watched as the couple stopped and started talking. More like arguing. He quickly thought of Madeline yelling and throwing her wedding band at him.

He saw the woman stop talking, screw her face into an angry expression and march toward the street that ran in front of the café. The man dropped his head, threw up his hands, said something toward the woman and started walking after her.

Then, in an instant three men appeared out of the shadows of one of the empty storefront doorways. One man wrapped his arms around the woman as a second tried to pull the car seat from her hands. Tasker couldn't hear her, but she obviously was screaming. One of the men backhanded her across the face, and a second man pulled a handgun. Still the woman held on to the handle of the car seat.

In an instant Tasker was up and moving to go help.

As he headed to the door Tasker saw the woman's husband running up to the three men. The man with the pistol didn't hesitate and swung the gun and hit the husband in the side of the head. He went down hard. The woman screamed once more, and the man who had backhanded her before, slapped her again.

She continued to scream and held on to the handle of the car seat with both hands.

As he ran out the café, Tasker yelled at the redhaired waitress to call the police. Jogging toward them he looked at the men and assessed the situation. All three looked young, maybe in their late teens or early twenties. They were all light skinned, with light hair.

None of the three was very big. Average height or less Tasker thought. And they were slight of build. As he headed toward the altercation, he could hear the woman crying and the men barking orders at her. The husband was still on the ground.

"Your money, now!" the man with the gun yelled. He had an obvious eastern European accent. "C'mon bitch, I know you have it somewhere."

Tasker could see the woman had no purse. If she had money, she had to carry it in her pants pockets.

"We're broke," she said in halting English, as she continued to try to keep the car seat away from the tallest of the three men. "I have no money."

"Bullshit," the second man said in the same Russian accent. He was wearing a red bandana around his neck, like an old-time cowboy. But he was no cowboy, that was for sure.

Gang colors? Tasker wondered. The man with the pistol had a red belt holding up baggy pants.

Because they were so intent on what they were doing the three men didn't see Tasker come up from behind them.

"Hey fellas," Tasker said making the three men jump slightly and turn immediately toward him. "What's this all about?"

"Get out of here sucker," the man with the gun said. "You might get hurt. This is none of your business."

Tasker got a better look at the gun. It was a dull black color, probably a .38 he thought. He had fired a similar gun at a range in Montana before he left for the Rangers. The one he shot was a five-shot Ruger. This one looked very similar.

"These are my friends, so it *is* my business," Tasker said. "The cops have been called so why don't you boys just run along?"

The whole time he was talking, Tasker was slowly moving toward the group.

"Back off," the guy with the gun said again.

"Listen," Tasker said. "You want money? These people don't have any. But I do. How about I give you some of mine, and we'll all be on our way?"

The three men looked at each other quickly. One said something to the other in Russian.

The husband moaned and moved his hand to his head. At least he wasn't dead. In the distance a siren blared.

"Give us your money," the gunman said to Tasker, pointing the revolver at him.

Tasker learned early on in his Army days to carry his money dispersed in smaller amounts in different places. He had the hundreds in his sock, some smaller bills in a front pant pocket and fifties zipped up in a side pocket near his knee.

He reached into his front pocket and pulled out all the cash that was there. He felt Madeline's wedding band. No way were they taking that. He hadn't counted his cash, but it was mostly small bills, probably less than a hundred bucks.

"Give it here," the red bandana guy said, and stepped forward.

This was the perfect time to take these guys. Tasker had worked it out in his mind. He would grab the arm of the man who was stepping at him, twist it around his back, forcing him in front of his body, between him and the gun. Then he would shove the guy at the man with the gun and follow it so quickly there'd be no chance to shoot. A good kick would separate the man from the gun and from there Tasker would take them out with quick, accurate punches to the face, throat, and ribs.

Plan for the best, prepare for the worst. His plan worked to perfection until it didn't. He threw the first guy into the man with the revolver, then kicked the gun out of the man's hand. But the guy ducked just before Tasker hit him and rolled into the woman. The force of the man coming into her, made the woman release the car seat, and the third man, who had been struggling with her over the seat, took off running with it.

"No" the young woman howled. "No!"

Tasker glanced at the man running down the street with the carrier and then back to the other two. They were quickly getting on their feet. He prepared for a counterattack, but the men took off running after the first.

He checked the woman, and her husband, who was now trying to stand, then Tasker ran after the men. They had run into an alley halfway up the block, but when he got to the alley's entrance and looked down it, the men were gone.

He listened for a vehicle, but didn't hear a thing. He stood and watched and listened for another three minutes. The only sound he heard was a police siren getting closer. It was like the men had vanished into thin air.

As he turned to head back to the young couple, he saw the husband was now on his feet, and he was consoling his wife. Tasker jogged back to them. As he ran, he thought about what had just happened. He hadn't heard the baby cry, even with the woman screaming and the car seat being jostled back and forth.

If the men were targeting people to mug them for money, the man and woman were poor targets. Both were dressed in raggedy clothes and wore shoes with holes in the toes. He had watched a dozen other people walk up and down that street just before the couple was jumped that would have been much better targets. They would have at least had some money. This couple looked as if they were down to their last dollar.

And why would those men want the baby so badly? Again, trying to kidnap their child for ransom seemed to be a fool's errand.

"Thank you for your help," the husband said. "You should not have risked your life for us."

Tasker ignored him and walked over to where the revolver had landed near the gutter on the sidewalk. He picked it up and looked at it. He was right. It was a .38 caliber Ruger LCRx just like the one he had shot years before. He checked the five-round cylinder. One round was missing.

"Was your baby in the car seat?" he asked as he stuck the revolver in his pants, behind his back. He pulled his shirt out and let the tail cover the gun.

The man and woman didn't answer, they just looked at him.

"There was no baby in it was there?" Tasker said.

The couple didn't say a word. If it had been a baby the woman would be hysterical, wouldn't she? But she wasn't. She had even stopped crying.

"Was there?" Tasker asked again.

Finally, the man and woman started to shake their heads slowly, but they said nothing.

"What was in there that those men wanted so badly?" Tasker asked.

"My family's life savings," the man finally said. "We were going to deliver it to my parents here. But they didn't show up."

The sirens said that the cops were just about there.

"What are you going to tell the police?" Tasker asked.

"The truth," the man said. "What else can we do?"

Tasker thought about it. Chances were the police might find the men, but it was likely they would never see the money again. He thought about what he would like to have happen if he was in their situation. If he couldn't get the money back on his own, but someone was there that could help him, wouldn't he want them to do it. His Ranger training gave him the chance to help, so Tasker decided he would do just that.

"Tell them they stole my money, just like it happened," he said. "But don't tell them about your money or the baby seat. I think I can get it all back for you."

Filing the theft report with the Spokane police took some time. Two uniformed officers had arrived in one car. One talked to Tasker while the other talked to the couple. They were professional and wanted everything in detail.

"We'll do everything we can to get your money back Mr. Tasker," the officer who had interviewed him said. He sounded sincere, but Tasker could see in the officer's eyes that there wasn't much chance.

When the cops left, the woman asked her husband, "What are we going to do now?"

"Let's walk over to the café and get something to eat," Tasker said. "And we'll figure this out."

When they walked into the café the bell on the door tinkled and Tasker looked at the waitress.

"Any chance I can get that meat loaf now?"

"Coming right up. What would you folks like?" she asked the couple.

"Just some coffee," the man said. "We are not hungry."

Tasker walked back to the same booth and sat down. The couple sat across from him.

After the waitress dropped off three cups of coffee, Tasker turned to the man and said, "Okay, tell me the whole story."

And the man did. His name was Nykolai Pavlychko. His wife's name was Maryia. They were from Ukraine. When Putin started placing his troops along the Ukrainian border in the months before he invaded Ukraine back in February of 2022, Pavlychko's parents sold all their worldly possessions and got out of the country. Worried that someone would steal their money, they left the bulk of it with Nykolai to get it out of the country if and when Putin invaded.

Nykolai had been a banker in Kyiv and had waited until his parents, along with several other refugees from Ukraine, had settled in the United States. Then, working through the banking system, he set up an account at U.S Bank, and transferred all his parents' money into the account. But he was the only person who could withdraw it from the bank.

Once he got to the United States, Nykolai was going to get the cash out of the bank and take it to his parents. He had tried to talk to them about just transferring the money into a new account at an established bank, but since they were not citizens of the United States his father feared the money would somehow be gobbled up in the banking system.

When he and Maryia arrived in the United States it had taken them some time to get to Spokane. They had just arrived earlier that day.

"Those men must have known we were coming and were getting the money out of the bank to give to his parents," Maryia said. "How else would they pick us out to attack?"

"Have you talked to your parents recently?" Tasker asked Nykolai.

"Yes," he said in Ukrainian accented English. "I spoke to them on the phone last night. They were supposed to meet us at a house near here. We were headed there when the men attacked."

"Those men spoke in Russian," Maryia said. "They said they would take your money and ours too."

The food arrived and Tasker started eating.

"You sure you don't want something to eat?" he asked the couple.

"No, I would like to go check on my parents," Nykolai said.

Tasker wolfed down the meat loaf and potatoes. The waitress was right. It was very good. Then he ushered the Pavlychkos to his truck and they drove to the house where the meeting was to take place.

As Nykolai got out of the pickup, Tasker could see someone looking out a crack in the curtains in the front window. A second later the front door opened and a short, slender woman with short gray hair stepped out and gave Nykolai a kiss on the cheek and a hug.

"That is his mother," Maryia said as she climbed out of the pickup and ran to the door. A second later a man, an older version of Nykolai, stepped out on the porch. They all hugged and kissed and then Nykolai waved at Tasker to come in.

After introductions inside, they talked about what had happened. Evidently, the senior Pavlychkos had told some friends about their son taking care of their money, and that he was bringing it to them today.

"I don't think our friends would have gone behind our backs," Nykolai's father said in Ukrainian. "But someone must have said something to the wrong person."

Nykolai translated for Tasker.

"So, he has no idea who those men were?" Tasker asked.

"No," Nykolai said. "But from their language, they are most assuredly Russian."

"Tell your mother and father, it might take me a couple days, but I am going to find those men, and I will get your money back."

Nykolai spoke to his parents in their native tongue. They turned and looked at Tasker with a look of hope and gratitude.

They both said "thank you" with a deep Ukrainian accent.

Tasker told Nykolai that he had no phone, but when he knew something, or found the money, he would come back to this house.

"Tell your parents to be extra careful," Tasker said. "And you and Maryia need to be, too. If anyone you don't know comes looking for you, or me, call the police. I will see you soon."

It was almost midnight when Tasker pulled back in front of the café. The little restaurant was closed. Before he climbed out of the truck, he grabbed his duffle from the back seat and pulled a black T-shirt out, which he exchanged for his white shirt. He also grabbed a black baseball cap from the back floorboards, and put it on.

Now he would be tougher to see in the dark, and if the trio of Russians did see him, they might not recognize him immediately.

Finally, after he climbed out of the truck, he pulled the snub-nosed Ruger out of the back of his pants, and double checked the cylinder. Still only four live cartridges in the five chambers He'd have to be prudent with his shots if he had to use the .38.

Tasker wandered around for two hours, from one block to the next, watching, listening. Since the men had been on foot, and he hadn't seen or heard a vehicle driving away when they disappeared in the ally, he figured the men had to live somewhere within a mile radius. So, he tried to stay within that rough perimeter.

He heard the music at 2:45. Russian music. Or what he thought was Russian music. Coming from an open window in an old apartment on 2nd Street. And he heard men singing along with the music. It was worth checking out.

He could see lights coming from a second-story window in the building but there was no way up to look into the window. So, Tasker climbed up on trash dumpster next to building across the street to get him just high enough to see the faces of the people moving around in the window of the apartment building. The first face he saw was of the man who had worn the red bandana. In fact, he was still wearing it.

"Bingo," Tasker whispered to himself.

He quietly dropped off the dumpster and went back across the street and stood below the open window. The music was loud enough that it was hard to distinguish voices. He wanted to try to figure out just how many people were in the apartment.

He had gone through doors many times before in Iraq and Afghanistan not knowing exactly who or what he was going to be facing, so this wasn't new to him. But in those times, he had other Rangers on his six. Going in alone was a much more dangerous situation. Knowing how many people were in the room would help immensely.

Finally, the men turned off the music. Tasker listened intently. There were three distinct voices, but what if there was another man or two who hadn't talked? He waited and listened.

After another ten minutes he heard no other voices, just the three men. Probably the three men who had jumped the couple for their money. A minute later the light in the window went out and the place went quiet. Time to move.

He walked around to the building's main door, which was made of glass and surrounded by thick metal. It was secured by an electronic lock system, controlled by a digital pad on the wall next to the door. He could wait for someone to go in the building, or come out, but at this time of night the odds of that were pretty slim of that happening.

Tasker studied the door and the lock, but about the only way he was going to get through it was to throw a rock through the glass. Not a good plan if he was going to get into the men's apartment without them knowing. The door certainly had an alarm system and he didn't need the thing to start blaring away.

As he worked his way around the building Tasker looked up at the windows in the four-story building. Some windows were open but he had to believe that all of those apartments that were occupied.

He got lucky when he got to the back of the building. Someone had slipped a small piece of wood in the jamb, keeping the metal back door just slightly ajar. Probably someone who had just left but wanted to slip back in without going through the front.

It didn't matter why, or who had done it, it was his way in. The back stairs were just through the door and Tasker slowly climbed to the second floor. As he watched the window earlier, he had figured out where apartment with the three men was in comparison to the others on the that floor.

Tasker had entered hundreds of buildings during his time as a Ranger and knew how to work his way through them. His footsteps were as light as a feather, and after each step he would stop and listen. He could hear a television playing somewhere down the hall. And he could hear someone snoring in the apartment closest to the stairs.

The hallway floor was covered in old linoleum, brown in color. The walls were probably painted white twenty years ago, now they were a dirty beige. Lights, with sixty-watt bulbs, dropped from the ceiling in between the doors in the hall. Half of them were burned out.

He hadn't pulled the snub-nosed .38, but he kept his hand on the butt of the revolver still held in the back of his pants. If he had to, he could have it out and ready to fire in less than a second.

As he slowly worked down the hall, he checked the numbers on the doors. He passed the snoring in B-1, then B-2, B-3 and then inched around the corner to a longer portion of the hall. It was clear.

Tasker counted doors down the hall. The men would be in B-7. He kept his eyes on that door, but continued to listen for anyone, or anything that might create a commotion.

When Tasker got to the door he stopped and listened. There was a TV playing somewhere inside the apartment. It sounded like ESPN SportsCenter. A person or persons could be awake watching the TV, or they could be one of those people who had to have a TV playing just to go to sleep.

He hadn't been able to see what the men were doing in the apartment from his perch on the dumpster across the road, but if he was to guess, the men may have been celebrating their heist with some shots of Vodka or some other mind-altering substances. He wasn't going to count on that. He had to believe and prepare for three men, fully ready to fight.

And he had to believe that somewhere in the apartment there were more weapons. Only one of the men who attacked the couple carried a gun, the Ruger that Tasker now had in his hand, but that didn't mean they didn't have more.

He looked at the door. It was old and abused. One of those doors he could open easily with one swift kick. But he didn't want to do that. He wanted to enter the room quietly.

The lock on the handle matched the door. A ten-year-old kid with a screwdriver could open that door in less than five seconds. Unfortunately, Tasker didn't have a screwdriver. But he did have a small pocketknife, with a thin, sharp blade. That would work.

Before he started working on the lock he tried the knob. To his surprise, it turned. The men either forgot to lock the door or figured no one would be dumb enough to break into their apartment. They were wrong.

Tasker slowly turned the knob and pushed. He waited for the inevitable squeak of the hinges, but none came.

It was dark enough in the room that he couldn't see much, so Tasker waited a minute, then two, for his eyes to adjust. The place smelled of fried sausage, beer and human body odor. As he waited, he listened. He could hear a sports anchor talking about the Seattle Mariners coming from a room next to the room he was now in. And he could hear muffled, deep breathing coming from that direction.

These apartments weren't large, so there must only be one bedroom. Could all three men be sleeping in the bedroom? Tasker didn't think so.

He was picking up more details in the room as he slowly looked around. A person was sleeping on a couch below the window. Tasker wasn't sure but he thought it was the man who had slapped Maryia Pavlychko twice on the street. He was sleeping on his side, facing the back of the couch.

Two on one were better odds than three on one, although Tasker wasn't really all that worried about the three men. He had surprise, strength and skill on his side.

Still, it was a chance to get this guy out of the fight before it began.

He looked around for something big enough, and hard enough to whack the man in the head. Tasker didn't want to kill the guy, just knock him out.

In the kitchen, which was just a corner in the main room, he found an iron skillet. That would do—although clanking it on the guy's head would most likely make a pretty good noise. Plus, if he didn't hit the man hard enough, he would wake up and start screaming in pain. It was a delicate game of hitting him too hard, possibly killing the guy, or not hard enough and have three pissed off Russians on his hands.

Tasker raised the skillet. He had decided he would error on the side of too hard. Having watched the guy slap Maryia helped him make his decision. The man probably wouldn't die, but he might be drooling in his borscht the rest of his life.

The skillet hitting the back of the man's head was less of a clanging sound, and more of a sickening thud. Like someone hitting a pumpkin with a baseball bat. Tasker didn't know if the guy was dead, but he was definitely out.

As he set the pan on the floor, he listened to see if the noise had awakened the other two men. No one stirred. The sports anchor was now talking about the Dallas Cowboys. Tasker rarely watched SportsCenter but it seemed to him when he did, most of the time they were discussing the Dallas Cowboys, no matter if it was football season or not.

He slowly crept toward the bedroom, and as he did, he pulled the little Ruger from the back of his pants and made sure the one empty chamber of the cylinder wasn't aligned with the barrel, guaranteeing he had a live round loaded and ready to go if he needed it.

Tasker peeked around the door frame of the bedroom and saw one man sleeping, face down in a double-sized bed, and another sleeping face up on a cot. The man on the bed was the one who had been holding the pistol on the street. Both men were wearing boxer shorts and nothing else. He looked all around the beds to see if there were any weapons within reach. All he saw were several empty beer bottles scattered amongst piles of dirty clothes.

Since the guy in the bed was the guy with the gun, Tasker figured he was the leader of this bunch. Best to control him if he was going to get the money back. So, he slipped up next to the bed and put the revolver next to the sleeping man's ear and pulled the hammer back. The clicking sound is distinctive and anyone who has spent any time around guns knows immediately what it is.

It took a couple seconds to register, but the man raised his head and started looking around. Tasker pushed the muzzle of the gun into the man's forehead and said, "Wake your buddy, now! And do it in English. If I hear one word of Russian, you're as dead as Stalin. Understand?"

The man slowly nodded his head and said, "Uri, wake up."

"What," the man named Uri said. "I'm sleeping."

Tasker pushed the muzzle into the other man's forehead again.

"Uri, wake up now," he said with some urgency.

"What," Uri said opening his eyes. He immediately saw Tasker holding a gun on the other man. Then he said, "You are the man from the sidewalk today."

"Yes I am," Tasker said. "I'm here for one of two things. I get the money back that you took from those people, or I kill you. It is as simple as that."

"We don't have the money," the man with the gun to his head said.

"Okay," Tasker said. "Then this will be easy. I've already taken care of your friend out on the couch."

Uri looked toward the bedroom door. The other man didn't move. The .38 between his eyes stopped him from moving, although Tasker saw him swallow hard, his Adam's apple moving up and down.

"So, are you going to stick with that story? That you don't have the money?" Tasker asked. "If so, let's get on with it."

Tasker pulled the revolver away from the man's head about six inches and made an overexaggerated move to aim the gun, closing his left eye and everything, at his forehead.

"Okay, okay," the man said. "We have it. We will get it."

"No," Tasker said, dropping the Ruger slightly. "I will get it."

Then he ordered the men to take the bedsheets off the bed and rip them into strips. It took them a couple of minutes to get the tears started, but once they got the strips going it didn't take long.

"Now, take two of the strips and twist them together," Tasker said.

They did that.

"Now, you Uri tie his hands together behind his back," Tasker said pointing at the man on the bed. "And make it tight. Not tight enough I will have to shoot you. I am going to check it."

Uri did as he was told. Tasker could see that he tied the man's wrists so tightly that it was cutting off the blood to his hands. They were going white.

"Good," Tasker said to Uri. "Now you sit there and put your hands behind your back. And don't think about doing anything because I can and will dislocate your shoulder so fast it will take a bit for the excruciating pain to hit."

Uri again obeyed. Tasker tied his hands with the rope made from the sheets. Then he looked around. There was a pair of dirty socks lying on the floor. He picked one of the socks up and stuffed it into Uri's mouth and then tied another strip of sheet around his head, holding the sock in his mouth.

"Please don't do that to me," the other man said. "I'll do anything you ask."

"Tell me where the money is," Tasker said.

"In the freezer," the man said. "We put it in the freezer in case this dump caught on fire."

"Get up and walk with me there," Tasker said. "Uri, you move and I shoot him first and then you."

Uri just nodded his head.

Tasker helped the other man to his feet and they walked out to the kitchen. Tasker saw the man look at the man on the couch, with the blood coming from the back of his head.

They stopped in front of the refrigerator and, still holding the revolver on the man, Tasker opened the freezer. There were ten six-inch tall stacks of one-hundred-dollar bills.

"Is that it?" Tasker asked.

The man didn't say anything, just nodded.

"If it isn't, I will be back, and next time I won't be so nice."

"It is all of it," the man said.

Tasker walked the man back into the bedroom and sat him on the bed. Then he grabbed the other sock and started toward him.

"No, please, not that, those are Uri's and he is the filthiest man in the world. I will catch a disease and die."

"Sorry," Tasker said and stuffed the sock in the man's mouth. He secured it with another strip of sheet. The whole time he was doing it the man was gagging.

"Don't puke, because it has nowhere to go," Tasker said.

Then he tied sheet strips around both men's ankles. Sooner or later, they would pull free from the fabric bindings Tasker knew, but it would hold them long enough for him to get the money out of the building.

He walked back out into the main room. Looked for the car seat, didn't see it, but found a backpack sitting in a corner. He grabbed it, dumped some cigarettes and other junk out of it, and filled it with the money.

Before Tasker left, he went over and checked on the man he had beaned with the skillet. He was still breathing. When he got the money to the Pavlychkos, he would make an anonymous call to the cops and they would get the man some medical help.

Tasker quietly and quickly made it down the hall, down the stairs and out the back door, which still had the wood in the jamb. He hustled to his pickup, fired it up and headed to the house where the Pavlychkos waited.

When he got there, they were overwhelmed. They thanked him at least fifty times and hugged him and shook his hand.

"You best get this in a bank where it is safe," Tasker said to Nykolai. Then he tried to give the .38 to the man.

"For protection," Tasker said.

The senior Pavlychko shook his head and said something in Ukrainian to his son.

"What did he say?" Tasker asked

"It is an old Ukrainian saying," Nykolai said. "Not to play with fire."

Tasker smiled.

He stayed at the house for another half hour, but he was getting really tired. What he needed now was some sleep. He finally told the Pavlychkos he needed to go. They thanked him and hugged him and shook his hand one more time as he left the house.

He climbed back into his pickup and for the first time in hours he thought about Madeline. He thought of heading back to Montana, to her. But he was too tired to drive any more. He headed down one of the main thoroughfares farther into Spokane. He needed sleep badly.

A few blocks later he spotted a sign for a mom-and-pop motel and pulled into the motel parking lot. Before he entered the lobby, he dropped the Ruger into the garbage can next to the door. He didn't need the gun anymore, and the old man was right, it was like playing with fire.

The dull black revolver had served its purpose, but he was glad to be rid of it. Now it was time to sleep. And Tasker did. Like he hadn't slept in weeks.

Las Vegas Always Needs Showgirls
Bobby Mathews

I don't even know where the gun came from. That's the funny part. I was drunk when I found it behind Mootsy's on West Sprague where we went sometimes to blow off a little steam. They'll tell you that they close at 2 but if you pay for your drinks ahead of time, Ashley behind the bar will let you stay while she closes up. Easy walk up North Washington from there to the east side of Huntington Park where you can score.

I'm sure that's what I was doing when the gun showed up, so I took it. Ugly old .38 snub-nose revolver with electrical tape wrapped around the grip and trigger so no fingerprints will show up. I figured it had been used sometime, somewhere, and that gun looked like money to me. So I checked the cylinder. Three bullets.

Well, I guessed that would be enough. I snapped the pistol closed and put it in my waistband. Went and scored and sat down on a hill in Riverfront Park to watch the ducks go back and forth in the Spokane River and the rippling wakes the reflected colors of the city lights in the water until the cold air coming off the river made me restless and I jogged back across West Main and up a few blocks to the Satellite Diner where they know me but still let me in. My head was full of cotton candy and the night full of stars.

The place was late-night crowded and hot the way a saloon always is when the food is cheap and good and it's shoulder-to-shoulder warm and sticky with sweat and talk and the bartenders are hotter than they have any right to be in their tight jeans and low-cut black tops. Krysta was working the stick, drawing pitchers and mixing old-fashioneds and shaking off the dirty jokes like "What's the difference between jelly and jam?" because she'd heard them all before. The sparrow tattooed over her left breast fluttered every time she lifted a hand and it was impossible not to watch it and wonder when it would take flight.

There wasn't space at the bar but I didn't care. Maybe the gun made me brave. I shouldered my way in and caught Krysta's eye. She came over, took one look at me and shook her head.

"I'm not serving you tonight, space cowboy."

"Why not?" The words sounded small and far away to my own ears. The place wasn't loud but I couldn't bring myself to raise my voice. Krysta just shook her head and put a plastic cup of water in front of me. I drank it down and gestured for another.

A few minutes later a basket of fries arrived without me ordering and I ate them so quickly I barely tasted them. I needed my regular vitamins and minerals: salt and grease. I was considering eating the wax paper, too, just for some roughage. I was up too far and out too deep and my orbit seemed permanent on a spaceship built for one. If I got any higher I'd be rocketing past Jupiter.

Maybe Colleen could bring me down. She was always the tether even if things weren't so good between us. She could reel me in like a lonely fisherman hauling in a big marlin before the sharks got to it. I asked Krysta if she'd seen her, but the answer was no so I went to the restroom and washed my face and tried to pry a little of the dirt from underneath my fingernails. It didn't help much. I left a five—my last one—on the bar for Krysta and stalked out into the night, my high turning as dark as the space my head was flying through.

The night felt like cold velvet and I could go anywhere or do anything that I wanted. I stopped a guy, little scrawny dude, two blocks away from the bar and asked if he'd let me have a cigarette. He told me to fuck off so I pulled the pistol out of my waistband and told him he could give me his wallet instead.

"Fuck off," he said again, but his eyes were wide and they stayed trained on the barrel of the gun. I can't blame him. I didn't know then what I know now, how that little black eye of death seems to follow you like the eyes in a haunted portrait. How once you see it, it's a staring contest you want to lose. You don't want to see that black eye blink and turn to fire and the rising smoke from the barrel and then you feel like you got punched in the gut and sit down to die.

"Give it to me," I said again, and he handed over a slim little eel-skin thing, real old-school cool. Steve McQueen would have been proud. Lots of plastic in there: debit card, AmEx, Visa, Discover. No cash. Nothing that would do me any good. I threw the wallet back and it hit him in the face before he could catch it.

"You ain't got no *money*? Seriously?"

"I'm sorry," he said. "I didn't know I was going to get mugged tonight."

This time I was the one who said to fuck off. I backed away and stuck the gun in my waistband again and went on down the street to find Colleen. She would bring me back. Reel me in. She always had before.

***

The house was dark. The only way I knew that someone was home was the generator chugalugging along in the back yard. I eased open the plywood panel that served as Colleen's front door and used the frayed rope nailed to the inside to shut it. There was one light on in the place, a clamp lamp that illuminated Colleen's bedroom. I whispered her name and she answered "Who's that?"

I told her it was me.

"Oh," she said and stuck her head out the door to make sure I was alone. "I'd tell you come in but you're already here."

I wanted to say that I was sorry about that but what was there to be sorry about? I stayed here a lot of nights, times when Colleen went out on "dates" with guys who paid her, made sure that no one else squatted in the house, and sometimes I woke up next to her after we scored something good and the nice feeling was on us and there was no one else to take it out on except the naked body of the person next to you. It was her squat, maybe our squat. I was never quite sure.

I went through the dusty living room with its warped floor and sagging popcorn ceiling and down the cobweb-choked hallway to the bedroom and leaned against the doorway. I was still high enough to wonder if the jamb was holding me up or the other way around and I giggled while I watched Colleen. She was something to see. An inch or so below six feet, great legs. Some of the money she earned she put back into her gym membership, and she got her money's worth. So did the guys who went on dates with her, but I tried not to think too much about that. Instead I watched that lithe tall girl with her back to me as she moved to and fro between an inflatable queen-sized mattress and a hard-sided rolling suitcase. Some clothes went in the suitcase. Some were tossed aside like extra ballast off a sinking ship. I couldn't make heads or tails of it.

"What are you doing?"

"What it looks like. Packing."

"Another date?"

Colleen shook her head.

"I'm going."

I didn't understand, so I didn't say anything. Just watched her move slow and rhythmic like a snake hypnotizing its prey. The single light was a spotlight and she moved in and out of its glow like a planet in orbit around a temporary sun. Finally I couldn't take the silence anymore and asked her what she meant.

"Vegas," she said. "I always wanted to go and now somebody wants to take me."

"Oh so it *is* another date."

Colleen shook her head.

"He'll come back, I guess he lives here."

When I first met Colleen in a bar—Ichabod's East, maybe?— where she was showing off her long stems in the mini-shorts she favored, drunk and going on about how she was going to make it to Vegas one day and dance on the Strip there.

"You know Las Vegas always needs showgirls," she told me, and I guess she was right. Colleen was twenty-two then, and that's young enough to hold onto your dreams. But now she was twenty-seven, maybe twenty-eight, and those dreams have a way of slipping off behind our backs when we're not paying close attention. She hadn't mentioned Vegas in a year at least and I thought she'd put the dream down the same way you toss a used Styrofoam container out the window of your car when you're finished with it.

"I don't think you should do that. Stay here."

"Why the hell would I do that?"

I didn't have an answer that Colleen wouldn't laugh at. Because I love you was close to the truth but she wouldn't respect it if I told her that. I had to dig around behind those words to find what I really meant, a racoon scraping through the trash to find the treasure of his truth.

"Because I need you," I said. "You leave, I got nothing."

Colleen didn't look at me.

"You can't blame me for that, you got nothing anyway." She barked a harsh laugh. "No money. No house. No car. No friends."

"Hey," I said, but my voice was low.

I was coming down now. I could feel Colleen reeling me back in. She wasn't trying to. Her sheer presence was enough. Pull me down from outer space, yank me straight through the radiation belt and into the burning atmosphere, hurtle through the clouds and watch Spokane come back in view from twenty thousand feet up and let the wind fly through my hair and the pressure disintegrate my eyeballs onto my cheek. And the ground twisted down there below me and who the hell really knows if that's Spokane or Coeur d'Alene, Idaho, and now the city streets rushed up to meet me and I crashed so hard back into my body that I nearly fell down.

"I'm going to get some money," I said. I was nearly gasping from my return from the intergalactic trip. I took the gun out and tossed it on the inflatable bed where it bounced a couple of times and lay motionless like a huge dead black insect.

"Jesus Christ," Colleen said. "Where'd you get that?"

I didn't answer because by then I couldn't remember. Just told her that I had a plan, and that the money would come.

"You don't have a plan. You don't even have the concept of a plan."

The phrase was a joke between us but I didn't remember where it came from. I couldn't tell her that I'd already tried phase one of my plan: rob somebody right there on the street. It hadn't worked and I couldn't admit that failure now. It would give power to the words she'd said about me, the things that I thought were my secret thoughts about myself. But she saw me. She knew me. Colleen picked up the gun and held it in her palm as if testing its weight.

"It's real."

"Course it's real. Be dumb to go around with a fake gun."

"Just the kind of thing you'd do," she said, and it hurt because she wasn't wrong. It wouldn't have mattered if the gun was a BB pistol. I still would have taken it.

"Give it back," I said and reached for it. Colleen moved her hand languidly and I missed my grab. I tried again and she skipped backwards a step.

"Stop it," she said. "You need to lie down and get some rest."

"Give it back."

"I will when you're sober."

"I said give it back, damn you." I turned on her and the anger rose in my heart and ballooned to my head. I could feel my hands swell to bursting with desire for the gun, with the need to take it away from her and—

—and do what? My fists flexed open and closed and I understood then that the only way that I would be able to keep Colleen with me was if I put my hands around that swanlike pale neck and squeezed. I could see the motion in my mind, feel my fingers around her windpipe, see the blue-going-on-black bruises that I would leave around her windpipe and then I was stalking her and she was backing into the far corner of the room where it was darkest. The eye of the gun followed me but it didn't scare me. Not then. In a moment I would pluck it from her hands and then it wouldn't matter. Nothing else would matter and I would have Colleen with me and I would eat her heart if I wanted to. I could keep her as part of my soul forever.

There were tears on her face and now I was so close that I could see gooseflesh standing out on her arms and then she pushed the muzzle of the gun against my belly and pulled the trigger.

I sagged back, my hands slapping weakly at my shirt where it was on fire from the gunshot. I smelled my own charred flesh and felt my strength seep out of my body slowly along with my blood. I slipped down to the floor, first on my knees and then on my back. The popcorn ceiling was low and ugly and gray now as whatever light the clamp lamp threw began to fade. I was there in the room with Colleen and I was somewhere else, too, out there floating toward the Spokane River and then Roosevelt Lake, over the mountains and sliding above the Pacific Ocean and out toward where the light could no longer touch me and the cold dark could finally take me.

Colleen took the gun with her. I don't know where. I saw her toss it into the suitcase. Zip the bag closed. I managed to turn on my side and watch her as she turned off the lamp and the room blinked into almost complete darkness. She was traveling now and so was I. Different directions, different destinations.

I was somewhere out past anger, the rage dribbling out of my body along with the dark and sticky blood on the floor. I couldn't believe how fast everything turned, like a snake twisting to make the fatal strike when you think you've got it by the tail. I wished her well, because Las Vegas always needs showgirls. I didn't want her to think about the rest of it, how the Strip used up girls like her and spit them out the same way Spokane had chewed me up and tossed me aside and now I lay dying in a house and no one besides her knew it.

I hoped she'd found something better, even if I doubted it would happen. The last thing I remember is hoping like hell that someday Colleen would find me no matter where I ended up and tell me that she came out all right.

Ninjas Don't Ride Bikes

Colin Conway

Bryce Hartley crossed his legs and rested his shoulders against the headboard. He spun a well-worn Rubik's Cube in his hands, not getting any closer to solving it.

Nearby, Everest Swenson sat at a small desk, playing a video game on the computer. He leaned toward the monitor as his left hand danced across the keyboard and his right hand jostled the mouse. Explosions came from the speakers on either side of the screen.

The two were in Bryce's basement bedroom. His dad reluctantly framed and finished it several years ago so Bryce wouldn't have to share an upstairs room with his older sister. The other side of the walls remained just studs, though. Bryce's father would only do so much work to help his son.

Natural light entered through a small window above the desk. Not that it mattered now since it was well after midnight.

"Summer sucks," Bryce muttered as he struggled to solve the cube.

Everest's tongue darted between his lips. "What's that?"

"Nothing."

Everest wore a black tank top that read *Yellowstone*—the TV show, not the national park. The guy was crazy about it. Everest's jeans were new as were his Adidas. His father had lots of money and supposedly paid huge child support to his mom. Everest never had to wait for school to start to get new clothes.

That's one of the reasons Bryce couldn't wait for summer to end. He'd get some new jeans for the upcoming school year. The pair he had on now were tight on his hips and high around the ankles. Bryce felt like a nerd.

He didn't know why his parents refused to buy him or his sister new clothes whenever they needed them. His dad had a good job, and his mom worked at a drycleaner. Bryce's sister said it was because their parents were selfish. He figured it had something to do with how much they drank.

Even though Everest's parents bought him almost everything he wanted, he could never have the freedom Bryce had. Everest's mother smothered him, while Bryce's parents barely paid attention to what he did until it was time to dole out punishment.

"No wonder you never beat this level," Everest said. "Your internet is glitchy. Hella lag."

"Tell me about it." Bryce looked up from his puzzle. "My dad's cheap as shit." He lifted the Rubik's Cube for his friend to see. "I asked for one of these and he gave me the one he had back in high school."

Everest glanced away from the game. "Rubik's been around that long?"

"Guess so."

"When you gonna beat it?" Everest asked absently. He jerked his head to the side as if to avoid incoming fire from the video game. "Can't be that hard."

"Think you can do better?" Bryce held out the puzzle.

Everest spied another look at the cube. "Analog over digital? Get real." He flopped back in his chair and slapped his hands. "Cheating son of a bitch cocksucker." Everest wasn't allowed to swear at his house because of his mother's church. Bryce's folks didn't care what he or his friends said as long as it wasn't directed at them.

The two boys met while attending the same middle school but became friends through karate class. The martial arts dojo they trained at was in a quasi-industrial building behind a U-Haul business. Bryce was almost a blue belt while Everest recently earned his orange. In a few weeks they'd start their freshman year at Central Valley High School.

Even though Everest's mom was hot, Bryce rarely hung out at his friend's house which was in a ritzy development behind the high school. She had too many rules for Everest which meant the boys could never have any fun there. Bryce had never met his friend's dad. Supposedly, the guy lived in the Five Mile area with a girlfriend still in college.

Bryce tossed the Rubik's cube to the end of his bed. "Wanna do something?"

"We are doing something." Everest put his hands back on the keyboard and mouse. "I'm trying to beat this level for you."

"I mean outside." He waved toward the small window above the desk. "Let's go ninja-ing."

Everest rolled his eyes. "Dude, all we ever do is walk around."

"We'll do something this time. I promise."

"I promise I'm about to beat this level." Everest motioned toward the monitor.

"You're not any closer than me," Bryce said. "Besides, you can play it some more when we come back."

Everest spun his chair to face Bryce. A goofy smile spread on his face. "What's your sister doing?"

"Ignoring you."

"Come on. I'm serious. Maybe she'll wanna go with us."

"Give it up, man. She only dates seniors. She's not giving a jackoff like you a chance."

Everest feigned hurt. "I could make an honest woman out of her."

"The hell does that mean?"

"I don't know," Everest said. "It's some stupid shit my dad says whenever he gets a new girlfriend."

"In that case, I'll make an honest woman out of your mom."

Everest rolled his eyes. "I don't think you're using that right."

"And you are?" Bryce hopped off his bed. "I'm going. You can stay here if you want."

"If we're gonna go, I wanna hit Zip-Zap and grab a Monster, maybe some nachos."

"You got money?"

Everest eyed Bryce like he'd lost his mind.

It was a stupid question. Everest always had cash.

****

The two crept up the basement stairs to the kitchen.

Bryce didn't expect his parents to be awake at this hour, since they usually went to bed well before eleven with bellies full of booze. If his dad happened to catch Bryce sneaking out, he'd slap him around. Not in front of Everest, but later when it was just them. His dad was smart like that. He knew how to smack a guy without leaving a mark.

The refrigerator hum was the only noise in the kitchen.

Bryce pulled open the back door and motioned for Everest to step outside. Bryce quietly closed the door behind them, then hurried around the side of the house opposite his parents' bedroom.

Neither boy spoke until they were on Fourth Avenue and headed toward Sullivan which was several blocks away.

"We should've grabbed our bikes," Everest whispered.

"Ninjas don't ride bikes."

"That's what you said about cell phones," Everest said.

Bryce left his cell phone in his room and made Everest do the same. At times, he hated the devices. Not because of how distracting they were, but for the symbol they represented. The cool kids always had nicer, newer phones. It would certainly be worse in high school. Besides, Bryce only had one real friend, and since Everest was with him, Bryce didn't need his phone.

A car turned onto Fourth Avenue from Sullivan, its headlights shining in the distance.

"Hide," Bryce whispered. He bolted toward the shadow of an overgrown maple tree.

Everest scampered behind a parked truck and knelt near its back tire.

The headlights grew until the car passed. Bryce remained hunkered until the red taillights faded into the distance.

Everest abandoned his hiding place first. "Nothing would've happened if they saw us."

"Nobody sees a ninja until it's too late."

"I mean, it's not like we're doing anything."

"Not yet."

Everest jumped ahead then turned around, backpedaling to keep pace with Bryce. "What's that mean?" Everest asked with an inquisitive smile.

"How do you keep a moron in suspense?"

"What are you talking about?"

"I'll tell you after Zip-Zap."

***

Bryce pushed the door and stepped onto the sidewalk in front of Zip-Zap Pump and Go. He carried a bottle of Gatorade Fruit Punch in his left hand.

"Hold the door," Everest said as he scooted by Bryce. He had a large Monster energy drink and a towering tray of nachos. The chips looked like they were drowning in gooey orange cheese.

Some old rock and roll song played through the convenience store's outdoor speakers. Bryce didn't know the name of the tune, but it was something he'd heard his father sing along with while they were in the car.

A homeless man with a shaggy gray beard sat on the sidewalk next to the trash can. His shoes were off, and he picked his toes. He looked up at the boys. "Anything to spare?"

Bryce shook his head. Everest glanced at the guy and hurried ahead. He stopped at the edge of the property, near a row of arborvitaes.

"Shit," Everest muttered.

"What?"

"I gotta piss."

"So?" Bryce shrugged. "Go in the bushes."

"I can't do that. What if I get caught?"

"You're not gonna get caught."

Everest said, "I'm using a restroom like a regular human." He studied his snacks. "You think they'll get mad if I bring these back inside?"

"Leave them here."

"What about him?" Everest lifted his chin in the direction of the homeless man.

"He's not going to bother me."

"Yeah. Okay." Everest set the nachos and Monster on the concrete curbing that surrounded the landscaped area. "Don't steal my chips." He hopped nervously as he hurried into Zip-Zap. The bright lights inside the store made it easy for Bryce to watch Everest until he hurried into the restroom.

Bryce leaned over and stole three cheese-slathered chips from Everest's nachos. Careful not to spill any of the orange goo on himself, Bryce shoved the chips into his mouth. He chewed them so fast he could barely enjoy them. Then he took three more.

While he chewed the second mouthful, he walked along the concrete curbing like a gymnast on a high beam. Better yet, Bryce thought, he was a ninja balancing on a tight rope between two buildings belonging to his enemies.

Something in the landscaped area caught his eye and he stopped his tight rope act. It looked like a gun. He stepped into the bark chips and bent to see it better. Maybe it was pretend, a plastic toy some kid left behind.

He kicked it, just to make sure. The toe of his ratty Converse hit something heavy. That sealed it for Bryce. The gun on the ground most definitely wasn't pretend. It was a snub-nose revolver like the one his dad wore around his ankle while at work. Someone had wrapped electrical tape around the gun's handle.

Excitement shot through Bryce's veins and his heart raced.

How did it end up there? Had someone robbed the convenience store and tossed the gun on their way out? Maybe a guy parked next to the curb after shooting someone, then threw the gun away. Bryce supposed a woman was as likely to ditch the gun. What if she dropped it by accident? Would she come back for it?

Bryce glanced over his shoulder. No one inside the store watched him, and the homeless man was more interested in his toes than Bryce. Nobody was at the gas pumps. Cars zipped by on Sullivan. If anyone happened to notice Bryce, it wouldn't matter because they were too far away.

He reached to pick up the gun but stopped, his fingers hovering over the small black revolver. Bryce had heard plenty about fingerprints and DNA at the dinner table. He knew better than to touch the gun with his bare hands.

Maybe he should tell an adult about what he'd found. Maybe even his dad who was a Property Crimes detective for the Sheriff's Department. Yeah, Bryce wouldn't do that. His dad would accuse Bryce of stealing the gun and smack him when no one was looking. Bryce learned through the years to not antagonize his father. The man's slap was harder than he'd ever been hit in karate class.

Bryce glanced over his shoulder once more before using his shoe to push the revolver fully underneath an arborvitae tree. He didn't have to decide what to do now. He could come back for the gun later if he wanted it or he could just leave it there if he changed his mind.

Maybe Bryce could even sell it. Score some cash so he wouldn't have to always borrow from Everest. Bryce had no idea how much he owed. His friend never made a stink about it.

"What're you looking at?" Everest asked.

Bryce jumped and turned. "What?" He moved in between Everest and the now hidden gun. "I wasn't looking at anything." He forced a smile. "I forgot to say thanks for the drink." He lifted the Gatorade bottle for emphasis.

"No problem." Everest picked up his nachos and energy drink. "Hey, did you eat some of my chips?"

"You're crazy."

"Looks like you did." Everest's brow furrowed. "Looks like you ate a lot of them, in fact."

"Not me, man."

Bryce hoped he didn't have nacho cheese on his breath.

***

The Appleway Trail ran parallel to busy East Sprague Avenue which was a couple blocks north. The paved path sat behind a slew of businesses and was used by runners, bikers, and citizens without a car. To the south were apartments and houses. Light poles lined the trail at intervals of twenty-five feet. This left plenty of shadows for Bryce and Everest to hide in.

Everest dropped his empty nacho container into a trash can. He took a final swig of his energy drink and threw that away, too. When Bryce finished his Gatorade, he tossed the bottle into a shadow.

"Litterbug," Everest said.

Bryce playfully punched his friend on the arm. "Narc."

They sparred for a minute. Everest desperately tried to hit Bryce, but he was inexperienced. Bryce easily blocked his strikes and lightly slapped his friend on the forehead. The boys stopped when they broke into laughter.

"Ready?" Bryce asked.

Everest bent over with his hands on his knees. "Where we going?"

"You'll see."

The teenagers darted along the path, sprinting from one shadow to the next, and stayed silent. Twice while they were running, Bryce saw homeless men sleeping on metal benches.

Twenty minutes passed before they arrived behind an old mobile home park on Sprague Avenue. Only three dilapidated aluminum trailers remained on the property. Bryce had noticed the nearly empty park while riding his bike a couple of days ago. During the light of day, the park looked sad. At night, it looked eerie like a place where evil lurked, especially since only a couple of light poles still worked.

Bryce left the trail and hurried toward a six-foot tall chain-link fence. He stopped and waited for Everest.

When his friend arrived, Everest hooked his fingers through the fence and peered into the nearly empty park. "Wasn't there a bunch of them before?"

"There's a sign out front," Bryce said. He'd seen it while driving with his mom to visit his aunt in Liberty Lake. "Supposedly, a new building is coming or something."

"They say what it is?"

"No, but it's probably a food place."

"Dude! What if it's In-N-Out Burger?" Everest glanced at his friend. "My mom took me to one in California. That'd be dope."

"I've never been," Bryce admitted. He jumped onto the fence. "Last one in is a homo."

"Hey," Everest protested, but he quickly climbed the fence.

The boys pulled themselves over and dropped into the mobile home park.

"What're we doing?" Everest asked.

"Getting you some action like I promised."

Everest grabbed Bryce's arm. "Wait. Are we breaking into one of them?"

"Don't worry. Nobody's living in them anymore."

"I don't feel good about this."

Bryce pulled his arm free from Everest's grasp. "Relax. This is gonna be fun."

***

The door to the first trailer was open. Even in the low light, it appeared someone had busted its lock. Bryce tried to be as quiet as possible as he pushed the door wider. He stuck his head into the mobile home to let his eyes adjust to the darkness. The place smelled like garbage.

"We should go," Everest whispered, his voice full of panic.

"You wanted action."

"Not like this." Everest glanced around the empty park.

Bryce was scared, but he wouldn't show it to Everest. His friend had nice clothes and the best video games, but Bryce had confidence. At least, the appearance of confidence.

"What if the cops show up?" Everest asked.

"They're not." Bryce stepped inside and his heart pounded harder. This was the first time he illegally entered a building.

While ninja-ing in the past, Bryce got on the roof of the karate school. He'd also run through plenty of yards. Once, a Rottweiler almost bit him. That was scary but made for a cool story. Everest hadn't been with him during those escapades. He usually kept it tame when his friend was around.

Bryce settled into a fighting stance—legs bent and hands raised. He was prepared in case anything attacked from the darkness. Nothing did.

He crept forward, shuffling slowly. The only sounds were from the cars whizzing by on Sprague Avenue.

"See anything?" Everest asked.

Bryce stopped moving and glanced back. Everest hadn't entered the trailer. Instead, he only leaned his head in.

"Well?"

Bryce shushed his friend, then continued down the hallway. He walked by an empty room, a bathroom that smelled like urine, and into the far bedroom. Nothing.

He returned to the front of the trailer and hopped out.

"What'd you see?" Everest asked.

"Take a look for yourself."

"I think I'll pass."

Bryce frowned. "Pussy."

"Call me whatever you want. I'm not breaking the law."

"Too late for that. We're trespassing."

Everest threw his hands in the air. "Great. Just great. What if my mom finds out?"

Bryce hurried to the next trailer which required him to briefly leave the shadows. Everest scampered behind him.

"Not another one," Everest whispered.

"I'm going in all three."

Bryce pulled on the second trailer's door. It gave slightly, but something wrapped around the handle stopped it from opening fully. Bryce stuck his hand through the crack and felt a small rope tied around the handle. His fingers pulled at a knot.

Everest grabbed Bryce's arm. "Someone's in there," he whispered.

"They're not supposed to be." Bryce felt the knot give.

"Dude, don't. It's dangerous."

Bryce paused as he heeded Everest's warning. If he stopped now, there'd be no big adventure. Nothing to tell the other freshmen about in the upcoming year. He'd remain the weird karate kid just like he was in middle school. Bryce tugged at the knot once more.

The rope fell from the handle, and he pulled the door open. Bryce leaned inside. It was dark and smelly like the previous trailer. He quietly entered and settled into his fighting stance.

On Sprague Avenue, a car honked twice.

Bryce moved deeper into the darkness, his heart racing wildly.

The layout of this trailer seemed like the first. Bryce stopped outside the first room and peered in. It was hard to make out anything in the dark. He waited for his eyes to adjust more before moving on.

He shuffled forward and his foot bumped into something soft. He poked it with his toe. It felt soft like a lump of clothes. Probably dirty, Bryce thought. He stepped over the small mound.

The bathroom door was open, and it smelled worse than the first. Like someone had crapped in the toilet and hadn't flushed. Bryce held his nose and moved onto the last room which had a closed door.

He thought for a moment about turning and leaving. Blood pounded in his ears and his mouth was dry. If he left now, there'd be nothing to brag about. Besides, Everest might call him a pussy as payback.

Bryce looked over his shoulder and could see his friend leaning in to see what was going on. It was too late to turn back. Bryce quietly pushed open the door to the last room.

Something moved to his left and Bryce pulled back into the hallway. A hammer slammed into the opened door, splintering the wood.

"Christ!" Bryce screamed.

An older man stepped into the doorway. His potbelly hung over his boxer shorts. The man used both hands to yank the heavy tool free of the door. Bryce couldn't get a good look at the guy's face. He did know the man was big. Much bigger than Bryce.

"Sumbitch thief!" the man yelled in a raspy, drunk voice.

Bryce punched the man in the chest and kicked him in the leg. However, Bryce hadn't planted himself so neither strike had much power. The man swung the hammer again. This time it banged against the door frame.

"Get outta there!" Everest hollered from outside the trailer.

Bryce backpedaled twice down the hallway before he turned to run. His foot snagged on the mound of clothes he'd stepped over earlier. Bryce lost his balance and stumbled forward. He caught himself on the wall, barely remaining on his feet.

"I got you!" the man yelled.

The hammer nicked Bryce's head before clanking against the wall. It felt like Bryce's head exploded. He careened down the hallway but stopped suddenly and turned. He kicked the old man in the groin, but it only seemed to slow the guy down.

"Lil' bastard," the man croaked as he marched forward.

Bryce scrambled toward the front of the trailer. He jumped through the open door and into the night. "Run!" he yelled at Everest.

The boys raced toward the chain link fence and clamored over it. When they landed, they turned around to see the half-naked man charging toward them with his hammer held high in the air.

"Get back here!" the guy shouted. "Thieves!"

Bryce and Everest sprinted along the Appleway Trail, not bothering to run from shadow to shadow.

***

When the adrenaline coursing through Bryce's body ebbed, a pounding in his skull announced its presence. Bryce stopped running and bent over. He felt nauseous, like he might pass out.

"What's wrong?" Everest asked.

"Guy hit me with a hammer. What do you think is wrong?" Bryce touched his head and stiffened from the pain. His fingers were covered with blood.

"Oh my fuck," Everest said. "Come into the light." Everest grabbed Bryce's arm and pulled him under a light pole. "Lemme see."

Bryce bent again.

"Dude, you're bleeding like crazy. This is why we should've brought our phones."

"My dad's gonna kill me," Bryce muttered.

"He's not gonna kill you."

Bryce looked up at his friend.

"Okay, yeah, you're probably dead, but we gotta do something about that bleeding."

"Hold up." Bryce pulled his white T-shirt over his head. The fabric dragging across his wound felt like sandpaper. He balled the garment and pressed it against his skull. "Let's go."

The two walked along the trail, staying in shadows as they went.

"What're you gonna tell you dad?" Everest asked.

"I'm not going to tell him shit."

"He's going to see your head."

"Whatever," Bryce said. "I'll worry about that in the morning."

"How can you not worry about that now?"

Bryce didn't answer. His thoughts were already elsewhere.

***

"I need a Gatorade," Bryce said as they neared Zip-Zap.

"You need a doctor."

Bryce waved his free hand. "No doctors."

Everest looked at him with concern. "What if you bleed to death?"

"I'm not gonna bleed to death. Jeez, you're as bad as your mom."

The boys entered the convenience store's parking lot. A couple of cars were at the gas pumps, and the homeless man slept next to the trash can. Another old rock and roll song played through the shop's outdoor speakers.

Bryce stopped and eyed Everest. "Spot me another Gatorade."

"Lemme see your head again."

"I'm fine. I just need something to drink."

Everest crossed his arms. "I'm not buying you shit unless you show me how bad it is."

Reluctantly, Bryce lowered his hand. His white T-shirt was covered in blood. He bent so Everest could see the top of his head.

Everest held Bryce by the temples and stood on his toes. "Oh shit, dude. There's a lot of blood."

"You already knew that."

"Is that your brain?"

Bryce tsked. "You can't see my brain."

"You'd have to have one for me to see it." Everest tugged Bryce's head down more which made Bryce even more nauseous. "I think I can see your skull."

Bryce pulled free of Everest's hands and held the T-shirt against his head again.

"I'm not joking, dude," Everest said. "I could see your skull. You need stitches."

"How about that Gatorade?"

Everest rolled his eyes. "Seriously, you're gonna get gangrene or something. They'll have to amputate your head."

"They won't have the chance because I'm about to die of thirst."

"We're gonna get in trouble for this," Everest said.

"If anyone was to get in trouble, it'd be me. You've got nothing to worry about."

"You don't know my mom."

Bryce smirked. "She'll forgive you when I make an honest woman out of her."

"C'mon, dude. I'm serious."

"Me, too. I seriously need a Gatorade."

Everest stared at him for a moment. "Don't go anywhere."

"Where am I gonna go?"

Everest walked slowly toward the store. It sounded like he was talking to himself.

The homeless man continued to doze against the trash can. Only one car remained at the gas pumps. The woman standing outside her car was on her phone and couldn't care less about Bryce.

He walked over to the landscaped area and sat on the curb. One final glance around, then Bryce flopped onto an elbow. He grabbed the gun from underneath the arborvitae tree, slipped it into his pocket, and sat upright. His pocket bulged so Bryce rested his arm on it.

His heartbeat raced once more, and he leaned forward, afraid he might pass out. Bryce sat that way for several moments.

Something bounced against his shoulder just as Everest muttered, "Here."

Bryce reached up and grabbed the Gatorade bottle. "Orange?" he said. "I hate orange."

"Beggars can't be choosers."

"The hell does that mean?"

Everest shrugged. "More shit my dad says."

Bryce stood. He held the bottle low to hide his bulging pant pocket.

"You know, man, I've been thinking" Everest thumbed over his shoulder. "I'm gonna bail."

"What?

"Go home."

"Why?" Bryce asked.

Everest crossed his arms. "I'm feeling pretty tired."

"You can sleep at my house." Bryce practically begged the guy. "We'll be there in a few minutes."

"I'm good," Everest said.

"What about your phone?"

Everest paused to seemingly consider the predicament. "I'll come by in the morning."

"Fine. Whatever. Go if you want."

"You really should get some stitches."

Everest turned and walked back the way they came.

***

Bryce sat on the concrete curb for a while. It might've been fifteen minutes as easily as it was an hour. His mind raced with possibilities.

He could take the gun home and hide it. If he did that, he risked his father finding it. There'd be hell to pay if that happened. If his father didn't find it, Bryce could take it out the next time his father laid a hand on him or his mother.

Bryce really didn't like the idea of hiding the gun like some savings bond his grandmother sent him. Instead, he wanted to use it now. He was angry at what happened in the mobile home park.

What if he returned to the trailer, confronted the homeless man, and shot him?

Bryce's gaze drifted to the homeless man sleeping next to the trash can. Maybe that guy was friends with the one who hit Bryce. Why not shoot him first?

No, Bryce thought, that guy wasn't bothering anyone.

He frowned. There were only two guys Bryce could think of to use the gun on—his dad and the guy in the trailer. He sipped the orange Gatorade and grimaced. It tasted like cough medicine. He sipped it again.

The longer Bryce sat there, the more worried he became about the gun in his pocket. If a cop showed up now, what would Bryce say? *Hey, I found this revolver and put my fingerprints all over it. I swear I was gonna call 911 and turn it in. I was just keeping it in my pocket for safekeeping.*

As Bryce's anger wore off, it was replaced by humiliation. He'd lost a fight to a homeless man—a goddamn bum. Bryce was almost a blue belt. He helped teach the kids class at his karate school. He should've been able to defend himself.

What would his instructor say if he found out? Bryce took another sip of Gatorade and frowned. He'd probably be more upset that Bryce broke into the trailers rather than losing the fight. He'd likely kick Bryce out of the dojo. His instructor was always talking about developing character, whatever in the hell that meant.

Maybe he should put the gun back under the arborvitae tree, but then a little kid might find it. Bryce didn't want that to happen.

He should just toss the gun in the trash and run for it. Then the homeless guy might grab it and try to rob the joint. Wouldn't that be something if the gun was used in two robberies? First by the guy who threw it away, then the bum. Bryce liked Zip-Zap. He didn't want anyone to rob the joint.

No, he decided. He needed to throw it away where no one would find it.

Bryce got to his feet and swooned. He started toward Sprague Avenue.

***

Tall pylon signs and streetlights lined the arterial. A digital sign in front of a bank displayed the time—1:51 a.m. Cars sped in each direction on Sprague.

Bryce shuffled along the sidewalk and pressed the T-shirt against his head. It was a hot night, so he didn't mind walking around with his chest bare.

He surveyed the businesses along Sprague. Probably the best option was to toss the gun into a dumpster. He left the sidewalk and crossed through a parking lot. Ahead was Kentucky Fried Chicken. That's where he'd do it. No one would want to pull the gun out of that dumpster when it was covered in grease.

A truck with a busted muffler roared along Sprague Avenue. Right behind it was a patrol car with its emergency lights whirring. The two pulled into the parking lot of the fast-food restaurant.

"Shit," Bryce muttered. He diverted his route and returned to the sidewalk. He picked up his pace as he walked by KFC.

The cop yelled at the driver of the old truck to stay in his vehicle. Bryce lengthened his stride and tried not to look like he was hurrying.

A car filled with teenage girls slowed and honked. One of them leaned out the window with her arms in the air. She shouted at Bryce, "Show me what you got!"

Up ahead, another patrol car raced in Bryce's direction with its emergency lights on.

Bryce's heart felt like it was about to burst from his chest. He stopped walking, then started again. Fear gripped him like a python. What if someone saw him pick up the gun at Zip Zap? Had they called the cops about a shirtless kid?

He should never have grabbed the revolver. He should have ignored those trailers, too. Hell, he should have stayed at home. Had he done that, Everest would've still been there trying to beat that stupid game.

The patrol car zipped past Bryce. He turned and watched it pull into the KFC parking lot.

His fear eased slightly, but he still had to do something with the gun and fast.

Bryce spun and trotted now, his hand still holding the T-shirt to his head. He got lucky. Those cops might've taken an interest in him had it not been for the noisy pickup.

The post office was on his left. Bryce wondered if they had a dumpster.

A third patrol car sped in his direction. This one had both its lights and siren on.

Bryce felt like he was about to suffocate. He needed to do something before he died. He left the sidewalk, yanked the gun from his pocket and dropped it into one of the blue mailboxes standing at the property's edge. It thunked when it landed inside.

Getting rid of the revolver released the tightness in his chest. Now, he just had to act like nothing was wrong.

The third police car zoomed by and silenced its siren. Bryce imagined the car was turning into the KFC lot, too.

He took a step and stopped. Bryce turned back to the mailbox.

"What were you thinking, you stupid son of a bitch?" It was the same question his father had asked him many times over the years.

Bryce yanked open the mailbox and stuck his arm in. His fingers only grasped air. Bryce shoved his arm deeper in, but he still couldn't reach the bottom. "This can't be happening."

He froze, his mind drowning in a sea of worry.

His fingerprints were on the gun. Maybe some of his blood, too. If the revolver was used in a crime, it could blow back on Bryce. If the cops managed to tie him to the gun, his dad would surely kill him.

Bryce slowly pulled his hand from the mailbox.

He could walk over to Kentucky Fried Chicken. The cops were probably still there. He could tell them how he found the gun, that he thought about keeping it, then got scared and tossed it into the mailbox.

The throbbing in his skull reminded him why that was a bad idea. The cops would surely ask him what happened to his head. They'd talk to the clerk at Zip-Zap who would likely tell them about Everest. Once that happened, Bryce would have to explain why he didn't tell his friend about the gun. If Everest cracked under pressure, the cops would know about him breaking into the trailers. Hell, maybe Everest had already confessed the break-ins to his mom.

No, Bryce decided. He couldn't tell the cops. He couldn't tell anyone.

The best thing he could do was go home, wear a hat for a few days, and avoid his father. He'd have to be a ninja in his own house. Bryce could do that.

His parents barely noticed him anyway.

About the Authors

Mysti Berry

Mysti's short stories have been published in *Ellery Queen Mystery Magazine*, *Alfred Hitchcock's Mystery Magazine*, and many other anthologies. Mysti is also the editor and publisher of *Low Down Dirty Vote*, three volumes of short stories. The third volume is an Anthony nominee. She lives in San Francisco with husband, Dale Berry.

Claire Booth

Claire Booth is a former journalist who has reported on high-profile stories all over the country, including that of a California cult leader who became the subject of her nonfiction book *The False Prophet: Conspiracy, Extortion and Murder in the Name of God*. After spending so much time covering crimes so strange and convoluted they seemed more fiction than reality, she had enough of the real world and decided to write novels instead. Her Sheriff Hank Worth mysteries take place in Branson, Missouri, where small-town Ozark politics and big-city country music tourism clash in—yes—strange and convoluted ways. www.clairebooth.com

Colin Conway

Colin Conway is the creator of the 509 Crime Stories, the Cozy Up series, and the co-creator of the Charlie-316 series (written with Frank Zafiro). He served in the U.S. Army and later was an officer for the Spokane Police

Department. He lives in Eastern Washington with his girlfriend and a codependent Vizsla that rules their world. Follow his journey at colinconway.com.

Libby Fischer Hellmann

Libby Fischer Hellmann left a career in broadcast news in Washington, DC, and moved to Chicago a long time ago, where she, naturally, began to write gritty crime fiction. She soon began writing historical fiction as well. Eighteen novels and twenty-five short stories later, she claims they'll take her out of the Windy City feet first. She has been nominated for many awards in the mystery and crime writing community and has even won a few. Her latest novel, *Max's War: The Story of a Ritchie Boy*, is the little-known story of German Jewish immigrants who escaped Hitler and joined the US Army to fight Nazis.

Cindy Goyette

Cindy Goyette is a probation officer giving her a front row seat to the criminal justice system. Her experiences helped her create fiction that mirrors real life situations. Her novel, *Obey All Laws*, A Probation Case Files Mystery, is part of a series, published in January of 2024. Book two, *Early Termination*, will be published in January of 2025. Book one of her cozy mystery series *Diamond in the Ruff*, A Wiggle Butt Manor mystery will release in May of 2025. Cindy lives in Washington State with her husband and two Cocker Spaniels.

Puja Guha

Puja Guha grew up and has worked all over the world, something she channels into her six novels, with settings from New York to Madagascar to Iran. So far, she has traveled to over 60 countries, each of which she hopes to someday include in one of her novels. Her spy thriller series *The Ahriman Legacy* is an Amazon bestseller, and she has been featured on TV and media, including Fox5, *Reader's Digest*, and the *London Post*.

James D.F. Hannah

James D.F. Hannah is the Shamus Award-winning author of the Henry Malone series, including the novels *Behind the Wall of Sleep* and *Because the Night*. His short fiction has appeared in *Best American Mystery and Suspense*; *Ellery Queen Mystery Magazine, Vautrin*; *Rock and a Hard Place*; and *Shotgun Honey*, and anthologies including *Eight Very Bad Nights, Playing Games*, and *Under the Thumb*. He lives in Louisville, Kentucky, where all the bourbon is. You can find him on all the socials at @jamesdfhannah and jamesdfhannah.com.

Curtis Ippolito

Curtis Ippolito is a two-time Anthony Award Finalist, a Derringer Award Finalist, and the author of the crime novel, *Burying the Newspaper Man*. His short stories have appeared in numerous publications, including *Ellery Queen Mystery Magazine, Vautrin, Tough, Mystery Tribune*, and *Shotgun Honey*, as well as being included in several anthologies including the Anthony Award-nominated *Trouble No More* and *The One Percent: Tales of the Super Wealthy and Depraved*. He lives in San Diego, California. Learn more about him at curtisippolito.com.

Bobby Mathews

Bobby Mathews is the Alabama Wildman whose fiction explores the bloody, still-beating dark heart of the modern South. He's the award-winning author of the novels *Magic City Blues*, *Living the Gimmick*, and the short story collection *Negative Tilt*. He won the 2023 Derringer Award for Best Long Story, and his work is included in *Best American Mystery & Suspense 2024*. When Bobby's not writing, he's procrastinating.

Jason Powell

Jason Powell is a FDNY firefighter and author whose work has been published in Slate and numerous online writing outlets. When he isn't at the firehouse or at a desk, he can be found out and about in New York City or lost in the pages of a novel. His debut novel, *No Man's Ghost*, is available for preorder and due to be released by Datura books in May 2025. Find him online at authorjasonpowell.com and Instagram @uh_thousand_words

Robert Lopresti

Robert Lopresti is a retired librarian who lives in the wetside of Washington State. He is the author of 100+ short stories and the editor of *Crimes Against Nature: New Stories of Environmental Villainy*.

Rob Phillips

Rob Phillips is an award-winning newspaper and magazine writer and the author of the critically acclaimed Luke McCain mystery series featuring a Fish and Wildlife officer who, with the assistance of his faithful yellow Labrador retriever Jack, patrols the mountains, streams, and trails of the Pacific Northwest.

Since the beginning of COVID in early 2020, Phillips has written and published eight books, including seven novels in the Luke McCain series, along with a book about his life with dogs, titled *A Dog's Life Well Lived.*

Rob and his wife Terri, live on a small cherry orchard in Yakima, Washington with a very spoiled Labrador retriever named Bailey. More information on the author and his books can be found at robphillipsoutdoors.com.

Frank Zafiro

Frank Zafiro writes gritty crime fiction from both sides of the badge. He was a police officer from 1993 to 2013, holding many different positions and ranks. He retired as a captain. Frank is the author of more than fifty novels, most of them crime fiction. His mainstream work (mostly hockey or humorous/heartwarming dramas) appears under the name Frank Scalise, while his science fiction and fantasy is written as Frank Saverio. In addition to writing, Frank has hosted the crime fiction podcast *Wrong Place, Write Crime* since 2017. He is an avid hockey fan, martial artist, and a tortured guitarist. He currently lives in Redmond, Oregon.